Bum
Steer

Books by Nancy Pickard

Bum Steer
Dead Crazy
Marriage Is Murder
No Body
Say No to Murder
Generous Death

Published by POCKET BOOKS

A Jenny Cain Mystery

Bum Steer

Nancy Pickard

POCKET

POCKET BOOKS, a division of Simon & Schuster Inc.
1230 Avenue of the Americas, New York, NY 10020

POCKET and colophon are registered trademarks of Simon & Schuster Inc.

Printed in the U.S.A.

Quality Printing and Binding by:
Berryville Graphics
P.O. Box 272
Berryville, VA 22611 U.S.A.

ISBN: 1-4165-8383-1
ISBN: 978-1-4165-8383-7

Author's Note

Yes, there really is a Kansas. But there really isn't a town of Rock Creek in a county named Hood, Kansas, or a hospital called the Kansas City Medical Center.

Acknowledgments

My heartfelt thanks to: Susan Dunlap and Sally Goldenbaum for their encouragement and writerly assistance; Larry King for critiquing the manuscript with a "reader's" eye; Nancy Short, R.N., for medical advice; Detective Herb Shuey of the Johnson County (Kansas) Sheriff's Department for police procedure; Kenneth I. Fligg, Jr., for legal advice about Cat's will; Jude Deveraux for properly landing Jenny's plane in Albuquerque; Judy Duhl and Edie Gibson for showing me around Winnetka, Illinois; and especially to Jim Link, associate director of the Ranch Management School at Texas Christian University, Fort Worth, Texas. If any errors of fact remain in this manuscript, it's my fault, not theirs.

Finally, special thanks to my parents, Clint and Mary Wolfe, for raising me in Kansas City, Missouri, to which I have finally, fictionally, come home.

This novel is dedicated,
with love and gratitude,
to my favorite cattle ranchers:
my mother-in-law, Eva Ann Pickard,
my father-in-law, Dr. Nicholas S. Pickard,
and especially to my husband,
Guy Pickard.

PART I

Crazy Little Women

Y ou know how the sound of thunder may first reach your ears from a long way off? So far away that it registers only as a rumble in your subconscious? There, for a moment, you felt something, an unease, but what was it? A truck going by on the highway, an airplane overhead? You shake your head, you go back to whatever you were doing. You shrug off the edginess that for an instant crept down your spine. The storm has to get closer and louder before you look up, startled: "Is that thunder I've been hearing?"

I didn't recognize the distant rumble when I heard it.

It came in the form of a long distance phone call on a Thursday, early one October afternoon. If I had glanced out my office window at that instant, would I have seen the cumulus clouds building into thunder-heads fifteen hundred miles west of me? If I had opened that window, would I have sensed a change in the weather, smelled rain in the air?

No, of course not. And anyway, I didn't.

"Port Frederick Civic Foundation," I answered.

"This is Dwight Brady. I'm calling from Kansas City, Missouri. I'm an attorney with the firm of Brady Buhl Freyer and Levinson."

I couldn't remember having ever received a call from anyone for any reason from Kansas City.

"Let me speak to your director."

His voice had a clipped, arrogant tone to which I immediately took umbrage. I clipped right back at him: "Speaking."

"Jennifer L. Cain?"

My, aren't we careful, I thought.

"Yes. What can I do for you, Mr. Brady?"

"Ms. Cain, I am instructed to inform you"—(Clouds building. Distant rumble. Look up, Jenny!)—"that one of my clients wants to make a bequest to your foundation."

I perked right up at that news. I was delighted to hear that some charitable soul had elected to will us the means to continue doing "good"—and perhaps even better—in our hometown. I thought fleetingly of the print gallery that one of my trustees wanted to fund at the museum. Maybe this new bequest would give us a boost in that direction. Would it be a direct transfer of funds? Five thousand, ten thousand, one hundred thousand? Probably not. Visions of stock certificates danced in my head.

"Well, how nice." I tried to sound grateful, but not greedy, always a bit tricky in my line of work. Most foundation funds derive from somebody's death, so it doesn't do to sound too eager. It is not considered seemly to shout, "Oh, boy, how soon do we get the moola?" Phrasing my curiosity as delicately as possible, I inquired, "Who's your client?"

"Cat Benet."

He pronounced it Ben-ay, so it sounded French. The stock certificates atomized into Seurat dots, which whirled into Van Gogh swirls. Impressionist paintings now danced in my head.

"And what is he, or she, leaving to our foundation?"

I pursed my mouth to utter a gracious *merci.*

"His cattle ranch."

2

"I beg your pardon?"

It nearly came out with a French accent: *pardon.*

"It's a thirteen-thousand-acre commercial cow/calf operation. Mostly Hereford, some black Angus and black baldies, a few longhorns."

At heart, I am a city girl. I understood scarcely a word of what this lawyer from Kansas City was saying. He might as well have been talking Chinese. Black angst? Black baldies? Was this some sort of racist slang? Ought I to be offended and to object?

"Where is this ranch, Mr. Brady?"

"In the Flint Hills of Kansas."

"*Kansas?*"

"It's pretty country."

"I'm sure it is." If you liked alfalfa. We'd been left some strange bequests before, but this beat them all. A ranch? In Kansas? What had I recently heard given as a standard for poor judgment—oh, yeah—poor judgment was going to Oz and preferring Kansas. "This is Massachusetts, Mr. Brady. We're a charitable foundation that serves an industrial seacoast town. We wouldn't recognize a cow if you ground it up and served it tartare. I hate to sound ungrateful, but what in the world are we going to do with a ranch in Kansas? We don't know anything about farming—"

"Ranching."

"Okay, we don't know anything about that, either. *Who* in heaven's name is this client of yours?"

"Charles W. Benet IV."

Now I got it: the name *was* French, the "Cat" probably being a bastardized pronunciation of *quatre,* the French word for "four."

"And who is he?"

"Cat Benet comes from a legendary Texas ranching family," Brady told me. "At one time, they had an empire of land, cattle, and mineral rights in Texas. He has liquidated those assets, however, and directed the money into trust funds to leave to his heirs. The only ranch he has left is the one you're getting, the Crossbones, that's the name of your ranch."

Our ranch.

"I should tell you, Ms. Cain, the Crossbones Ranch is worth a great deal of money."

I was still too stunned to be tactful. "How much?"

"Three to four million."

Omigod. "That's a lot of cows."

"Oh, that doesn't include livestock, equipment, or improvements. That's just the land. That's what you might get if you could sell it today." He paused. "Which you can't."

"Why not?" We would want to unload this white elephant (brown cow?) as quickly as possible and invest the proceeds in nice, quiet, trouble-free Treasury bonds. "Are land prices too low?"

"Well, they are depressed."

So was I going to be if I got stuck managing a cattle ranch. I had a feeling he was hedging.

"Is there more to it than that, Mr. Brady?"

"Well, the will forbids it."

"Forbids us from selling the farm?"

"Ranch."

"Ranch! Why the hell—excuse me—can't we sell it?"

"Because you have to provide lifetime employment for two of his ranch hands."

"What?"

"And I suppose I might as well tell you right now that the will forbids the heirs from so much as setting foot on the ranch or interfering with its management. If they disobey, they will forfeit their inheritances."

I was stuck on: *"What?"*

"And, to get their money, they'll have to agree not to contest the will. I'd rather let Mr. Benet explain this to you, himself. I have taken the liberty of making airline and hotel reservations for you this evening—"

"I beg your pardon?"

"—so that you can see Mr. Benet tomorrow."

"Mr. Brady, that's not possible."

"He's dying, Ms. Cain."

"I'm sorry to hear that." I meant it sincerely: the sooner this unknown benefactor died, the sooner we might have a cattle ranch on our incompetent hands. Given the state of American agriculture as I

4

knew it, which admittedly wasn't well, a farm was no prize even to people who knew how to run one. "What's the matter with him?"

"Lung cancer, emphysema, liver disease, you name it, he has it. He took a turn for the worse last night. His doctors told him he may not live out the week. That's why you have to come tonight."

I removed the receiver from my ear and stared at it in lieu of staring at him: *Are you crazy?* I was furious at the sheer gall of these people, expecting me to drop everything to fly off to sit at the deathbed of a total stranger. A totally crazy stranger who wrote impossible terms into his will and then tried to place me in charge of them. I put the receiver back to my ear and said, "No, Mr. Brady."

What I didn't say was that my husband and I had vacations beginning the next day. I could postpone mine if I had to, but I knew Geof couldn't change his. The police department, where he is a lieutenant, is not that flexible. We were invited to join friends for a week at sea on their 42-foot Cheoy Lee. No way was I going to Kansas City, instead.

"But what if he dies, Ms. Cain?"

I was annoyed enough to be crass. "Would that cancel the bequest?"

"No, but he needs to explain things to you."

"I'll figure it out."

"But—"

"Write me a letter, explaining everything in *great* detail," I said firmly, "and *then* I'll see if my trustees will approve a trip."

"I have already done that." The arrogance and confidence slid back into his voice. "Your trustees will get their copies this afternoon."

He refrained from adding: touché.

"You'll have to go, Jenny."

That's what Roy Leland said when he called later that afternoon. Roy is one of my bosses, the new president of the board of five trustees who run the Port Frederick Civic Foundation. He is also the chairman emeritus of United Grocers, a man accustomed to dealing with dock workers and yelling at people over heavy machinery.

"I've talked to the other trustees," Roy said. "We're unanimous: after reading Brady's letter, it is clear that this bequest is too large, and the circumstances are too unusual and too critical, to brook any delay." I had read the same letter, and I could not in good conscience disagree with him. "I'll get the lawyers to check the legality of the goddamned thing. In the meantime, we want you to get out there and meet this screwball Benet, find out why he picked us, take a look at his ranch. Investigate these two men we're supposed to employ for the rest of their lives. If that isn't the most goddamn ridiculous thing I ever heard—"

"Quentin Harlan," I interjected, "and Carlton Everett."

"Those two. Find out how the hell we're supposed to keep Benet's relatives off the ranch, and *why,* for Christ's sake. And Jenny . . ." Roy softened his tone a bit. "The trustees want you to know that they, uh, we are sorry about your vacation."

"Thanks, Roy."

"If it's any comfort," he said gruffly, "remember that everything's up-to-date in Kansas City."

"Right, if the date is 1950."

He laughed more heartily than I.

I closed my eyes and watched a Cheoy Lee sail off into the sunset without me. What was that other old song about Kansas City? Something about going to Kansas City, where they had some crazy little women . . .

And it looked as if I would soon be one.

2

Ms. Cain?"

Dwight Brady, who picked me up at the Kansas City International Airport at eleven-thirty that same Thursday night, was a tall, pale man, slim as a runner, with prematurely thinning blond hair. He looked about my age, which is to say early thirties. Brady wore wire-rimmed glasses, an immaculate pin-striped blue suit, white shirt, blue-and-red-striped tie, black wing-tipped shoes. At eleven-thirty at night. He managed not to raise an eyebrow at my rumpled sweat suit and tennis shoes.

"How was your flight?"

"Long." I had changed planes in Atlanta. "The airlines seem to believe that the straightest line between two points is a triangle."

He did not smile; neither did he apologize for the inconvenience he and his client were causing me. He only said, "I'll take those," and reached for my briefcase and my carry-on suit bag, which was the only luggage I'd brought. I did not intend to linger in the Midwest—I'd spend tomorrow in Kansas City, the weekend at the ranch, and then I'd take an early flight home on Monday so that I could catch up with my husband and our friends in Provincetown, before they sailed beyond my reach.

"My car's this way," Brady said.

In the few short steps it took us to walk from the gate to the curb, we established ourselves on a first-name basis. Dwight. Jenny. Outside, the smell of jet fuel made me feel sick to my stomach. I experienced a moment of intense longing for the salt air at home, and I recalled with resentment the weekend weather report for the entire northeastern seaboard: unseasonably warm and sunny, light winds, calm seas. In Kansas City, it was raining and chilly. I had been carrying a lined trench coat; now I put it on. Swallowing my nausea and disappointment, I stepped into his car while he held the door open.

"You're staying at the Hyatt Regency, Jenny."

His car, a late-model, silver Mercedes, was as immaculate as he was, but it had the black-tinted windows I usually associated with south Florida or drug dealers. Or is that redundant? From inside the car, the rainy night seemed even gloomier. Just before closing the door in my face, he said, "I'll pick you up at eight-thirty in the morning, after you've had breakfast at the hotel, and then I'll take you to KCMC to meet Mr. Benet."

"KayCeeEmCee?"

"Kansas City Medical Center."

Slam.

I thought about asking him if he'd like to set my alarm clock. *Try to think of him as efficient, rather than arrogant,* I suggested to myself as he placed my luggage in the trunk. Right. And try thinking of black as white. *Well then,* I countered as I heard him close the trunk lid, *try thinking of yourself as tired and cranky.*

Okay. That was easy.

What was not easy was making conversation with Dwight Brady on the way to the hotel. Every question about Mr. Benet, he deferred to "your own opinion when you meet him tomorrow." When I asked about the Crossbones Ranch, he said, "I don't know, I didn't handle his other business affairs, only the will." But when I inquired about the odd terms of the will, he said, with the only touch of irony I was ever to hear from him, "You'll have to ask Mr. Benet about that, and good luck to you. He is not a man who confides why he does things, he just does them. Or rather, I do what he tells me to do, like writing the will as he dictated it to me. He gives directions, not explanations."

A lot like his lawyer, I thought.

I finally gave up the effort, leaned back against the seat, and took a deep breath, inhaling the scent of leather upholstery. *Right now, I could be snuggled into a berth with my husband,* I thought, *nuzzling into his neck, smelling his Old Spice.* Weariness, horniness for Geof, regret for my days of lost vacation, seeped through my skin, down through my muscles, and deep into my bones, finally settling into a ball of self-pity in my gut. For some reason, I thought of my sister. "Poor Jenny," she would have mocked me if she had been there at that moment, "poor, poor Jenny."

The heater had warmed the car sufficiently for me to remove my trench coat, but I kept it wrapped comfortingly around me anyway.

Brady turned the radio on to a soft-rock station.

We drove (and drove and drove) through a monotonous landscape, passing clots of commercial buildings and packs of tract houses. There was no city in sight. *Maybe Kansas City is only a figment of a songwriter's imagination,* I mused. *That would be a relief. I could go home.* But then it appeared: a cluster of skyscrapers rising out of the plains like a three-dimensional cutout in a children's book.

"This is the Missouri River," Dwight said as he paid a toll on a bridge called Broadway. "That's the Kaw River flowing into it from Kansas." He pointed right. "That's Kansas City, Kansas, over there." He jerked his left thumb over his shoulder. "That's North Kansas City back there. And that's Kansas City, Missouri, straight ahead of us."

I hoped there wouldn't be a pop quiz on this later. It all looked the same to me as the rain washed the cities into a single watercolor painting in dark tones. The lights in the buildings looked like glitter tossed at the canvas.

The city we drove into, Kansas City, Missouri, was surprisingly hilly, even downtown. We drove along a deserted avenue called Grand, which was indeed, where tall, green streetlights glowed eerily in the rain. Dwight pulled into a circle drive in front of a Hyatt hotel with one of those revolving restaurants on top. This was unaccustomed luxury to me. On business trips I usually stayed at modest quarters the foundation could more easily afford. Our benefactor, Cat Benet, was paying for this trip. Through the front doors, I glimpsed a spacious lobby.

"Wait a minute." I nearly put my hand on Brady's arm. "Isn't this the hotel where all those people died when some skywalks fell down?"

"Yes," he said. "It happened right there in that lobby."

I remembered now: concrete balconies had come crashing down during a dance, killing more than one hundred people. Nausea rose in my throat again as I looked in. I felt as if Brady were asking me to sleep in a crypt. If I had been less tired, or less afraid of looking foolish and oversensitive, I might have asked him to take me somewhere else to stay.

"You don't need to go in with me, Dwight."

I did not want to make small talk in that lobby.

"Thanks, I do need to get home."

He retrieved my suit bag and briefcase from his trunk and handed them over to a bellman. Standing there in the circle drive, Brady and I bade each other polite good-nights.

As I followed the bellman to the reception desk, I picked my feet up quickly from the red tiles in the lobby. I felt as if I were walking disrespectfully on graves, although the shiver that crawled down my spine suggested someone walking on my own grave. It struck me as ghoulishly appropriate to stay in this hotel before meeting a dying man.

Such a comfort, that thought was.

I dreamed that night of falling from a great height. I jerked awake at four-thirty in the morning, just before my dream body hit bloodred tiles.

I couldn't get back to sleep, so I stayed up, propped against pillows, reading and rereading Brady's long letter regarding the bequest of the Crossbones Ranch, looking for clues as to reason or cause. Brady's letter detailed the assets we would inherit, including tractors and post-hole diggers (equipment, I assumed, not people), horses and barns, even natural-gas wells, which I could only hope might keep the ranch afloat during the inevitable lean years when cattle sold for less than it took to raise them.

It did not explain why the Benet family was barred from the ranch, though it did name them and list their addresses: there was an Alice Lawrence, a Merle Lawrence, a Lilly Ann Lawrence, and a Margaret Stewart, all from right here in Kansas City; there was an Anna Railing, Mark Railing, and a Suanna Railing, all of Winnetka, Illinois; there was a Marvalene Podhurst and a Daniel Zeller of San Diego, California; a Judy Benet and a Ladd Benet of Fort Worth, Texas; and a Frederica Sue Gomez of Santa Fe, New Mexico.

Neither did the letter say why Charles Whitepaw Benet IV, famous cowman from Texas, had picked the Civic Foundation of Port Frederick, Massachusetts, to receive his largess.

"That's the first question I'm going to ask you, Cat Benet, when I meet you in the morning," I said aloud, and then I noticed the light oozing in around the edges of the draperies.

It *was* morning. Friday morning.

3

At six-thirty, I ordered room service to avoid eating breakfast in the mezzanine café that overlooked the lobby where all those people had died. The waiter who brought up my rolls, coffee, and scrambled eggs told me the orchestra had been playing "Satin Doll" when tons of concrete buried the dancers. He'd been on duty that night. The lobby, he said, had been ankle deep in blood and water from burst mains.

He removed the silver cover from my plate of scrambled eggs. The aroma gagged me. I put the lid back on.

"What caused the disaster?" I asked him.

He shrugged cynically. "Nobody ever said, officially."

"But that's appalling!"

"Yeah, it was like being bombed and never finding out who was flying the airplane. It sure looked like a bomb hit." His hands on the silver coffeepot were steady, but the cuticles around his nails looked painfully raw, as if he picked at them all the time. "I still get nightmares. My psychiatrist says it's because wounds that don't close can't heal."

It was a thought I was to recall, ironically, in the days and maybe even years ahead. But for the moment, all I said was, "Why do you keep working here?"

He shrugged again. "It wasn't Hyatt's fault, we do know that. Anyway, who else'd want me, nerves shot to hell and all."

I signed a two-dollar tip onto the bill.

"Thanks," he said. "*Bon appétit.*"

After his story, I never did manage a bite of those eggs, but I consumed the whole pot of coffee before I checked out. Then I escaped from that haunted lobby and waited outside under the canopy for Dwight Brady to arrive. It was still raining, with some clearing to the west.

"Sleep well?" Brady inquired when I slid in.

"Like a log," I lied.

The Kansas City Medical Center was in a picturesque area of town that Brady called Old Westport. KCMC was one of those ancient red-brick hospitals—every big city has one—that has a vaguely sinister appearance because of its massive size and Victorian style of architecture. Reinforcing the idea that this was, indeed, a big city was the fact that there were three police cars parked in the emergency lot.

"So much firepower," I said. "It makes you wonder if they've brought in a suspect instead of a victim." Or worse yet, and I felt my chest constrict at the thought, maybe they'd brought in one of their own.

"What?" Brady gave me a funny look.

"I'm a policeman's wife. My mind runs to assaults instead of heart attacks."

He let me out before going off to find a parking space. When I stepped out of his car, it was right into a puddle. In revenge, I slammed the door harder than a Mercedes owner likes to have his door closed. I stepped up onto the sidewalk and looked down at my soaked leather shoes. They had started out the morning red; now they were deepening to wine. They had been very expensive. There in the rain, I sighed. *Welcome to Kansas City, Jenny. You crazy little woman, you.*

Inside, the hospital seemed almost cozy compared to the weather conditions outside. It was by now nearly nine A.M. (*Ten A.M. back home, and they're rounding Pebbly Point by now.*) I avoided the information desk, which was three-deep in inquiring people, and found my way to room 1080 by following signs.

Straight down the hall . . .

Through double swinging doors.

There was a nurses' station directly ahead of me.

The morning hospital bustle was in full swing: Orderlies wheeled groggy patients to surgery, nurse's aides stacked trays from breakfast, doctors were interminably paged on the loudspeaker, families huddled in waiting rooms, nurses conferred with one another over phones and charts and IVs. Being flat on your back was a very busy occupation in hospitals, as in certain other trades. I sensed an especially strong undercurrent of the excitement, disguised as tension, that electrifies the air in medical centers.

Nobody paid any attention to me until I turned right, at the nurses' station. Then I felt, not as if people were talking behind my back, but as if they had *stopped* talking. I almost stopped, myself, to look back, but I shrugged it off, attributing it to the fact that tall women of Swedish descent attract attention that's way out of proportion to our relative importance to the world.

I kept my line of vision focused on the room numbers.

1072. 1074, 1076. 1078.

1080, across the hall from the closed door of 1079, was just this side of a stairwell exit. A sign on the door said NO SMOKING. OXYGEN IN USE. So it was odd that the first thing I smelled when I pushed open the door was cigarette smoke.

A uniformed policewoman blocked my path.

"You can't come in."

"Why not?"

"Police business."

Over her shoulder I glimpsed two plainclothes detectives. How did I know that's what they were? I have lived with one, that's all I can tell you, and I knew.

"Isn't this Mr. Benet's room?"

"Step back, please."

"Wait," said one of the detectives, the one who wasn't smoking. He walked around the bed in the room and came toward me. "I'll go with you."

The policewoman moved aside to let the detective through, then quietly closed the door to the room again. But not before I'd had a chance to get a glimpse of a bed with rumpled sheets. A single pillow lay in the middle of the bed, and I was pretty sure that I saw an irregular circle of blood and mucus on the pillowcase.

4

My fingertips were suddenly ice cold, just as my palms began to sweat. My teeth started to chatter, so I clamped my jaw shut. When the door was firmly closed against the smells lingering in that room, I took a deep breath that was shakier than I had expected it to be. All I could think of for a moment was, *Damn, I knew I should never have come to Kansas City!* I leaned against the nearest wall to give my knees some extra support. (I don't have calluses from the other deaths I have seen; I have, like that waiter, jumpy nerves and nightmares, and undependable knees.)

The detective put out his hand for me to shake as he introduced himself. I took it as an act of kindness, frankly, feeling that he knew I needed steadying at that moment. I absorbed enough strength from his firm grasp to allow me to step away from the wall, and I told myself to be cool.

"I'm Detective Luis Canales of the Kansas City, Missouri, Police Department." He gave his name a Mexican pronunciation. Canales was about my height, five seven or eight, skinny, with an acne-scarred face, and eyelids that drooped so far over his brown eyes that they almost hid the intelligence that gleamed there. He had heavy bags under those eyes, an overnight growth of black beard, and his black suit was rumpled—all signs of a cop who has been summoned out of his bed. He wore a wedding ring. I felt a flash of sympathy for the wife who'd been asleep beside him and who was probably worrying about him right now. Canales had waited politely for me to open my mouth again. My silence forced him to ask, "Would you mind telling me who you are?"

I cleared my throat. I blurted, "A cop's wife."

"Really."

"You're homicide, aren't you?"

"What makes you think so?"

"That's what my husband used to be. Correct me if I'm wrong, Detective Canales, but it seems to me that the message here is that Cat Benet is dead, and that you think somebody smothered him with that pillow on the bed. Am I right?"

I was not showing off. I was anxious to know—*now*, immediately, at once—exactly what was going on, even if I had to put the words in his mouth in order to find out.

I had caused his eyebrows to raise.

"Are you a relative?"

"No."

"A friend?"

"No, you don't have to break the news gently."

He smiled slightly. "You have it all figured out anyway."

I must have flushed, because my face suddenly tingled, as if somebody had applied a hot washcloth to my cold skin.

"Tell you what," he said. "Let's try this again." It finally dawned on me that Canales was trying to take charge of the interview and that I was not making it easy for him. Me and my smart mouth. I hadn't meant to be obstructive. "I would appreciate it," he continued, "if you would tell me who you are, and why you're here." Dwight Brady had walked up beside us during this last exchange. Canales included him in the query. "You, too."

"Dwight," I said, "Benet's been murdered."

"Well, now wait a minute," Canales said.

"He's *what*, Jenny?"

"He's dead, Dwight, somebody killed him."

"Please, ma'am, slow down."

Dwight looked flummoxed. "*When? Why? Who killed him?*"

"My questions, exactly," Canales said wryly. "You took the words right out of my mouth."

In a nearby waiting room, which Canales emptied by the simple expedient of asking everyone else to leave, he took out a notebook and a ballpoint pen to make it official. We sat at a knotty pine table littered with open copies of *Family Circle* magazines from which recipes and coupons had been torn out. I understood that need for busy hands when you're feeling absolutely helpless.

"Jennifer Lynn Cain," I repeated for him. My own hands were under the table, busily rubbing themselves together.

"From *where* in Massachusetts?"

Dwight had already provided his name, rank, and serial number. Now, while he occupied himself with compulsively closing those magazines and putting them all in one neat pile, I answered the basic questions one at a time, exactly as Canales asked them. I knew better now than to try to anticipate him.

"Would you mind telling me your business with Mr. Benet?"

"He wanted to make a bequest to the foundation, and he had asked me, through Mr. Brady, to come to Kansas City today to discuss that bequest."

"Which is?"

"A ranch, a thirteen-thousand-acre cattle ranch in the Flint Hills. That's in Kansas."

He smiled slightly. "Yes. But it's a big area; where exactly?"

I looked at Dwight for help.

"Hood County," Dwight said. "Near Rock Creek."

"Okay." Canales nodded. "How long have you known Mr. Benet, Ms. Cain?"

"I didn't know him."

He didn't alter his expression. "No?"

"No, I realize this sounds strange, but I had never heard of him or his ranch until Mr. Brady called me yesterday to tell me about the bequest. And I don't know how Mr. Benet ever heard of me or of the foundation, either."

The detective glanced at Brady.

"I don't know, either," the lawyer said.

"How much is the ranch worth?" Canales asked him.

"Three to four million for the land."

Canales raised his eyebrows at that and looked back at me. There was an old acne scar in the middle of his left eyebrow, slicing it in two. "And you never heard of him before? You're saying he was leaving a ranch worth three or four million dollars—"

"Not counting livestock, buildings, or equipment," Dwight interjected. Bless his accurate little heart.

"Really?" Canales asked. "What would all that add to its value?"

Brady shrugged. "Half to three-quarter million."

Canales tugged at his left earlobe. Even it was pitted, as if somebody had repeatedly and unsuccessfully tried to pierce his ears. "I've got a car worth about fifteen hundred dollars, and I wouldn't even leave *it* to a stranger. So how come he was leaving all this to"—he shifted his gaze abruptly to me—"you."

"Not me," I corrected him. "The foundation."

"Still. How come?"

"I don't know how come," I said irritably. *Or even why.* Canales was extremely polite, but those dead-steady brown eyes made me nervous. How did a man with a complexion like that get so self-confident? Because, I thought, he had a sureness within, because he respected his own intelligence and integrity. Such a man, if he were to draw a wrong conclusion, I thought, such a man could get stuck to it. Canales's line of questioning frightened me, and that made me cranky. I tried not to let it show again.

"Other beneficiaries?" he asked Brady.

The lawyer nodded his head.

"He was a rich man?"

"Yes."

Canales thought about that for a moment, then he looked with great interest at me.

A beneficiary.

So to speak.

Of a wealthy, murdered man.

"Were you thinking of returning home now, Ms. Cain?"

"No. The original plan was for me to meet Mr. Benet this morning and to visit the ranch for a couple of days." I decided now was the time to make a stab at being totally cooperative. "Would you like the phone number there in case you need to reach me?"

Canales smiled at me. "Yes."

It was the small, private smile the hunter gives the deer when she helpfully steps out from the bushes, right into the line of sight of his rifle.

I blurted, "Are you going to tell us how he died?"

Canales shrugged. "You had it right the first time. He was smothered with his own pillow between the times the nurses looked in on him."

"What times were those?" I asked politely.

I expected him to ignore that question, and he did. But hell, it never hurts to ask! "He'd been sedated, but he must have awakened as it was happening. You saw the shape the sheets were in. It couldn't have been much of a struggle, as weak as he was, but he did try to fight off his assailant. When did you get into Kansas City, Ms. Cain?"

"Now wait," Brady started to object on my behalf. About time, I thought, but I stopped him anyway.

"I arrived at eleven-thirty last night. Dwight picked me up at the airport and took me to the Hyatt Regency Hotel where I stayed until he picked me up at eight-thirty this morning. I don't suppose there's anybody who can vouch for that, but nobody saw me leave, either. I mean, I *didn't* leave, and so nobody can say that I did . . ."

That hadn't come out right, at all.

I watched Canales scribble all that into his notepad, then click his ballpoint pen and put it back into his inside coat pocket.

On wicked impulse I said, "Don't you want to know where Mr. Brady was?"

Dwight stared at me.

"Mr. Brady will say that he went home directly from the Hyatt," Canales said. "He will say he stayed there until it was time for him to pick you up this morning. His wife will vouch for him, right, Mr. Brady?"

"It's true!" Dwight said.

"I never said otherwise," Canales murmured, and then, probably on an equally wicked impulse, he turned to me. "Anything else, Ms. Cain?"

I stared at my hands, shook my head.

Canales stood, and we followed his lead.

"Do either of you know a Carlton Everett and a Quentin Harlan?" he asked. "They're listed on Benet's admittance forms as the people to notify. They have a three-one-six area code and a rural post office box. I've tried calling, but all I get is a machine."

"Yes," Brady said. "They're Benet's hired hands."

"Funny he didn't list you, his lawyer."

"Quentin Harlan would have called me."

"Or a member of his family."

"What?" Brady said.

"I say it's funny he didn't list any family members. Parents living?"

"No."

"Was he married?"

"Divorced."

"Where is she?"

"The first one died some years ago; the other three live in Chicago, San Diego, and Santa Fe.

"*Four wives?*" I exclaimed.

"Four wives." Canales shook his head slightly and smiled a little. He took a card out of his breast pocket and passed it to Brady. "I would appreciate it if you would call and leave their names and addresses for me, as well as the names and addresses of any heirs and other beneficiaries." Canales took out a second card and handed it to me. "If you think of anything I should know." Then he put his notebook away. "Thank you."

It was clear that we were dismissed.

After Canales left the waiting room, I used the telephone there to place a credit card call back home to the president of the foundation. "Roy? It's Jenny."

"Well?" Roy Leland had such a booming voice he could practically have raised his window and hollered to me from Port Frederick, dispensing with AT&T altogether. "Is it legit, are we getting a ranch?"

"I'm afraid we've already got it, Roy. Our benefactor is dead, he's been murdered."

"No!" He had the forbearance not to refer to me as Typhoid Jenny, but he did say, with a heavy-handed attempt at macabre humor, "Well, if that isn't the most discouraging word I've ever heard. What happened?"

I told him the little I knew, then added, "I think I'd better keep my appointment at the ranch, don't you?"

"Hell, yes. I'll call the other trustees and then get back to you." I did not tell Roy I was a potential suspect, because I felt that would sound so absurd to that solid, practical man that he'd only think me paranoid. Well, all right, that's not entirely the truth; the truth is that my bosses have put up with a lot from me, and I just couldn't bear the idea of telling them, "Guess what, your executive director is now suspected of a murder in Kansas City." I liked my job; I didn't want them to pass it on to somebody with a slightly less "exciting" life than mine. I'd tell him later, if I had to. Which I certainly hoped I wouldn't. Therefore, Roy's only instructions were: "Call me back tonight, Jenny."

"I will."

The person I really wanted to call was on a boat in Cape Cod Bay. It was a comfort to know I'd be catching up with him in three days.

I looked up at Dwight, who had been standing in the doorway with his hands in his pockets, pretending not to eavesdrop as he waited for me.

"Okay," I said, "now we can go."

He led me past room 1080 and on to the stairwell, where we walked down one flight, then traversed a long corridor of hospital offices to a covered parking lot. (All of those office doors would have been closed last night, I thought, with nobody watching who came and went by that staircase.) I probably should have apologized to Brady for my impertinent question to Canales. He certainly should have apologized to me for not leaping to my defense any sooner, or any more strongly. But neither of us said a thing. I don't know how he was feeling, but I was scared and furious. We walked the long corridor silently, but I turned on him the minute we reached the privacy of his Mercedes.

"Why didn't you tell him about the family feud, Dwight?"

"What family feud, Jenny?"

"The one that prompted Benet to bar his family from the ranch, *Dwight!* That one! It couldn't have anything to do with the fact that the old reprobate was married four times, could it?"

"I don't know any more than you do," he claimed as he backed out of the parking lane. "And he wasn't all that old, fifty-four. He told me he got married and had his first child when he was only seventeen." He straightened the tires and put the Mercedes in forward gear. "May I point out, it is not my job to create murder suspects for Canales."

"It's not your business to help convict me, either!"

"I think you're exaggerating my role."

He turned left onto a two-lane street, narrowly missing a taxi coming from the right. The cabdriver used his horn to express his opinion of Brady's driving. Through the Mercedes's tinted windows, the rainy day looked like a bleak evening.

"Jenny." There was feigned patience in Brady's voice. "The police will see Benet's will. They'll draw their own conclusions. It's ridiculous for you to think you're a suspect."

"I am, even if indirectly, a beneficiary to a murdered man's will, Dwight. I just happened to come into town the very night he is killed. The fact that he was so weak means that even if he struggled, he still could have been killed by almost anybody, big or small, male or female. And I haven't a hair of an alibi for the probable time of his death. The only thing I'm missing is a few feathers from that pillow stuck to my suit! If the police don't suspect me, they're asleep!"

"I have a favor to ask," he said.

I stared at him. "What exquisite timing you have."

"One of Mr. Benet's families lives here in town. I'd like to drive by their house and tell them the news of his death, personally, before we take you to the airport."

"And you want me to go with you?"

"It's on the way. I'd appreciate it."

"I thought you didn't know these people."

"I don't. But I know they're here, and it seems only considerate."

It also seemed to me like a way for an ambitious young lawyer to ingratiate himself with potential clients.

"You're a case, Dwight, you know that?"

"That's more or less what my wife says."

"Poor woman," I muttered as I leaned my head against the seat rest. "When she asks you to take out the trash, do you tell her it's not your business to empty other people's refuse?"

The look he gave me at that moment could have peeled the tint off his windows. *Good Jenny,* I thought, *make an enemy out of the only friend you have in Kansas City. Nice going. Hang yourself.*

I stroked the leather upholstery of the seat. "This is really a beautiful car, Dwight."

5

We drove through the rain into the Country Club Plaza, an area of streets lined with chi-chi restaurants and luxury stores. Brady called it the "first shopping center in the country," a claim to fame I wasn't sure I would care to make. This project looked as if it had been imported brick by brick from Seville, however, and was very pretty. The hands of a huge clock on a Moorish watchtower pointed to ten o'clock. We then proceeded west along a creek where the water rushed fast and deep along a cement bed, then south, up Ward Parkway, a winding boulevard lined with museum-sized mansions.

Brady pulled into a circle drive in front of one of them and parked parallel to its front door. I looked up at the immense brick house and thought: Either they still keep slaves in Kansas City, or else they have some horribly overworked housewives.

The woman who answered our ring was no maid.

"Mrs. Lawrence?" Dwight inquired.

"Yes, I'm Alice Lawrence."

"I am an attorney for your father," Brady said, and I watched her elegant eyebrows rise. She wore the most beautiful red suit I'd ever seen on anybody outside of Nancy Reagan. She was not tiny like the former First Lady, however, and I decided the suit must have been custom-tailored to fit her matronly figure that well. "My name is Dwight Brady, of Brady Buhl Freyer and Levinson."

"Oh, yes?" she said coolly. "I know the Freyers."

I nearly smiled—in Port Frederick, everybody knows everybody else, too.

"I have been handling your father's will, Mrs. Lawrence," Brady told her in deferential tones he had never used with me. "We have just come from KCMC where he has been a patient for the past few weeks. I am extremely sorry to tell you that your father passed away this morning. I felt someone should tell you personally."

"Oh, my." She pressed her right hand between her breasts. "Oh, my goodness. What a thing to hear right out of the blue, and from a stranger." She took a breath, composed herself. "I'm sorry, but why should I take your word for this, Mr.—"

"Brady." He pulled out his wallet and attempted to give her a business card. "Dwight Brady. I certainly don't blame you for wanting to be sure. If you'll call our office, Mr. Freyer will vouch for me."

"I'll find the number," she said.

And closed the door in our faces.

I refrained from looking at Brady, since I was taking a certain amount of pleasure from the reception he was getting. Which was a good thing, since the weather afforded me no pleasure at all. Luckily, we stood under a copper overhang, so only our backs got rained on. Water ran down the tops of the heels of my shoes, spreading under the soles of my feet. I looked at my watch. *Ten-fifteen. Eleven-fifteen back home, and they'll be barefoot, in jeans and T-shirts, deciding whether to eat on the boat or to tie up somewhere for lunch.* It seemed a longer time than it probably was before she returned.

"You can hardly blame her," Brady said.

"No, no, of course not."

Finally, the door opened again.

"Come in, please."

We walked into a foyer that looked like a wing of a thirteenth-century museum. Swords and tapestries adorned the stucco walls, and a full suit of armor stood in a corner. Mrs. Lawrence took our dripping trench coats from us and hung them on pegs. Since I couldn't very well ask her to hang my shoes there, too, I squished my way into the living room behind her, hoping Dwight Brady's black socks were as soaked as my hose. Walking across the tiled floor, we sounded like three drummers out of sync, but all was silence when we crossed onto the wall-to-wall carpeting in the living room.

There were two people sitting there, a man and a woman, who were looking up expectantly as if they knew we were coming in. As, how could they not, considering how we had clattered across the tiles? A lush arrangement of fresh flowers, mostly white orchids, stood in a black vase on a brass-topped table between them and us. I could smell the orchids from the doorway, that's how profuse they were.

"This is my younger sister, Margaret Stewart," Alice Lawrence said, "and my husband, Merle Lawrence. And this is Mr. Brady and his secretary, Miss . . . ?"

"Cain," I said. "Jenny Cain. I am the director of the Port Frederick, Massachusetts, Civic Foundation, to which your father has bequeathed the Crossbones Ranch."

"Oh, forgive me." Alice did not look particularly contrite, although she had warmed up since receiving Dwight's bona fides. "Is that one of the Texas ranches?"

"No, it's in Kansas."

"Kansas!" She glanced across at her husband, then at her sister. "I didn't know Father owned a ranch so close to us. Won't you both sit down?"

We did, in chairs upholstered in silk.

The younger sister, Margaret, was prettier and thinner than Alice, with the fine-boned features of a lady in a tapestry. Her blond hair was twisted into a thick French braid; she wore a creamy-white, full-skirted wool dress, with creamy hosiery and matching high heels. If I had been a man, I suspect I would have thought she looked good enough to lick. The husband, Merle Lawrence, appeared to be older than the two women. He had the long-boned, aristocratic, hollow-eyed look of Franklin D. Roosevelt. In fact, he did sit in a wheelchair with a plaid wool blanket draped over his knees, continuously stroking a beautiful Burmese cat. His hand, with its long, graceful fingers, nearly covered the cat from ears to tail.

"What a lovely cat," I murmured, to break the ice.

"Thank you," he said.

Margaret smiled, quick and catlike herself.

"Now," Alice said. "Please do tell us everything."

She was probably Cat Benet's first child, I thought, which meant she was only about thirty-seven, but she acted and dressed older; they all did, in fact, as if their wealth had brought them, like some investment bonds, early maturity.

Brady leaned forward, clasped his hands sincerely between his knees and said, "Your father died early this morning at the Kansas City Medical Center. He had been a patient there for several weeks."

In the moment of silence that followed, I waited for him to tell the rest of the story.

Merle's hand lay still on the cat's back.

"Dead?" Margaret said. "At KCMC?"

"My goodness." Alice frowned. "You'd think he could have let us know he was here in town! I hardly know what to say about this." She seemed to force a smile for my benefit. "You must think we're very coldhearted, Miss Cain, but you see, we hardly knew him, did we, Meg?"

The sister shook her lovely head.

Merle resumed stroking the cat.

"We weren't Father's only family, you see," Alice continued. "We were his first family. Our late mother, Emily, was his first wife, that is. But he does have—had—one other family and two wives with whom he had no children. Four families in all, I suppose you'd say. He has four children that we know of, and I'm ashamed to admit to you that I don't know how many grandchildren, besides my own Lilly Ann. We are not in touch with the others, you see."

"Father was a character," Margaret put in.

"Father left Mother when we were toddlers," Alice said. "But his parents, our grandparents, made sure that he didn't leave her destitute."

Margaret waved her right hand gracefully as if to indicate the sumptuous room and smiled her quick cat-smile. "As you can plainly see," she said.

"Oh, yes," Alice agreed. She was evidently the earnest one, while Margaret played the witty beauty. Merle, meanwhile, contributed nothing to this, but only sat watching us, smiling pleasantly and petting the Burmese. I had never seen such a placid cat. "And later, when Father had money of his own, he was always quite liberal with us. Father was a fair man," Alice added, "and a generous one. But he had a wandering soul."

Her sister smiled. "Some might say philandering."

"Mother never said so," Alice chided her.

"That's true," Margaret conceded. "I was joking. Mother always said he didn't leave her for another woman. He left her, and *then* he found another woman."

Alice laughed at that, but it sounded hollow.

"And then another and another," her sister added with a mischievous air.

The man in the wheelchair finally spoke, in a gently cynical tone. "Well, he could afford to, couldn't he?"

Margaret smiled.

Alice nodded. "He was fortunate to be in ranching when he was. There aren't many men like him anymore."

"No," Margaret said, "a rancher today would have a hard time keeping his ranch, much less four wives."

We all chuckled politely.

Margaret smiled her cat-smile at me again before saying, "Especially if he had a foundation to support, as well."

"I beg your pardon?" I said.

It had come so quickly, her little knife had sliced through the sweet cake of courtesy so cleanly, I had nearly missed feeling the wound.

"You're the director of a foundation that's getting one of Father's ranches, you said. We have our own family foundation, Ms. Cain."

"Meg," Alice's tone was soft, warning.

"No, I didn't know that," I said.

Merle scratched the cat's head so roughly I was amazed the Burmese didn't scratch him back, or at least jump down from his lap.

"Our foundation was established a generation ago by our grandparents." Margaret walked over to a bookcase and pulled out a volume, then handed it to me. I looked at the title: *Barons of Branchwater*. "You may have this book. It will tell you the long and illustrious history of the family with whom you are dealing. Our foundation—you may have heard of it—is the Longhorn Foundation."

I had. It was enormously rich, one of the big ones.

"I am naturally wondering," she said in the same wryly courteous tones, "why Father would choose to leave a ranch to a small . . . obscure . . . unimportant foundation—"

"Meg!" Alice pleaded.

"—like yours, rather than to the Longhorn . . ."

Margaret's voice trailed off gently, a parody of sweet courtesy. I noticed that there were two battle-axes crossed on the wall behind her. How appropriate. Alice avoided my eyes, but Margaret didn't, not for a second, and neither did Merle Lawrence. Dwight Brady examined the tips of his shoes. I wanted to trod on those shoes, jump up and down on them, stomp them into sandals. The man was developing a very bad habit of getting me into nasty situations, then not lifting a hand to help me out of them.

I knew what was going on here because I'd run across it before—these wealthy people didn't begrudge the ranch for their personal gain, they begrudged the power and control that comes with having ever-more-vast sums of money to dispense as you please through your own foundation. Altruism breeds its own form of greed when donors start competing to give the most and the best.

I waited them out.

Alice finally looked up, although she was a little pale, and so did Brady. Now they were all gazing at me with looks of polite expectation. As if Margaret hadn't just gratuitously insulted me.

"Beats me," I said finally.

"Ah," the lovely Margaret murmured. I glimpsed the disbelief in her light blue eyes a moment before she glanced away from me. I had the feeling of being something distasteful from which she averted her gaze.

"Where is this ranch that Father left your foundation?"

"In the Flint Hills."

"How large is it?"

"Thirteen thousand acres."

She glanced over at Brady. "What is that worth?"

"Three to four million," I said. I was getting quite good at reeling off the essential facts of the inheritance by now. "Not including livestock, equipment, and, uh, improvements."

"And I suppose," she said, "that you think we're just going to let this ranch, this last remaining ranch, go out of the family."

"Yes," I said, "because your father's will says you each have to sign an agreement that you will not contest the will or interfere with the management of the ranch, or even attempt to go onto the ranch."

She straightened her spine. "Or what?"

"Or you lose your inheritances."

They all looked over at Brady, who nodded.

I said, "I'm curious about something myself."

"Uh, Jenny," Brady said.

"Were all of you at home last night?"

"Jenny!"

"Were you?" I insisted.

Merle stroked the cat. "Yes, of course. Why?"

"That's good." I smiled at him. "You'll want to be sure to tell the police that, when they investigate your father's murder."

They stared at me.

I stared back.

"Mr. Brady?" Alice asked.

"That's true," he admitted. "I was getting to that."

It was while Dwight was explaining to them about the murder that I realized that the cat on Merle Lawrence's lap wasn't a real one. At least, not a live one. It was either an amazingly lifelike stuffed toy or an actual stuffed animal. I hadn't felt such a chill go down my spine in a very long time.

At the end of Brady's recital, Alice, exuding false briskness, got up from the chair where she had been sitting. "We've been so rude! We haven't offered you a thing to drink. Miss Cain? Mr. Brady? A Bloody Mary perhaps? Tea? Would you like some coffee?"

"Coffee," I said.

"Good! Why don't you come out to the kitchen with me, and I'll show you more of the house, Miss Cain."

Clearly, she was also getting me out of the room so the other two could talk to the lawyer behind my back, probably about their inheritances. Well, that was fine with me. When they talked to my front, I got altogether unnerved. A nest of cobras, they were, mesmerizing their victim with politeness and then spitting their poison. And what the hell was the story on that cat, anyway?

I slipped the book into my briefcase.

My tour of the mansion consisted of following Alice through a dining room that featured a great carved oak table from which I could imagine drunken lords tossing gnawed, roasted deer legs to hungry serfs and slavering hounds. From behind her, I admired the cut of Alice's suit. This was definitely not my idea of a cowboy's daughter. I had expected something more along the lines of a country-western singer in tight jeans and rhinestones.

And found her, minus the rhinestones, sitting at a counter in the kitchen.

L illy Ann!"
Alice clapped her hands at the sight of the girl, who flinched at the clap but didn't look up. I thought that took a bit of highly disciplined disregard. Was the woman given to clapping for attention? Was the girl given to ignoring it? She sipped from a can of Dr Pepper and leafed through a magazine, acting as if she had not heard a thing. In front of her, there was an open sack of potato chips and a waxy carton of dip. I was suddenly so hungry I wanted to scoop my. bare fingers into that container.

"I'm glad you're here, darling," Alice said.

The girl raised her glance, but not her head.

I lusted for those potato chips.

"Hello, Mother."

She flicked her gaze at me before returning it to the magazine. Her face revealed her to be a little older than her slim body suggested, maybe eighteen or nineteen. Here at last was someone in blue jeans and a cotton shirt, even cowboy boots and a fringed suede jacket. Her blond hair was pulled severely back into a ponytail that was secured with a rubber band at the nape of her neck. She wore no makeup that I could detect. But she didn't need any, having (as John D. MacDonald might have titled one of his mysteries) a tan and lovely skin. The expression in her eyes—which were blue and large, like her mother's and aunt's—matched the sulky look of her mouth.

"Dear, this is Jennifer Cain. Miss Cain, I'd like you to meet my only child, Lilly Ann."

"Hello," I said, dragging my glance up from the dip.

"Hi."

If there ever was a girl who didn't look like a Lilly Ann, this was the one. She should have been a Kate or a Carla, names as lean and abrupt as she was.

"Lilly?" Alice waited until the girl was forced to look at her. "Lilly, your grandfather Benet died last night, dear."

The girl dropped her gaze again.

"He bequeathed a ranch in Kansas to a foundation that Miss Cain runs, back in Massachusetts."

This time when the girl glanced up, I saw a glimmer of real interest in her eyes. "My grandpa had a ranch in Kansas? Can I go there?"

I regretted what I had to say next.

"I'm sorry, but your grandfather's will bars his family from the ranch." This was embarrassing to say. "If you so much as set a foot onto it, you'll lose your inheritance."

Lilly glanced angrily at her mother before quickly looking down again.

"I'm going to the ranch when I leave here," I said, trying to cover the awkward moment. All the while, I was inching closer to the potato chips. "Maybe I'll find out what that's all about."

"It's the strangest thing I ever heard," Alice said, and her amazement sounded genuine. "Why would Father do this?"

"Because you didn't give a shit," Lilly muttered.

"Lilly! Don't you have a hair appointment . . . dear?"

"I'm not going."

"Oh, Lilly." Her mother's voice softened. "Please."

The girl turned a page.

I sneaked a potato chip and ate it.

"My hair's clean," she said.

"But you will look ridiculous in that ponytail and a ball gown." Alice turned to look at me, catching me in midcrunch. "She's 'coming out' tonight at a benefit ball. Our Lilly's a debutante this season."

"Lilly's a hypocrite this season."

"You're not, darling."

The girl looked up. "I am, Mother!" She slammed the magazine shut. "I hate it!"

"But it's such a lovely evening, dear."

"Yeah. All the white girls in our white dresses."

At that, I expected her mother to say, "That's enough, Lilly Ann." But she surprised me. She reached over to gently touch her daughter's fist, though she drew back quickly before she could be rebuffed. "It's too late now, darling. You can't expect years of tradition to change between now and the time the ball starts tonight. You've already accepted this responsibility, Lilly, months ago . . ."

"You accepted it for me!"

"You've been to the parties, now all that's left is the ball, dear. Just this one more night and then it's over and you can go back to riding your horses. Lilly, you can't let your escort down, really you can't, and besides, his poor mother would kill me. Please, darling. Try to do this with some grace, if not for me, then for your father."

"That's a great guilt trip you're laying on me, Mother."

Alice's smile held a touch of guilt. "I know, I probably should have been Jewish."

"Mother!"

"Oh, Lilly." She sighed. "Does everything I say offend you? I wish you were more . . . flexible."

"*Me* inflexible! I'm not the one who—"

But now her mother did stop the argument. "Lilly, it's too late for this, and I'm sure we re making Miss Cain feel quite uncomfortable."

No, just ravenous.

"I feel a lot worse than uncomfortable, Mother, I feel—"

"You have a hair appointment, dear."

The girl clamped her lips together in a ferocious scowl. She slid off her stool, stomped over to the refrigerator, and jerked open the door with such force that I thought she might pull the whole thing down on top of her. There were covered dishes inside that I wanted to grab and consume whole. I cursed myself for being such an oversensitive twit and not eating my breakfast eggs. Lilly extracted another Dr Pepper, butted the door closed, and wrenched open the can with one angry pull. The aluminum tab fell onto the carpet with a soft tap. Without another word, she walked out of the kitchen and out of the house, via a back door. The suede fringes on her jacket swung angrily.

"I apologize," Alice said to me.

For which offense, I wondered. I grabbed a handful of chips and mumbled something. She bent to pick up the tab and put it into a wastebasket, and I took that opportunity to shovel some dip. She poured a cup of coffee and handed it to me. Since my right hand now had potato chips stuck to it, I had to take the coffee cup and saucer in my left. Every time I raised the cup to my lips, bits of chip snowed to the kitchen floor.

Alice poured herself a cup, too.

"Cream or sugar?"

"No, thanks."

"Sometimes I think my daughter is a throwback to my father." From Alice's sigh, I gathered she considered that a splintery cross to bear. "She wants to be a large-animal vet, of all things. You can't imagine what that does to her fingernails. The child looks and smells like a stable hand, most of the time. Lord." She stopped abruptly, looking slightly horrified. "I hope she gets a manicure while she's at the beauty shop."

The little scene had given me an edge, and I took it.

"Mrs. Lawrence," I began, "I didn't know your father. I didn't know anything about this bequest until Dwight Brady called me yesterday. I can't imagine why your father gave the ranch to our foundation instead of to yours, and I swear I don't know what we're going to do with it now that we've got it!"

She seemed to bite back a smile, a real one.

"I believe you," she said. I thought I heard a faint emphasis on the first word. "That's how I feel about ranches, too."

"Why do *you* think he did it?"

Her smile instantly metamorphosed into the one she kept for company. "I can't imagine." She set her cup and saucer on the counter and turned away, as if to lead me back into the living room, and so I followed. Behind her back, I rubbed my hands together remorselessly; where I walked, potato chips crunched under my shoes. Too late, it occurred to me that it wouldn't be Margaret who had to vacuum, it would be a maid. We reached the foyer just as sweet Margaret was pushing Merle Lawrence's wheelchair clatteringly over the tiles to the front door. They were accompanied by Dwight Brady, who handed me my briefcase.

Merle still had the stuffed cat on his lap.

Well, I thought, maybe he felt about cats as the settlers in these parts once felt about Indians, as in, the only good Indian is a—

I finally recognized in myself the signs of incipient giddiness, a prelude to hysteria.

"Good-bye," I said firmly to them.

They smiled and thanked me for coming. They didn't ask me to come back. I was more than glad to oblige. Brady seemed to want to linger under the copper overhang to exchange more conversation (probably offering a cut rate on *their* wills, I thought), so I excused myself and scuttled back down the front walk through the drizzle to his car.

I opened the door and got in.

"*Hi.*"

7

The girl, Lilly Ann, was in the driver's seat.

"My God! You startled me! I do not need any more surprises today!"

"I'm sorry," she whispered.

Her legs were pressed together at the knees and she was clutching her own arms.

I took a deep breath. "You scared the *hell* out of me."

"I want to go to the ranch with you," she said in a stronger voice. "I won't get in your way, really."

The fright she gave me was a good thing—like shock treatment on a mental patient, it had the reverse effect one might expect, calming me down, cooling me out.

"Didn't you hear what I said about the terms of the will, Lilly?"

"I know! I won't go on it! I just want to see it."

"But what about the ball tonight?"

"I'm not going. Please!"

I gazed at her for a moment, observing how pretty she was and how unhappy she looked. There was nothing artificial about this girl, either in appearance or attitude. Lilly Ann Lawrence displayed her feelings all over her face, and she blurted them uncensored from her mouth. I felt sorry for her, but I couldn't help her.

"No," I said. "For one thing, it would be incredibly unethical of me to encourage you to violate the will. Furthermore, if you don't go to the ball tonight, that's your business. But it's none of mine. I'm not going to put myself in the middle of a fight between you and your parents. So, I'm sorry, but no."

"Thanks a *lot.*"

She got out of the car, then ran with swift, scissoring steps across the street. Lilly Ann was already halfway down the block—her head down, her shoulders hunched, her hands stuffed in the pockets of her jacket—when Brady slid into the seat she had just vacated.

"Where are we going now?" I asked him.

"Downtown Airport. Sorry we can't stop for lunch, but this visit put us behind schedule, and the pilot will be waiting. That was Benet's granddaughter, wasn't it? What'd she want?"

"She wanted—to look at your car."

"More boy than girl, that girl."

I thought that appraisal grossly unfair, but I didn't say so. I didn't want to argue with him about her. I didn't want that much more involvement with these strangers. Still, I had ample reason to be curious about them.

"Dwight, what do you think happened to Merle Lawrence?"

He glanced in the rearview mirror before pulling away from the curb. "The wheelchair? I've heard that was a horseback-riding accident."

"Is Margaret Stewart married?"

"She told me she's a widow, that her husband died in a hunting accident a long time ago. No children. Hard luck all around, I guess."

"I guess. She lives here, too?"

"You might say so. On the third floor. Margaret has her own suite up there."

Margaret? "A close family."

"Evidently."

The rain accompanied us down the Southwest Trafficway, back across the Broadway Bridge to a little airport just across the Missouri River from the downtown skyscrapers. With the weather conditions as bad as they were, I thought maybe the plane wouldn't be able to fly, but Brady told me there was enough clearance and the pilot was instrument rated.

"I guess you think that's reassuring," I said.

He actually smiled. "Afraid to fly?"

"Not in jets, but I don't know about small planes. I guess it's like the old joke—I'm not afraid to fly, I'm afraid to crash."

"You won't."

"Then why aren't you going, too?"

"I can't, Jenny. I have to get those names and addresses to Detective Canales. Besides, you won't need me. I don't know enough about ranching to fill one side of a legal pad. You'll learn everything you need to know from the people down there. They're the cowmen, not I."

"I feel as if I'm flying to the moon, Dwight," I confessed. "This whole thing is so alien to me."

"I sympathize." He didn't look sympathetic, he looked smug. "Believe me, if you scratch a Kansas Citian, you do not find a farmer underneath. All it takes is one generation away from the farm, and we forget everything our grandparents ever knew. I hardly know the front end of a cow from the back."

"I'll send pictures."

He smiled again. It occurred to me that Dwight might be as glad to be rid of my company as I was to be leaving his.

Brady drove the Mercedes right up to the wing of a single-engine, propeller-driven aircraft. It looked like a toy that ought to be connected to a remote-control device operated by a ten-year-old boy on the ground. To board, I'd have to climb up the wing to a little door on the passenger's side. The pilot, a heavy-set blond man wearing a dark windbreaker, was already in his seat, one of only four in the plane. From the ground, I could see him reading a thick notebook that looked like an instruction manual of some sort; I hoped the title was not "How to Fly This Thing."

Brady opened his car door, but then paused with one foot on the pavement. "This area you're going to visit, the Flint Hills, it's not like the rest of Kansas. It's more like some parts of Wyoming or Montana, real ranchland. Hardly any farming at all. Most people have never heard of it, much less ever been there. I didn't know much about it, myself, until I met Mr. Benet."

Ol' Dwight was certainly turning loquacious, I mused, like somebody who was getting a load transferred from his shoulders to somebody else's: *mine.*

The pilot was talking into a tiny microphone that was attached to headphones, and he merely nodded at me when I climbed in. Suddenly, I thought of something. I leaned out and called down the wing, shouting over the whiny vroom of the engine, *"Dwight, will there be a funeral?"*

He shook his head. *"No, the will forbids it."*

Of course, I thought, shaking my own head as I pulled myself back inside the cockpit, why should anything about this bequest be standard operating procedure?

"Jenny?"

I leaned back out again. Dwight had his hands cupped to his mouth. *"You may have to tell the men about Mr. Benet!"*

Just as I opened my mouth to echo Lilly Ann's *Thanks a lot!* the pilot leaned over me. I jumped back in my seat, startled, until I figured out what he was up to, which was merely to close my door. "Excuse me," he said. He flipped the door handle up until it clicked twice, and then he belted me into the seat. A few minutes later, as we taxied down the runway, I looked back, expecting to wave to Dwight Brady, but all I saw was the red of his taillights in the rain. I didn't even like him, but now I felt bereft, as if he had been my last link to civilization as I knew it. A ranch, for God's sake. What the hell was I doing, going to a cattle ranch in the middle of Kansas. I sighed and turned around in my seat, only to gasp with horror. We were taking off, heading straight into those tall buildings downtown. I closed my eyes, convinced this was the last minute of life (as I knew it). When I opened my eyes again, we had swung safely to the west and were now flying over river bottoms.

For the next hour, we flew on instruments at 8,000 feet over landscape that all looked the same to me when I got glimpses of it through the clouds: flat, gray, and wet. But then the weather and the land both began to change: we passed the back edge of the front, so to speak, and the sun appeared, shining down on rolling terrain. On top of the hills, there were gray circles that looked like salt on the rim of enormous margaritas. When I asked the pilot what they were, he said, "Limestone." Ah. Gray rocks. As in Flint Hills. I saw brown dots that I assumed to be cows. No trees. Or, practically no trees. Water holes. In fact, lots of water standing in pastures where the rain had passed through. A barn here and there. Even fewer houses. As we descended, I saw long, long fence lines.

It looked like no country I'd ever seen before.

Suddenly, I felt as if I were flying into another century, the one with sod houses, covered wagons, and cowboys.

We landed in a pasture and rolled bumpily down a dirt strip to a stop a few yards from a barbed-wire fence. I breathed again and looked around. Straight ahead was a metal airplane hangar with a tin roof. Farther left, there was a green pickup truck with a cowboy standing beside it, and to our right were a few red cows. That was it.

Welcome to the real Kansas, I thought.

Also: *What* am *I doing here?*

The pilot got me unharnessed and unloaded. By the time I started trudging across the damp grass toward the truck, the plane was already rolling back down the dirt strip for takeoff. I put down my bags long enough to wave when he lifted off, and he waggled his wings in reply.

My heels were sinking into mud, but I didn't care, and it wasn't because my red leather heels were already ruined. I felt exhilarated. Maybe it was the simple rush of joy at being alive, maybe it was the country air that smelled so fresh, so pungent after the rain. At any rate, it was with some vigor that I trudged on toward the truck. The cowboy—a real one in boots, blue jeans, a checkered shirt, a yellow slicker, and a cowboy hat—met me halfway there.

PART II

Home on the Range

Hi, there." The cowboy stuck out his left hand for my bags and his right hand for me to shake. The hand was hard and callused, the handshake firm.

"Hello. I'm Jenny Cain."

"Well, I hope so." He grinned, producing a faceful of deep lines in his tanned skin. "I'd be mighty surprised if you weren't. I'm Quentin Harlan. Pleased to meet you, Ms. Cain. This all you brought with you?"

"Yes, that's all, I won't be staying long."

"Our loss."

"I guess you've heard from the hospital?"

"Got a call from a detective name of Canales."

Like the detective himself, Harlan gave the name its rich Mexican pronunciation: Cahnahlays. *Thank goodness he knows,* I thought, *so I won't have to break the news to him.* "I'm sorry about your boss."

"Thanks. The son of a bitch who killed him is going to be a hell of a lot sorrier."

Harlan hoisted my suit bag and briefcase and casually tossed them over the side into the bed of the pickup truck. I winced, although I didn't hear the expensive leather come to any harm.

"Smooth flight?"

"Yes."

"Well, I'm sorry, but this half-ton limo ain't likely to give you such a nice ride." He opened the door of the truck for me and I did my best to climb in without hiking my skirt up to my waist. One of the first things I was going to have to do now that I was officially in the country, I decided, was to change my clothes. As Quentin Harlan settled himself behind the wheel, he asked me, "Ever been to Kansas before?"

"No, although I've flown over it many times on my way to somewhere else."

He started the truck. "It may surprise you."

I gazed out at the rugged, rocky landscape and admitted, "It already has." There was so much open land, so much sky. I'd been here five minutes, and already I felt a world away from Kansas City and an entire dimension in time away from Massachusetts. "Please, call me Jenny."

"All right, I will. You can call me Slight, if you want to; it's an old nickname."

It seemed a funny one for a tall and well-built man, but then I had once known a dour woman named Sunny and a skinny man named Fats. I sneaked glances at him as we started off across the pasture. He didn't exactly look like the Marlboro Man, but Quentin Harlan, occupation cowboy, had that same air of rugged attractiveness about him. I couldn't place his age with any confidence. His skin was so weather-beaten it could have belonged to a man of seventy, but he moved with the easy grace of a much younger man. His deep tan made his eyes look almost unnaturally blue. Under his big hat, I glimpsed graying brown hair, but it was very thick. Was he in his fifties, maybe? Older than that? Younger? I couldn't tell. It mattered, too, because this was one of the men we were supposed to employ for the rest of his natural-born life, however much longer that might last. So far, it didn't seem like such a bad idea.

"Slight, about Mr. Benet's death—"

"If you don't mind, I don't feel much like talkin' about it yet."

"Oh. Sure. You bet."

We drove for twenty minutes through a world painted russet: red cattle, red autumn grass, and nearly everything else blended to deep rust by the long shadows cast by the flat, pewter clouds in the enormous expanse of sky.

"So what do you think of these wide-open spaces . . . Jenny?"

He had lit a cigarette and rolled down his window to let the smoke escape. The air blew chilly around my legs in their thin hosiery.

"Well, it's so enormous and empty it makes me think of an ocean. And this color! 'Red sky at morning, sailor's warning; red sky at night, sailor's delight.' I suspect a person could feel pretty small and inconsequential out here, just like at sea."

"Funny you'd say that." His smile curved around the cigarette in his mouth, but then he removed the cigarette to talk. "This part of the country used to be called the Inland Sea. Those were the days when the native grasses grew higher than a horse's head and when the wind blew the grass looked like waves rolling on a sea." He looked a little embarrassed at his own flight of poetry. "There's some folks, mostly city folks, of course, who want to turn all this into a national park." He smiled. "Guess they think the tourists'll come out to watch the grass grow. Now there's a thrill for you. Hell, there's nothin' to do out here if you ain't workin' cattle. Besides, the prairie frightens a lot of people. Just scares the p—hell—out of 'em. Don't know why. I guess it's all these miles of nothing. I see them driving by, staring out of their cars, and their windows are all rolled up and their doors are locked. I don't know what they think's goin' to get them out here, coyotes maybe. Indians." He flicked the ash off his cigarette and laughed.

"Aw, you're just trying to scare a city girl."

He laughed again and turned left toward a padlocked gate that bore a wrought-iron sign that said CROSSBONES RANCH. Below that was a wooden sign that said POSTED: NO HUNTING, and below that a painted metal sign that warned trespassers they would be prosecuted . . . "Or Shot," somebody had spray-painted in red letters over that.

Slight got out of the truck, unlocked the gate, came back to the truck, drove through the gate, got back out of the truck, locked the gate again, and returned to the truck.

I began to think they *could* keep the relatives out.

He drove down the slope of a bowl and then straight ahead toward a cluster of buildings and fences. Just before the sun disappeared, I got a good look at the ranch headquarters, which was composed of a house, a barn, a long, low wooden structure that stretched out to the west of the house, and three smaller wooden buildings. The house was a two-story rectangle constructed of huge stones, without even a porch to soften its stark lines. The barn was a masterpiece of masonry, a magnificent four-story structure built from the same quarry as the house, with a huge "front door" that gaped like an open mouth.

"Here we are," Slight announced. "You can stay in the main house or the bunkhouse, it's up to you."

The buildings gave me the creeps. With their stones as big as tombstones and of a similar dead-gray color, they irresistibly raised images in my mind of spiders hiding between rocks, of dirt and moss, of witches. There was something a little run-down and neglected and lonely-looking about the place. I tried to tell myself I was only disturbed because the scene implied expenses to the foundation, but it was more than that. It was a feeling of dread. I didn't want to go into those buildings. The chill running down my spine was just like the one that stuffed cat had produced in me. I didn't want to spend the night anywhere on this property.

"I have reservations at a motel, Slight."

I saw from the look he gave me that he understood perfectly well that I didn't want to stay here alone with him and the other man.

"Dwight Brady arranged it," I said quickly. "Besides, I wouldn't want to get in your way."

"You're not likely to."

"Well, thanks, but I'll keep the motel room, if it's not too much trouble." Of course it *would* be more trouble for him to drive back and forth to fetch me.

He shrugged. "You're the boss."

Slight parked the truck on the grass in the front yard of the house, beside an old black Cadillac. I grabbed my purse. When we got out of the truck, he hauled my luggage and briefcase out of the back.

"I'll take this in," he drawled, "in case you need anything before I drive you into town."

I felt I had been somehow outmaneuvered.

Slight carried the bags inside the house, with me reluctantly following him.

"*Carl!*"

He yelled the name in a loud, deep voice as he set my bag on the floor near the front door. It was dark and cool in the stone house, like walking into a cellar, though it didn't smell like one. It smelled like an old brewery, as if the stones were steeped in beer. Still, I felt better about the house once I was inside it. I decided it only seemed spooky from the outside, because of the way it stood tall and stark and lonely against a prairie that seemed endless. Inside, where we were surrounded by solid walls, the world felt smaller, safer, more manageable. The rooms I could see—the living room where we stood, a dining room beyond that, a bit of the kitchen, a hall, and the first three steps of a stairway going up—were sparsely furnished. In the front room, there was a divan, a coffee table, a floor-model cabinet TV set, a couple of end tables with reading lamps, and two brown leather rocking chairs of the reclining type. There was a pile of books by one of the rockers, and a mess of newspapers and magazines by the other. A massive dark-wood table and three mismatched dark-wood chairs nearly filled the dining room. That was it. There were no carpets, no pictures, not even a calendar on any of the painted white walls. It was grim. There was, however, a spray can of furniture polish and a gray rag on top of the television cabinet. Somebody had made an effort to dust the place for company.

"So, how do you like it?" Slight inquired.

Disconcerted, I looked over at him and discovered that he was squinting at me in an amused kind of way.

"It's lovely," I said, straight-faced.

He laughed, then made me jump again by yelling, "*Carl, goddammit!*" In a normal tone of voice he said, "I suppose you're

thinkin' this is what you get when you got men livin' without women."
That had been exactly what I was thinking, but I didn't say so. He went
on, "It ain't that I wouldn't like to make it pretty. I don't know, what do
you think? Flowers, maybe, and curtains? Hell, I haven't got the first
idea and Cat never did and Carl ain't either. We've just been
three-fourths of a barbershop quartet peckin' in the dirt. I hope you can
stand us for a day or two."

"I probably can manage," I said in a dry tone to match his. "But don't
expect me to crochet any doilies for you."

He squinted his amused smile at me again in a way I was beginning to
recognize as characteristic of him. I suspected he was putting me on
about his alleged male incompetency. I suspected that whatever he gave
a damn about looked just fine, as the fields had seemed to, and the
cattle, at least as far as I could tell.

"Now don't tell me you know what doilies are," he said. "You're too
young to know that."

"Not so young."

He gazed at me a second longer than was perhaps necessary. I felt as
if he'd received a message I hadn't sent. Or had I? Slight Harlan, with his
snug jeans, his creased, tanned face, his amused blue eyes, and his sly
sense of humor, would have been an attractive man at any age. I didn't
look away from him, but I shifted my feet. And the subject.

"How long have you worked for Mr. Benet?"

"Thirty-two years this August, and Carl a little longer than that." He
walked into the dining room, peered up the stairs, then into the kitchen.
"Don't know where he is, probably out talkin' to his horse. You
remember those movie cowboys who'd rather kiss a horse than a
woman? Well, you're gonna meet one, Jenny. He's the goddamest fool
you ever met. If you want to get on the good side of Carl Everett, just
take along a carrot to feed him, maybe a couple of sugar cubes—"

"Talk about your goddamn fools."

I turned, to see that a second man had come in the front door behind
us. He swept off his cowboy hat and took the hand I offered to him to
shake.

"Glad to meet you, ma'am," he mumbled.

"That's Carl," Slight said unnecessarily. "This is a lady, Carl. Try to remember to spit outside."

The object of his needling had a wide, fleshy face with a large nose that flushed purple at Slight's gibe. Carl Everett looked to be in his sixties, a big man who looked as if he might be heavily muscled beneath his checked shirt and blue jeans. Some of the muscle had turned to paunch that bulged over his silver belt buckle. He glanced at Slight and then shook his head, turning his mouth down at the corners in a look that might have been mock or real disgust.

"I'm glad to meet you, too," I said.

"Well," Carl mumbled.

He nodded at me again, then headed back out the front door he'd just come in. He reminded me of an overgrown adolescent, eager to get back to the boys, uneasy around the girls. I had the impression that he'd bolt in a panic if I ever tried to get past "hello" with him. I had no such impression of his old friend Slight, however. I suspected that one would abandon the boys in a minute at the first whiff of perfume. He and Benet must have been quite a pair of tomcats at one time.

"Cowboys come in two varieties, Jenny."

I looked back at him.

"There's silent," he said, grinning, "and there's gabby."

"Let me guess which one you are."

He chuckled as he bent down to pick up my luggage again. The phone rang on the wall right beside him, but he ignored it, which was just fine with me, since I was afraid of being summoned back to Kansas City by Canales. "You don't want to let Carl talk your arm off." The phone rang a second time as he started up the stairs. I saw then that they had an answering machine, which took the call. "You might like to get out of those city clothes. I'll put your stuff in the spare room."

"But Slight—"

He disappeared from my view.

Well, he was right, I did want to change clothes. But I waited until he had come back down again before I went upstairs to do it.

9

Supper that evening (I called it dinner, but Slight corrected me: "It's supper in these parts. Dinner's what you eat at noon.") was broiled steak, pinto beans, and Tater Tots served at the big table in the dining room of the old stone house. Carl, who was one beer into a six-pack by the time he set the pack on the table, had done the cooking. The steaks—T-bones—were charred on the outside, nearly bloody inside, and more tender than any beef I'd ever tasted. It was "ranch beef," they told me. I resolved to send some back for my trustees; good steaks might console them for all the trouble this bequest was going to be.

I'd never eaten pinto beans before, and after the first bite I was certain I never would again. Carl had cooked the light-brown, oval beans with chunks of jalapeño peppers that set my tongue on fire. As for the Tater Tots, I had known they lived in the freezer sections of supermarkets, but the idea of buying them had appealed to me about as much as buying frozen French toast. Now I discovered that I kind of liked the fat, crunchy pegs of reconstituted potatoes—proof, as if any were needed, that I was not, and never would be, a gourmet. The steak knives were bone-handled, the dinner plates were wood with metal inserts. I drank my beer from a tall glass with "Hacker's Amoco" printed on it, which was what Carl offered me in place of drinking from the can. I would have preferred the can, but Carl seemed to be trying to play gentleman to my "lady," and I didn't want to spoil that for him.

I decided we had to talk about it.

"I was at the hospital today," I said.

Slight glanced up at me; Carl didn't, but he did stop eating and lay his utensils on his plate.

"I had an appointment to see Mr. Benet at the hospital this morning. He was killed before I got there."

Neither of them said anything.

The phone rang, and they let the machine get it.

For a few minutes we sat in total silence. Then Slight started eating again, but slowly, as if he were forcing himself to do it. Carl picked up his beer can and drained it, though he didn't eat any more of his dinner. It seemed an eternity before Slight finally said, in a slow, calm drawl, "Well, he had an awful time dyin', but he had a good life. Good, I mean, if you can take the droughts and the blizzards and all the rest of the bullroar that goes with ranching. Good if you like the smell of cow manure." He glanced at Carl and laughed, briefly. "Good if you like ownin' land, and if you like havin' money. Old Cat kinda liked the green stuff, right, Carl? On the ground and in the wallet, both. So I guess he was happy. I'll bet he had in his lifetime probably a half a million cows and a couple hundred horses and four wives and a passel of children. Don't know what more a man could ask for, right, Carl?"

Carl crushed the beer can in his fist.

"Four wives," I said, in much the same wondering tone that Detective Canales had used.

Slight nodded with mock solemnity. "And damned if he wasn't faithful to every one of them."

I smiled and found myself saying to these virtual strangers, "I have a husband like that. This is Geof's third marriage, and he's not even forty yet. But just as you say"—I smiled again, as much to myself as to Slight—"he's been faithful to every one of us. I think there's a phrase to describe men like Mr. Benet and my husband—"

"Yeah," Slight drawled, "lucky bastards."

I laughed out loud and immediately felt tactless for doing so. "Well, I was thinking of serially monogamous."

Carl was frowning at Slight, which Slight noticed.

"Carl is offended at the levity we are showing at this moment—"

"Oh, I'm sorry—"

"Also, he wants me to watch my language," Slight said in that mock-solemn way that was becoming more familiar, and more amusing to me, all the time. I did wonder if Slight wasn't something of a bully toward the older man. Slight had the quick wit and quicker tongue that Carl did not and that could be as advantageous as a longer reach is to a boxer. "Why, Carl's a more sensitive man than you might think by looking at him, Jenny. Carl's got very delicate sensibilities. I apologize, Carl. Lucky buzzard, how's that? Poor old Cat, may he rest in peace. How's that, that better?"

"Fool," Carl pronounced.

Surprisingly, that seemed to annoy Slight.

"Aren't you finished eating that damned steak of yours yet?" he said, looking tight around the mouth. It was an unjust charge, considering Carl had long since stopped eating. "I'll swear, you take longer to eat your food than you do to cook it. If you took as much trouble over your cookin' as you do over your chewin', we might get a decent meal every now and then. You got to eat faster, if you want me to ride out and check on those pregnant heifers tonight. I ain't about to leave Jenny here alone with you at the table. Poor girl'd die of loneliness before you finally set your knife down."

Carl's response was to make an X of his knife and fork across his plate. He threw his paper napkin on top of them and then pushed himself away from the table.

"Excuse me," he said politely to me.

"Pardon moi," Slight mocked.

Oh, knock it off, I wanted to say.

Carl carried his six-pack away with so much dignity that I realized he was drunk. A big man like that, on two beers? Maybe this wasn't his first six-pack of the evening. I had the feeling that Slight was observing me as I watched Carl lumber off down the hallway and into the kitchen. Out of our sight, a screen door slammed.

"You've known each other a long while," I said.

"Obvious, ain't it?" Slight reached over and picked up the crushed empty can Carl had left behind; he tapped it up and down on the table, beating out a nervous rhythm with it. "I guess we're like an old married couple, always carping at each other. When Cat was around, I think we were probably on better behavior. He was the peacemaker, I guess, maybe because he was the boss, maybe because that was his nature. A man's got to be a natural born diplomat to stay on speakin' terms with his ex-wives, don't he? Well, Carl and me and Cat, we was together a long time, probably longer than you been alive, I expect." Slight's grammar dropped in and out of school, I noticed, just as his drawl deepened when he wanted to say something sly and then practically disappeared at other times. I didn't interrupt, hoping he'd keep talking.

"Me and Carl worked for Cat Benet all those years, we've seen some times—" He stopped, and suddenly squeezed the beer can, turning it even more into trash in his hand. His voice turned hard, and I felt my stomach clench, as he said, "A man's got a right to die when it's convenient for him, and not for somebody else. If I find the murderin' sumbitch who did this, he's gonna be calf fries by dinnertime."

I sat frozen, hardly breathing.

He opened his hand, letting the destroyed can fall to the tabletop, and then he took a deep breath, and said in a milder tone, "Well, I'm sorry he's dead. But I've been missin' the old bastard ever since he got sick, so that ain't nothin' new. At least he's at peace now." His smile was sardonic. "If there's any peace in hell, 'cause that's where he sure got told to go often enough by enough women."

Slight pushed himself back from the table.

"Well, life goes on. Mine anyway. Come on, Jenny, you might as well come with me."

He stood up and hitched up his jeans.

"Calf fries?" I said. "What's that?"

The amused squint returned. "Fried bull balls."

"You must be kidding. People—eat—them?"

He grinned. "Sure do."

"Oh." I swallowed, hard. I was appalled and amused in about equal measures. What I wanted to say next was, "My God, that's the most disgusting thing I ever heard!" What I did say, trying to be nonchalant, and clearly not fooling him for a minute, was, "Well. And where are we going now?"

"To check on some cattle."

I glanced at the darkness outside the windows. "Not by horseback, I hope."

He smiled. "No, we'll take the truck."

I started to pick up my dinner—supper—dishes.

"Leave 'em," he said. "Carl'll get 'em. Sometimes I 'spect he just gives 'em to the cats to lick clean, but it sure as hell beats washin' them myself. Got a jacket upstairs? Good. Go on up and grab it, and I'll meet you outside."

"For an employee, you are pretty darned bossy."

He grinned. "Sorry, ma'am."

I ran upstairs, laughing under my breath.

I was beginning to regret that I would never meet Cat Benet. I wished I could have seen the three of them together, Slight, Carl, and Cat. I had a feeling this was like meeting the Three Musketeers without D'Artagnan. Peter and Paul without Mary. The Kingston Duo. The Two Stooges. I was still smiling when I ran outside to join him in the truck.

10

We bounced over the yard and down onto a dirt road that led into pastures behind the house. Between the first pasture and the house, we drove through an open gate.

"Aren't you afraid the cows will get into the yard, Slight?"

"Nope," he said. "Feel those rattles and bumps? That's a cattle guard. If it weren't so dark, you could see the metal bars stuck in the ground. Cattle won't cross it, not unless they're panicked. A lot of cowboys think cows are smart, but me, I think that's more a case of a dumb cowboy. The other day, I heard about some psychologists who tried paintin' silver lines on the ground, and the cattle wouldn't cross them, either."

"Maybe they lack depth perception," I suggested.

"They lack depth, all right." He smiled, keeping his eyes on the bumpy dirt-and-gravel road ahead of us. "In my opinion, a cow's about

as smart as your average chicken, which ain't no compliment." After a
moment he said, "I like 'em, though." After another moment he added,
"But hell, there are a lot of dumb cowboys I like, too."

We both laughed.

Soon we had climbed a hill and dropped down on the other side.
The house and other buildings were now out of sight. In fact, I couldn't
see much of anything except what the headlights picked up—the road,
grass at the side of it, a bit of fence now and then. It was dark like this
on the road to our new house back in Port Frederick, but I still wasn't
used to total darkness. I would have felt more secure in the city, under
streetlights.

"*Hold on!*" Slight braked the truck so suddenly that I slammed into
the dash and then slid toward the floor. He honked and leaned out his
window. "*Get outta the way, you big old dummy!*"

"Christ," I muttered as I worked my way back into a sitting position
again. I felt my limbs to make sure everything was all in one piece. Ow.
My right shoulder announced it would be bruised by morning. I looked
out the window and finally saw who—or what—he was shouting at.
An enormous cow blocked our path. She appeared to be blinded by our
lights, which illuminated her broadside. On her rump I saw a darkened
area amidst her curly red hair and realized it was a cattle brand.
Curious, I leaned forward to get a better look at the brand "our" cattle
bore. What I saw made me gasp.

"You all right?" Then Slight noticed where I was staring. "Oh, that."
He chuckled. "Cat's idea."

The cattle brand for the Crossbones Ranch was a human skull
outlined over crossed bones.

"Skull and crossbones?"

"You think it's weird?"

"I sure do."

"Yeah, everybody does."

The skull grinned malevolently at me from its nest on the cow's ass.
So this was to be the brand owned by the Port Frederick Civic
Foundation. I could just see it on the cover of next year's annual report.
If I had thought about it ahead of time, I suppose I would have

imagined that we would have a quaintly western brand, one of those rolling M's or rocking Z's or Q-Bar-T's or whatever. Not this evil-looking thing.

"*Why, Slight?*"

"Because he was dying." He edged the truck closer to the cow. "And so is she, when you think about it, only she don't know it yet." He nudged the cow's side with the truck. I held my breath for fear he meant it literally, and that he was going to slice up fresh steaks right then and there. But she merely flicked her tail and trotted off.

"I'm sorry," Slight said. "I should have seen her coming up on us. You okay?"

I rolled my shoulder to see if it still worked. "Sure. Fine."

I thought of the bumper sticker on city cars: I BRAKE FOR ANIMALS. Given the size of these beasts, any sensible person would. But would any sensible person have burned a skull and crossbones into their hides?

I shivered under my thin suede jacket.

After a few more minutes of rough driving, our headlights picked up a closed gate. Slight pulled right up to it, but then he switched off both the engine and headlights. In the sudden darkness inside the truck, I saw him shift his body around until he faced me. I felt as if somebody had thrown a sheet over me. For an instant I was blind with terror. I had an insane impulse to start flailing around with my arms and legs, to fight my way out of that confining truck. *Stop it,* I commanded myself. *Dwight Brady knows you're here. The pilot knows you're here. The trustees know where you are. For God's sake, even the cops know you're here! Nobody would dare to hurt you. Stop this. You are safe.* But that moment brought to full consciousness the thought I'd been suppressing simply because I liked Slight Harlan: This man was not above suspicion. Even he might have killed Benet.

"Ready for your first lesson, Jenny?"

I swallowed and said, "In what?"

In the flame of the match that he struck to light a cigarette, I saw him glance at me and grin. Leave it to Slight Harlan to find a double entendre in the most innocent question. Suddenly, the fear seeped out of me; in its place poured a sense of coziness, almost of intimacy, caused by that grin and by the fact of the two of us being closed in together in that small, dark space.

"In ranching, you mean?" I said quickly.

"That's what I mean," he deadpanned. "So ask me any questions you want to."

"Do we have to keep that brand?"

"No," he said a shade coolly, "but I wouldn't like it if you didn't."

"Why not?"

"Because." He shifted in his seat, as if to relieve a discomfort. "I don't know. Because Cat picked it. Because this is the last ranch. Because it's our last brand together. Because I guess it means something to me."

I didn't pursue it.

"Next question?"

"Why are his relatives forbidden from coming here?"

He hesitated, then said, "These aren't exactly the kinds of questions I had in mind, but fair enough. Well, he did it to keep them out of our hair, to tell you the truth." He lifted his hat and ran a hand through his own thick hair, as if to illustrate the point. "They weren't any of them interested in the ranches when he was alive, so why should he let them interfere with us now?"

"Still, it seems . . . vindictive."

"Yeah, he could hold a grudge."

"Is that why he didn't leave this ranch to them?"

"Well, it embarrasses me to say this, but I think ol' Cat, he wanted to provide somethin' for Carl and me, and if he'd left his family in charge, they would have sold this place, and then Carl and me'd be out of a job at what you might call awkward ages in our lives."

"Why didn't he just leave it directly to you then?"

"I 'spect he knew we didn't want that much responsibility, and maybe couldn't even handle it if we had it."

Hmmph, I thought, you *could handle it.*

"But why leave it to *us,* Slight?"

"Guess you got a good reputation."

"All the way out in Kansas?"

He shrugged.

"Why didn't he tell Alice and Margaret that he was in a hospital in Kansas City?"

"Didn't want to impose."

"On his *daughters?*"

"They weren't close."

"I guess not," I said dryly. "But *why* not?"

"Hell, Jenny, he had three wives after he left their mother! That'll create a little distance between a father and his children, don't you think?" He stubbed out his cigarette on the door of the truck, then flipped the butt to the dirt. "You know, I thought he'd live a little longer than this, I really did. Old cowboys are tougher'n stringy chicken. I thought he might have had a few million more breaths left in him. I don't say he would have enjoyed 'em, but I don't say he wouldn't have, either."

"So he was bitter because they didn't love ranching as he did? Or because they didn't love him?"

"Stubborn, aren't you? And now you're putting words in my mouth. Well, I don't know anything about psychology, but I do know a few things about cows. So let's see how much you know, Jenny."

I decided it was time to play along. "Uh-oh. I'm in trouble already." I made out his grin in the dark.

"What's a steer?"

"Something you do with a car?"

"It's a bull with his balls cut off. We do it when they're little." I heard laughter in his voice. "That's how we get calf fries. And fat cattle to sell for a bigger profit."

I winced. For the poor little bulls. "Eunuchs," I murmured.

"Yeah, but they don't sing at the Vatican."

I glanced at him. He was squinting at me again, obviously highly amused. It occurred to me that I might be providing even more amusement for him than Carl did. Right then I decided never to underestimate this man's sophistication.

"What's the difference between a heifer and a cow, Jenny?"

"I don't know, but I'm afraid you're going to tell me."

"A heifer is a cow that's never had a calf; she's a sort of a virgin until she's about a year old and gets bred. A cow is—"

"I've got the idea."

"If we get lucky here tonight, you might even get to see one of these heifers drop a calf. We got a whole mess of calves due right about now."

I was almost afraid to ask the obvious. "Drop a calf?"

His squint deepened until I couldn't see his eyes at all. "A cow, she don't have her babies in bed, Jenny. She has 'em the natural way, standin' up—"

"Yes, I see."

"You got any kids, Jenny? You and that lucky bastard serially monogamous husband of yours?"

"No."

"Seems to me you could have answered that by saying not yet."

"I could have, yes."

"Well, I'm going to get out and open the gate. You drive the truck on through. Just pull up and wait for me on the other side. Think you can drive this thing?"

"Sure."

He lit another cigarette after he got out and slammed the door. The noise set off some mooings in the pasture ahead of us. I heard a nearby rustling. Until I switched the headlights back on, all I could see of Slight was the glow of his cigarette. I slid over to the driver's side and looked down at the gear knob on the stick shift, hoping it would tell me how to get the truck into first gear. The mechanism was looser and more difficult to slot than any automobile transmission I'd ever operated, but after a couple of false starts in neutral, I managed to get it going.

As I drove through the gate he had opened, a rock flew up and hit the little window behind the passenger's side of the front seat. I braked instinctively and looked back. The glass was shattered. I drove on through and pulled up, waiting for Slight. He ran up to the cab.

"*Goddamn hunters.*" He looked furious as he flung open the door on the driver's side. "Scoot over—"

"That was a *gun*shot?" I slid quickly to the other side. "In a *pasture?* I thought hunters stuck to woods and duck blinds, places like that."

"That was two goddamn gunshots, and I think one of 'em got a heifer. We've got deer and coyotes and prairie chickens people like to hunt for, but you'd think the goddumb fools could tell the difference between a cow and a coyote, wouldn't you? Even at night." He drove the truck in a circle, playing his lights over the cattle, most of whom were scattering in confusion. Slight hollered out the window, *"There's people and cows out here you idiots!"* Finally, the headlights picked up the figure of an animal lying on the ground.

Slight stopped the truck, leaving the lights on, and we both got out and started running.

"Oh, Jesus."

It was one of the heifers, who was giving birth at the moment she was dying.

11

L ittle hooves and legs were emerging from between the hind legs of the heifer, though she seemed senseless of it.

"The head's still stuck inside her," Slight said. "We gotta hurry, or he'll suffocate! Come on!"

I followed him, running, back to the truck where he had me help him lift down an apparatus made of a metal Y-fork, winch, and chains. He directed me to help him force the Y part of it over the cow's rump and then to attach the chains to the forelegs of the calf. He was not satisfied with the result—we couldn't lift the dead cow to get the Y on well enough to please him, but he started frantically winching up the chain anyway. As Slight strained and groaned with the effort, I held my breath, partly because the rich, awful animal odors of death and birth were overwhelming to somebody like me who'd never smelled them before. But I also held my breath from sympathy and suspense—I desperately wanted to take hold of those little hooves myself and pull until the calf popped free . . . and breathed.

"Damnation!"

The Y slid off the cow's rump, making the chain slump and the winch useless. I got to the cow before he did this time. Together we pushed and shoved until we had it pressed onto her again. I lost all awareness of how bad the animals smelled or how primitive we looked and sounded as we grunted with the effort; now all of my senses, my civilized city senses, were focused on *push pull lift strain*. This time I straddled the cow and grabbed onto the apparatus where I could get a handhold, trying to increase the resistance against the winch.

He started winding the chain again.

"Come on uh you little bastard uh come on uh you little sucker."

An agonizing minute of intense struggle passed in which only a couple of lengths of the chain wound up into the winch and the calf moved only a couple of inches out of its mother. *"Come on!"* he yelled. My fingers grew white and numb with their puny effort to hold on. Another minute passed, filled with the sound of Slight's grunting and cursing. The calf wasn't moving at all; I was afraid it was already dead. *"Come on!"* I screamed. *"Come out, come out! Please! Come on!"*

Another half-minute later, the calf's head popped free, another minute and Slight had most of its body out, and then, unbelievably fast, the whole animal emerged. Slight dropped the winch onto the ground and ran to the calf, which lay sopping wet and limp on the ground. "Oh, God, it's dead," I cried. "Poor little thing, poor little thing." He removed a handkerchief from his pocket as he fell to his knees beside it. Quickly, roughly, he wiped its nose, eyes, and mouth clean. Then he began to beat on its back with the flat of his gloved hand. *"Help me, Jenny!"* He ripped the chains from its forelegs, and between us, we stood the calf up. Slight whacked its back, its side, its chest. It convulsed into breath! One breath. Whack. Two breaths. Whack whack. Three breaths, four, five, six, it was breathing on its own . . .

"Hold him, Jenny," Slight said, and then he ran off.

I tried, God I tried, but the calf was slippery with blood and feces and surprisingly strong, and I didn't know how to hold him securely. He slipped out of my grasp and tottered away. I made a grab for him, he slipped away from me again, and now, already stronger on his feet, trotted drunkenly but quickly away from me. I felt simply desolate with failure until I saw that the baby was only trying to get to its mother. He nudged her, looking for an udder to nurse.

I began to cry.

"Don't cry, Jenny," Slight said gently, coming up behind me. He put a bloody arm around me. "She never knew what hit her, and we're going to take care of him. Help me now."

He'd gone for a rope from the truck, and together we put it around the calf's little neck and led him away from his dead mother to the pickup truck. Slight had lowered the gate to the truck bed, and now he lifted the calf and put it in there. The calf's little hooves skittered on the metal truck bed, and down he flopped onto his front knees. Slight handed me the keys.

"I'll stay back here with this little one."

"What about the winch?"

"I'll come back for it."

I followed the ruts back to the gate—which I opened and closed by myself—and then I followed the dirt road back to the house. When we arrived, I helped Slight lower the baby from the truck and lead him into a straw-filled pen in the huge old stone barn.

We locked the calf in, then we stood back and stared at our little orphan.

"We'll bottle-feed him tonight," Slight said, "and then we'll see if we can get one of the other cows to take him tomorrow. It doesn't always work, but this little guy's been lucky so far, so maybe it will." He turned toward me. "Thank you for your help. It would have been hell by myself, and I might not have managed to save him. You do good work, Jenny Cain from Massachusetts." He smiled. "But you look a god-awful mess right now."

My leather jacket, wool slacks, and silk blouse were ruined, and I couldn't have cared less.

"You think it was hunters?"

"Sure." He walked me out of the barn. "We got this place posted everywhere you look, and we don't allow anybody to hunt on it except a few friends now and then. But you can't keep out somebody who really wants in, especially at night. God, I hate poachers."

We had reached the truck again. I was so exhausted I couldn't even speak, so I touched his arm to get his attention, and then I pointed at the shattered window behind the passenger's seat.

"That shot must have hit a rock," he said.

"I'm going to change clothes," I mumbled.

As I stumbled toward the house in the dark, I heard him yell, "*Carl!*" several times. I walked on in and started upstairs. His voice carried clearly, "*Carl! Goddamit! Where are you when I need you!*" In the upstairs bathroom, I stripped off my ruined clothing and stuffed it, with no real regret, into the metal wastebasket under the sink. There was no dry cleaner in the world who was going to successfully get that much cowshit out of green suede, white silk, and gray wool, and no way I was carrying it back home in a sack anyway. My flat leather shoes I saved, planning to resurrect them later.

I then stepped under the shower.

When the water stopped running red and brown, I soaped myself down, rinsed off, and then wrapped a towel around me. I ran to the room where my luggage was, put on my sweat suit and tennis shoes, and combed my hair off my face and let it hang wet on my shoulders. I was back downstairs before either Slight or Carl returned. Then I had to wait for Slight to wash and change before he could drive me to my motel. I was, by that time, so deadly weary I felt as if *I* had been shot, and that all of my life's energy was draining away out of some bullet hole in me, and I was just too darned tired to feel it.

Thirty-nine dollars a night bought me a plain and clean room at the Rock Creek Motor Inn five miles from the ranch. Slight let me off at the motel office with the admonition to be dressed and "ready to ride in the morning." He said he was going back to the ranch "to round up Carl and go look for the fools who mistook a truck for a buck."

I called Roy Leland from my room.

"Any news, Jennifer?"

"I helped deliver a baby calf from a dead heifer."

"What? Did somebody murder a cow, too?"

"No, Roy." I laughed, then stopped. Much more slowly I said, "Well, I guess you could say that. Uh, have you and the other trustees decided what you want me to do, Roy?"

"Is it dangerous for you down there, Jenny?"

Roy said it in a shocked tone of voice; clearly, the idea had not previously occurred to him. Knowing me as well as he did, it probably should have. But then, although Roy's a very smart businessman, he's a bit obtuse about people, seeing all of us mostly as means to ends. I hoped he wouldn't order me home, not yet.

"No, no, and I've got plenty to learn here."

"Find out anything about that damn will yet?"

"One of the hired men, Quentin Harlan, seems to think Benet banned his relatives because he resented their lack of interest in his business."

"Huh," Roy snorted, but then everybody knew he had a long-standing feud with his sons over the management of United Grocers. "Benet didn't know when he had it good!"

I reported everything I knew to that point.

At the conclusion, Roy said, "Well, I—the trustees that is—think you might as well stay over, come back on Monday, like you had planned. But listen, anything else gets killed out there, I don't care if it's a goddamned squirrel, I want you on the next plane out of Kansas City."

"That's a deal, Roy."

I thought I would collapse after that, but found, instead, that I was too keyed up to sleep. The motel didn't have a coffee shop, but across the highway there was a Pizza Hut that looked pretty good to me.

12

What I really wanted was a drink, but coffee would do, even hot chocolate—something to put my hands around, something warm and comforting to grasp. Like my husband. I realized with some guilt that I had not thought about Cape Cod Bay for the last couple of hours. And it flew right out of my head again when I trotted across the two-lane highway, after looking *very* carefully in both directions. So far in this day I'd survived a murder rap, a ride in a small airplane, and an alleged hunter's bullet; I wasn't about to let some trucker squash my good record.

When I opened the door to the restaurant, the hostess inquired, "One person?"

"Yes." I looked around the room, which had the usual red Pizza Hut booths and salad bar and smelled of pepperoni. A surprising number of the booths and tables were occupied, but then, this was probably the only open restaurant for miles around. "I'll be darned, there's someone here I know." I pointed to a booth that was occupied by a young woman in a fringed, suede jacket. "I'll sit with her. I'm only having coffee."

"I'll bring it over," the hostess promised.

I slid into the booth across from Lilly Ann Lawrence before she realized I was there. She looked startled at first, then apprehensive, then guilty, then proud and defiant, then stubborn, all in a row. Her mobile face betrayed the full range of her conflicting feelings. It was like watching a young actress desperately try out for every role in a play. Finally, she settled on wary.

"How'd you know where to come, Lilly?"

"I called that lawyer and pretended to be your secretary, and I told him you'd walked off with all the papers and I needed a mailing address for the ranch."

I laughed, a response she didn't seem to expect.

"So, how was the ball, Lilly?"

"Screw the ball."

"You didn't go?"

She shook her head.

"What about your parents? Screw them, too?"

She sat in silent rebuke of my limited adult view. It was odd, but I felt as if I knew this girl well. Our words, their underlying tone of blunt familiarity, had the quality of long acquaintance.

The hostess brought my coffee, for which I expressed such heartfelt gratitude that she laughed. After the woman walked away again, I said, "You can't go to the ranch with me, Lilly."

"I told you I know that."

"Then why'd you come?"

"I just want to see it."

"The ranch? You could do that anytime, if all you want to do is stand across the highway and stare at it. So why tonight, Lilly?"

"You know why," she said sulkily.

"Sure, I know why. How's this? You were afraid the pumpkin might turn into a coach and you might turn into a woman?"

"That's bullshit."

I thought about it a minute and then grinned at her. "Yeah, I guess it is. Although, what do you think those things are if not initiation rites? Listen, Lilly, putting on glass slippers for a night beats having to stalk a lion or having a bone stuck through your nose."

"I'd rather stalk the lion."

"That's too bad—they still save most of the best lions for the boys. Well, anyway, it's done. What will your parents do now?"

"What do you mean, do?"

"I mean, will they disown you? Lock you out of the house? Lock you in the linen closet when you go home? Cut the fringe off all your suede jackets?" She smiled a little at that, a good sign; maybe she did have a bit of perspective about herself. "I mean, what will they do to punish you?"

"Oh," she said casually, "nothing."

She tore a large hunk off her pepperoni pizza and began to eat it. Suddenly I was very hungry. I unwrapped my knife and fork from the paper napkin in which they were rolled and cut off a piece myself. I ate a couple of bites, holding the piece in my hand, before I said, "Nothing? Won't they be furious?"

Lilly shrugged. "They'll get over it."

"They'll get over it," I said in a tone that mocked her own. She flushed. "I'll bet you have no idea how lucky you are. You get to keep your principles and your parents, too. Not many revolutionaries get to do that, you know."

She glanced up, looking pleased. "You really think I'm a revolutionary?"

I wasn't going to let her preen on it. "I think you're a pain in the ass."

She looked deflated, but that quickly reverted to defiance. "Are you going to send me back?"

"Don't be ridiculous. You're at least eighteen—aren't you?—so you can do as you please. Which you certainly have done tonight."

"Are you going to call them?"

"No, but I hope you are."

She turned her face to the window.

After a few more sips of my coffee and a few more moments of her stubborn silence, I said, "Say, Lilly, what's the story on that cat?"

"What? Oh." She laughed a little. "Daddy's Little Darling?"

"If you say so."

"That's Spot, my Aunt Meg's idea of a joke on my mother. My dad wants a cat, but Mom's allergic to them, so Aunt Meg found that thing at an estate sale and gave it to Daddy, and they bring it out for company. I guess he thinks it's funny."

"How very amusing."

"Yeah."

"Can he get around on his own, Lilly?"

"Daddy? Oh, yeah, he's got a specially outfitted car he drives and he can walk a little bit on canes, enough to get himself in and out of his chair, at least. He gets around okay. He was going to use the chair tonight to present me . . ." Sudden tears sprang to her eyes and she covered them with her hands. "Oh, shit. I don't want to feel guilty."

"Then don't sneak onto the ranch, okay?"

Behind her hands, she sniffed.

"Please. Don't."

She wiped her eyes with her napkin.

"Really," I said. "You may not think you want your stupid old inheritance now, but you'll be awfully glad you have it when you're forty."

"I told you I wouldn't!"

"I guess I don't believe you."

She glanced away. "Well, it's true!"

I shrugged. If she was going to do it, she was going to do it, like those hunters Slight couldn't keep out. I hoped I wouldn't catch her at it, because I didn't want to have to decide whether or not to turn her in. In the meantime, rather than let her pizza go to waste, I ate the rest of it. Lilly wasn't opening her mouth anymore, either to speak to me or to eat.

I finished my coffee and then drank a refill. Still, she sat there silently. She could have left at any time, so I figured she must want company, even if it was mine. When I had finally finished consuming her dinner, I decided to take a chance, and to hope that she wouldn't call my bluff.

"Lilly."

She looked up.

"If I see you on the ranch, I'll report you."

She pretended to stare at the trucks going by.

I resisted the impulse to grab her shoulders and shake her until the fringe on her jacket shimmied. I said good-bye to her and walked over to pay her bill and mine. Then I left the restaurant and ran back across the highway to my room. Why, I asked myself, had I been so tough on the girl? The truth was that I felt a lot of sympathy for her, even for her desire to see the ranch she was forbidden from entering. So why the hardass act? The obvious answer—that she reminded me of myself, and that I wanted to force her to be smarter than I had been at her age—didn't occur to me then.

It did occur to me to wonder, as I brushed my teeth, what her family had found to do that evening, instead of going to the debutantes ball. Had they indulged their macabre sense of humor by taking potshots at pregnant heifers? Maybe wanting to add a stuffed cow to their collection of dead lap pets? Hard to imagine that trio traipsing across pastures, but Brady had said that Margaret Stewart's husband died in a hunting accident, so it was possible there was at least one hell of a poor shot in the family.

Nah, maybe they went bowling. I could just picture swishy Margaret down at the lanes with all the gals.

But why was I connecting the cow killing with the murder of Cat Benet, anyway? Whatever the reason, I was too exhausted to think of it. My brain was fuzzing out on me. I hung up my toothbrush and went to bed. Under the covers, I wiggled my toes.

G'night li'l doagies.

13

Next morning, I put on my sweat suit again, since it was the only thing I had left to wear besides my business suit. Slight Harlan took one disbelieving look at my tennis shoes, however, and said, "Nope. You're not gettin' on a horse in those. You'd rub your ankles raw, for one thing, and the horse'd laugh, for another. I'm taking you into town right now to buy you some self-respectin' *boots.*"

"I'm not buying boots just for one day's ride."

"The snake's aren't all hibernatin' yet."

"What?"

"Snakes. In the tall grass. Boots."

It took me a minute, then I said, "Right."

We drove three miles in the green pickup, through a morning as bright and shiny as a copper cowbell, until we reached a tiny town that was one commercial street surrounded by a few blocks of small frame houses. I saw a one-story brick building set off by itself at the end of the main drag: the sheriff's office.

"Slight, did you call the sheriff last night?"

"Sure, and the game warden. Why are you smiling?"

"Game warden."

"Don't have much call for them back home?"

"Not much."

"There won't be a whole lot they can do, but it won't happen again anyway. The idiots who did it probably scared themselves more than they scared us."

"I sincerely doubt that."

He smiled. "We'll keep our own watch, maybe padlock a few gates." His wide shoulders rose and fell in a heavy sigh. "I hate to do that, because it makes it damned inconvenient for *us* to get in and out of the pastures, too."

If he wanted me to absolve him of that responsibility, he was going to have to wait a long time. When I didn't say anything, he jerked the truck roughly from third into second gear.

He parked the truck in front of a two-story building with a sign that said BOBBY LEE'S DRY GOODS. Its front windows displayed male and female mannequins wearing matching blue jeans, western belts, checked shirts, bandannas, cowboy hats, and boots. Just the outfit for your basic Saturday-night square dance back home in Port Frederick, I thought. If he thought he was going to dress me up like some country & western Barbie Doll, like Barbie and Ken Go to a Dude Ranch, well, he was going to have to think again. I would tolerate the boots for practical reasons, but I would, by God, draw the line at a leather belt with the letters JENNY burned into it.

In Bobby Lee's Dry Goods store, I refused even to try on the elephant-skin boots that Slight pressed on me, and I rejected the ostrich-skin pair, as well.

"Ostriches are not endangered, Jenny."

"This one clearly was."

I insisted on buying their cheapest pair of plain, brown, cow-leather work boots, as these were not items of apparel I was likely to wear past tomorrow. Their prices on shirts and denims were so good, however, that I ended up carrying several sets into a dressing room to try on. The store had an old wood-plank floor that creaked when you walked on it, and a pleasantly musty aroma that mixed the smells of new leather, new clothes, and old dust.

When I emerged—feeling like Dale Evans—I saw Slight in what appeared to be casual conversation with the store's only other customer. It was Lilly Ann Lawrence, who also wore the same clothes she'd had on the day before.

Uh-oh, I thought, and hurried toward them.

He was leaning against a counterful of men's underwear while Lilly thumbed through a rack of women's shirts. Slight was talking—no surprise there—and Lilly appeared to be smiling as she listened. I'd never seen a full smile on the girl's face before, and I didn't get to see it for long, because it vanished the moment she spotted me.

Slight gave me an appraising look, top to bottom. In fact, he focused rather overlong on my bottom.

"The shirt's fine," he said, "but you got enough room in those jeans for you and me, both."

I plucked at them. "They're comfortable."

"They look it."

Lilly laughed. Her jeans, I noticed, were skintight. So far, neither of us had given any indication that we were acquainted with one another. I didn't want to play that game of collusion, however, so I said, "Slight, by odd coincidence, this is Lilly Ann Lawrence, one of Cat's grandchildren. Lilly, this is Mr. Quentin Harlan, who works at the Crossbones Ranch." That last bit wasn't meant to put Slight in his place, but rather to warn her.

They both looked thunderstruck, although Lilly's expression seemed to combine fury at me (for giving her identity away) with the shock of meeting him. Or was it such a shock? She could have followed us from the motel, with the idea that we might lead her to the ranch. If so, she was awfully brassy about walking right up next to him. I decided it had to be a coincidence. It was natural, after all, for a girl with horsey interests to come looking for a store like this.

Slight was the first to recover his equilibrium. He put out his hand. After a moment's hesitation, she took it.

"Alice's daughter?"

She nodded, looking defiant and scared.

"What are you doing down here, Ms. Lawrence?"

He said it casually, politely, but there it was, the most loaded question of all, hanging right out there in the air between us. And he hadn't wasted a minute in asking it. What would she say? She'd be crazy to lie, because this man was no fool. What finally came out of her trembling mouth took me by complete surprise.

"I want to get to know my grandpa."

Slight looked startled. "Your grandpa's dead, child."

She stuck her hands in the pockets of her jacket and sniffed. "He never gave me a chance to know him while he was alive. I would have liked him, I know I would, and he would have liked me. I know it! My mother's always saying I'm a throwback to Grandpa. I could have come to the ranch a lot, I would have loved it, he could have taught me all about it."

Slight folded his arms over his chest. "So where have you been all these years?"

"I was a kid!"

"How old are you?"

"Eighteen," she said mulishly.

"You get your driver's license at sixteen?"

"Yes, but—"

He shrugged. "You could have come down on your own."

"But that lawyer told me Grandpa didn't buy this ranch until last year! You were still way down in Texas somewhere, and . . ." She trailed off in the face of his skeptical expression. But then she blurted, "It isn't *fair.*" Lilly glared at me, then at him. "He never even *asked me* if I would like to run the ranch! I could have gone to ranch management school, I could have done it, I could! Instead, he gave it to *strangers*"—she threw me another hateful glance—"who don't know *any*thing about managing animals, or land—"

"And you do?" Slight drawled.

"That's not the point! I could have learned! It isn't fair!"

"But it is the way it is," he said firmly.

"Can't I just *see* it?"

"Come on the ranch, you mean?"

"Yes! Please!"

"The way I understand it is that Cat left you a nice trust fund. Set you up for life, all of you." Slight looked resentful; there was an edge to his voice as he said, "But that's not enough for you, I guess, you think you ought to have his last ranch, too."

"You can't love a trust fund," she blurted.

"Oh, I don't know." His tone was wry. "I think I could learn to get pretty fond of one myself. And I think you'd be better off goin' on back home, Ms. Lawrence, before you get yourself in a heap of trouble."

Lilly clamped her jaw, but then her face crumpled, and she burst into tears. Blindly, she turned away from us and stumbled down the aisle to the counter, as if to pay for the blue jeans that were stacked there. But she couldn't pull it off. She ran out of the store. The bell on the front door jingled as it closed behind her. The clerk behind the counter, who'd been tactfully trying to ignore us, gave it up and stared openly, first at the door, then back at us.

"Her grandpa was a pisser, too," Slight said.

"A pisser?"

He nodded, still gazing at the door. "Impulsive, headstrong, emotional. Exasperating as hell. Except maybe for Carl, Cat Benet was the most goddamned emotional man you'd ever want to meet. He'd yell at you one minute and then get all teary-eyed and sentimental the next. I 'spect that sentimental streak, that's how he came to get married so many times. Not to mention bein' impulsive." He laughed a little. Then he faced me. "Did you bring her?"

"No, of course not."

"I didn't think so. She seem a little young for her age?"

"I don't know, yes, maybe."

"Lot of city people got romantic notions about livin' in the country. They think it's all sweet cream and fresh eggs and bluebirds. They don't know anything about the reality of it day to day." He glanced again at the front door. "Pretty little thing, though."

"A child," I said sternly.

His gaze, when he turned it on me, was offended. "I can tell the difference between you and her, Jenny."

Did he think I was jealous? Good grief. I opened my mouth to defend myself, but thought better of it, and just wandered away, among the rows of denims and twills. But that didn't detach me from Slight, who followed me all around the store, jabbering away the whole time. Did I think the girl would try to get on the ranch? What did she want down here, anyway, really? How could she get to know her dead grandpa by coming down here? Why wasn't she in school someplace the way a rich kid ought to be? What did she mean, she would have loved the ranch? Was she a horsewoman? What did I know about her? Didn't I want to do something about her, to make sure she really did go back home? Didn't I want to make sure she didn't do anything stupid that might hurt her or her family?

Finally, I held up one hand.

He raised his eyebrows.

I held up a pair of blue jeans in my other hand.

"I'm going to try these on," I said.

He nodded grudgingly. He couldn't very well follow me into the women's dressing room, although he talked to me all the way to the door of it. And then he tried to talk to me *through* the door, but I told him to go away. When I came back out—wearing a smaller size this time—he was gone.

I paid for my purchases—which included in addition to my new boots, three pairs of jeans, a couple of long-sleeved cotton shirts, socks, and work gloves that Slight had recommended for riding, all of which I could also use back home for gardening—and then I carried what I wasn't already wearing out to the truck.

Slight was nowhere to be seen.

I dumped my old and new clothes on the backseat and checked my watch. It was past eleven. My how time flies when you're spending money. I was hungry, and there was a café across the street. But first, I had some fiduciary responsibility to exercise.

14

I strolled down the street toward the sheriff's office. Cars and pickup trucks were angled into the curb the old-fashioned way. No parking meters. Along the way, I passed a hardware and kitchenwares store, a grocery store, and two closed and boarded businesses. Their empty display windows gave that side of the street the look of a set of uppers with its two front teeth missing. When I glanced at the other side of the street, I noticed other gaps denoting failed businesses. This little town in Kansas, founded in 1902 according to the sign at the city limits, was like an old man who'd lost his bite. There was a little bank, and a tiny liquor store. Rock Creek was down to the essentials, all right: cash, clothes, screwdrivers, frozen food, and booze.

The stiff morning breeze kicked up little tornadoes of dust that swirled around my boots, making me feel for a minute as if I had walked into Oklahoma in the Dust Bowl days of the thirties.

The sheriff's office was a neat little square of red brick, with azalea bushes bordering the clean cement sidewalk that led to the front door. There was a sign on the door: HOURS: 12 P.M. TO MIDNIGHT. KINDLY DO NOT COMMIT ANY CRIMES BEFORE NOON. It listed a long-distance emergency number that was probably the highway patrol. I looked at my watch: eleven-thirty A.M. Well, shoot. As I started to walk away, a female voice called, "Can I help you, Miss?"

I turned to look just as a young woman in a brown uniform, complete with gun and belt, came around the corner of the building. She wore a badge on her chest and she had hedge clippers in her hands.

"I'm Sheriff Pat Taylor," she said, and smiled.

"Jenny Cain." I smiled back and stepped toward her. She let the clippers hang from her left hand while we shook right hands. "I represent the new owners of the Crossbones Ranch."

"Oh, yes?" She grinned as she lifted the clippers in a kind of salute. "Well, I represent Hood County, where we got a whole lot of land but not a whole lot of taxpayers. Part-time sheriff, part-time gardener, mother, wife, Sunday school teacher, that's me. What can I do you for?"

"I wondered if you were going to investigate that hunting accident we had on the place last night?"

"Don't believe I've heard about that one."

"Didn't you get a call from one of our men?"

"Don't believe we did, and I believe I'd know." Sheriff Taylor had a solid, feet-apart stance, brown eyes that looked straight into mine, and shoulders that strained the fabric of her short-sleeved shirt. I was willing to bet her own kids behaved themselves, and that very few of her Sunday school charges ever ended up in her jail. "What is it happened? You want to come in, make an official report on it?"

"I don't know." I felt confused, embarrassed by Slight's lie, and more than a little betrayed. "Quentin Harlan and I were out in a pasture last night, about eight-thirty, and somebody shot a couple of bullets in our direction. One of them hit a rock and shattered our truck window, but the other one hit and killed a heifer as she was giving birth."

The sheriff made a tsking sound with her tongue. "D'ya lose the calf, too?"

"No, we saved it."

"Well, thank God for that. I tell you what, let's go write it up, you'll want the report for the insurance company, I 'spect. And I'll try to get out there to take a look. You never know, I might even get lucky and catch 'em."

"Really?"

"Sure, if they're from this county, I could prob'ly tell who they were just by lookin' at their tire tracks." She smiled. "Well, maybe not quite."

Sheriff Taylor unlocked the front door and turned the sign over to read OPEN. When we went in, she discovered to her "tsking" dismay that she had failed to switch her phone answering machine to "on" the night before, so there couldn't have been any message from Slight. That made me feel better, though not entirely, because hadn't he distinctly told me he'd talked to the sheriff? Or had he just said he'd "called" her? After I filled out the report, I headed back toward the center of town (which was only the center of the block) to find out. But Slight still wasn't at his truck.

I crossed the street to the Rock Creek Café.

I pushed open the front door, only to find Slight and Lilly Ann seated at a table together. I sighed to myself in my best put-upon manner and walked over to sit down at their table with them.

The café was as plain as they get. Just past the door was a glass-front counter with a cash register on top and one flavor of Life Savers (wintergreen) for sale below. There were only about ten tables, each with silver metal legs and a gray and silver-flecked Formica top rimmed in metal, each with its own two-sided silver paper-napkin dispenser, salt and pepper shakers shaped like Hawaiian dancers, plastic catsup and mustard containers, and honey in a plastic bear wearing a yellow dunce cap with a hole in the top. The kitchen was in the back behind wooden swing doors.

I threaded my way between two tables of three men each, all of them wearing coveralls and dirty baseball-type hats, most of them staring curiously at me. A couple of the older ones nodded politely. Their conversations recommenced once I had passed by.

Slight's squint was a richly amused one.

"Now *those* jeans fit," he said.

The look Lilly Ann gave me was as sly as his.

"I think I know what you're up to," I said to her as I sat down. I glanced at Slight. "I never have any idea what *you're* up to." I opened a menu. "But neither of you knows what I'm going to do next, and if I were you, I'd start wondering." I looked up as the waitress appeared. "I'll have a grilled cheese sandwich on whole wheat, a dinner salad with Italian dressing, and coffee black, please."

Their sly grins had faded.

That pleased me.

But nothing could still Slight for very long. Soon, he was regaling Lilly Ann with wild tales of her grandpa's escapades when Cat had been as young as she was now. It was all highly amusing, especially to hear Slight tell it. But I kept my eyes on my sandwich, pondering this odd little luncheon group. Just what was going on here, I wondered, and just what was I going to do about it? The girl was obviously trying to ingratiate herself with Slight, probably in the hope that he'd relent and allow her onto the ranch, in spite of the will. By the time I'd polished off the potato chips and dill pickles, I had decided to be direct.

"Where are you going to go now, Lilly?"

She had grown relaxed listening to Slight, but now she visibly tensed again.

"I don't know," she mumbled. "Back to the motel."

"Where are we going?" I asked Slight.

"Riding," he told me, and I had the impression that he was just about to say where when he stopped to eye the girl. "Don't know where, exactly, we could ride just about anyplace on the ranch today, I suppose."

It was a warning to her: Do not trespass, for we may see you do it.

"Bye," she said abruptly, and got up and left.

I turned toward Slight, to discover him staring after her with a strange expression on his face, one I couldn't decipher.

"Goddamned old fool," he muttered.

"Who? Cat?"

"Me. You payin'?"

I laughed. "You're not so foolish."

He squinted that grin of his at me.

I paid the bill for all three of us and even bought him some Life Savers for dessert.

84

15

We were almost the only traffic on the two-lane highway going west toward the Crossbones Ranch. But whenever we did pass somebody driving east, Slight and the other driver would raise their right index fingers off their steering wheels in a kind of salute. Sometimes, they nodded as well. Once a man driving a tractor-trailer rig waved with his whole arm—clearly a demonstrative type, probably cried at funerals.

When a large dark car came over the horizon and drew near to us, I expected Slight to give the driver the same cool one-fingered greeting. Instead, he slowed and then came to a complete stop in our lane. The Caddy halted in its lane, too, and both drivers rolled down their windows.

It was Carl Everett.

"Where you goin'?" Slight inquired.

"Flywheel's in," Carl said cryptically.

"Well, pick up some bacon."

"I wasn't plannin' on grocery shopping."

"Now don't get any more of that thin, skinny bacon, either. Make her cut you off some thick-sliced. We could use some more instant coffee. And buy me a *TV Guide,* will you?"

"You need diapers, too, do you?"

"No, Dad, just the bacon and the coffee and the *TV Guide.* You plannin' on stopping by the liquor store, Carl?"

"I could," the other said with a bit more enthusiasm.

"You could drown in your own beer piss, too. I didn't ask it to encourage you, Carlton, I asked it to discourage you. We got us enough empty cans as it is now to set up target practice for Fort Riley. I think you ought to drink what you got left if you have to, and then give it a rest for a while. I expect your liver's looking more like Swiss cheese every day."

"I expect you got a tongue made of baloney."

Carl drove off in a bad-tempered cloud of dust.

"Man's going to drink himself to death."

"What's a flywheel?" I inquired.

"Tractor part."

"Sure," I said. "I knew that."

After we drove a bit further, I said, "Did I tell you I saw the sheriff this morning?"

"Um, you may have."

"At least now she knows about the shooting."

"Um."

Slight shook a cigarette loose from the pack he kept on the dashboard, stuck it in his mouth, and reached over to push in the car lighter.

"You tried to reach her last night?"

"Uh-huh." He pulled out the lighter before it was quite hot enough, so strands of tobacco stuck to it after he finally managed to get the cigarette lit. "Well, shit." He pushed the lighter back into the dash and sucked on the cigarette to keep it going.

"Why couldn't you reach her?"

He blew smoke out his window. "Couldn't get through to her."

"Why not?"

"Because nobody answered the goddamned phone. Shit." He picked a loose strand of tobacco off the tip of his tongue. "You'd think they'd answer the goddamned phone at the sheriff's office, wouldn't you?" Slight spit out the window, as if trying to dislodge other bits of tobacco. He was certainly having a difficult time with that particular cigarette.

So he'd called, but nobody had answered. It was one of those defenses anyone could claim.

"So you were going to try her again today?" I asked.

He smiled slightly. "Now that you mention it."

"She's coming out to take a look."

"Always glad of company," Slight said, and turned in toward the padlocked front gate that seemed to contradict those very words.

16

But company had already come calling.

When Slight and I drove up to the house, there were two extra cars parked on the gravel out front, two sedans, one white and boxy, the other tan with long, silver antenae sticking out of it and a thin man in a blue suit leaning against it. I saw smoke curling up out of the open window on the driver's side, and as we approached, I could see that the man sitting there was the one who'd been smoking in Benet's hospital room. A slim, young black woman wearing a plain, gray business suit got out of the white car.

"How'd they get in?" I said.

"There's an old gate with only a cattle guard down the road apiece and around the bend. It's pretty well hidden by cottonwood trees, but if you poke around, you're bound to find it. I guess they poked around, all right. Offhand, I would say those are probably not insurance salesmen."

"No, they're Kansas City homicide detectives."

I was only two-thirds right about that.

The thin man in blue was Luis Canales.

"Detective Ben Krulick," the other man said after he emerged from the sedan. He appeared to be in his late twenties, taller and thinner, looser-limbed than the intense and older Canales. The young woman stopped beside the front bumper of Slight's truck and said, "Fran Bradley, KBI." She remained there, not coming any closer, so we had to turn our heads to see her. I had the feeling of being "surrounded" in an old-fashioned "lawman" sort of way.

Kansas Bureau of Investigation. I felt as if she'd applied a lug wrench to my breastbone and tightened my ribs.

"Why KBI?" Slight asked, sounding no more than curious.

"Because," Krulick cut in, "the victim was murdered in Missouri, and this is Kansas we're standing in." The detective made a point of gazing around and widening his eyes at all the empty space. "Definitely Kansas. So how you folks doin' this afternoon?"

"Doin' pretty good until you three showed up," Slight said with a wry smile. "I'm Quentin Harlan. Carl's gone into town, if you're lookin' to talk to him, too. Your bein' here reminds me of what I'd just as soon forget, that ol' Cat's done used up his ninth life. Come on in the house, why don't you?"

But Krulick inhaled deeply and shook his head.

"We don't get much time in the open air," he said. "Do we, Lou?"

So we remained in the gravel drive, Slight and I leaning against his truck, the two detectives leaning against their car, both of them taking notes now and then in their own little pads. Canales, I saw, had one of those spiral-bound jobs with lined pages; Krulick (and my own Geof) preferred the flip-top variety, unlined. The KBI agent stood so quietly beside the bumper, just out of our line of vision, that it was easy to forget she was there.

"When did Mr. Benet purchase this ranch, Mr. Harlan?" Canales inquired.

" 'Bout a year ago."

"I understand he'd always operated before in Texas."

"That's right."

"So why the move up here?"

"Detective, have you ever worked cattle in August in Texas?"

Canales smiled slightly. "Kansas is not known for its mild weather, either."

"It wasn't just the summers," Slight said with an air of remembering hard times, "it was the droughts and the mesquite and the sheer amount of land it took to feed just one goddamned cow. You can feed a cow and calf on ten and a half acres up here, Detective, and you need thirty acres to do the same thing down there. That's a lot of hours on a horse. That's a hell of a lot of fences to maintain. It's just a hell of a lot of hard work, and we weren't any of us gettin' any younger. A man's butt gets thin after thirty years in a saddle, Detective Canales, that kind of work, it gets to wearin' down your bones."

"How sick was he when you moved here?"

"Not too bad, good enough to make the move."

"One of the best cancer treatment centers in the world is in Houston," Canales said.

"You mean, so how come we moved him away from it?" Slight was squinting slightly, but I didn't think it was because he was amused. "Because he didn't want to be 'saved' just so's he could keep gettin' sick. He just wanted to finish bein' sick, and then die. They couldn't of cured him, not even in Houston; all they could of done was to prolong his life. That didn't sound real interestin' to him. And he didn't want a fuss made over him, the way it would have been if he'd stayed in Texas. He wanted to go by himself and he wanted to go quiet, Detective."

"So you made that possible."

Slight stomped out his cigarette under the heel of his boot before he looked up. "What are you sayin'?"

Krulick spoke up. "Lifetime employment. That's a pretty sweet deal for you. Can't be easy to find this kind of employment anymore, with so many farms and ranches goin' belly up."

"Shit," Slight said, and folded his arms on his chest. "That's the most piss-poor excuse for killin' a man I ever heard, and I've heard a few of them."

"Where were you and Carl Everett two nights ago?" Canales asked.

"Here."

"I suppose you'll vouch for each other."

"You got that right."

Canales glanced at me. "You ever meet her before?"

"Nope."

"Why'd Mr. Benet leave this ranch to her foundation?"

"He was a philanthropist."

"Why didn't he want his relatives to come here?"

"He wasn't much of a family man."

Krulick said, "You got any ideas about who killed him?"

Slight smiled thinly. "Probably one of those crazy nurses who goes around putting patients out of their misery."

Canales smiled that hunter's smile of his and said, "There have not been any other cases of smothering by pillow reported from that hospital."

Krulick laughed. "But we'll watch out for it."

"Where can we find Carl Everett?" Canales asked.

"He's gone for supplies. If you wait here long enough, he'll show up, but you won't get much out of him."

"Oh?" Canales said.

Slight looked at his watch. "It'll be the middle of the afternoon by then, and Carl'll be well on his way to drunk. He gets things confused when he's drinkin', and his memory's not so good, either. But hell, you can stick around if you want to."

Krulick and Canales exchanged glances.

"Do you have anything to add to any of this, Ms. Cain?" Canales inquired.

"Just that Mr. Harlan and I were out in one of the pastures last night, checking on pregnant heifers"—I caught a hint of a smile in Slight's blue eyes—"and somebody took a couple of shots in our direction. One of them killed a little heifer that was giving birth."

"Goddamn poachers," Slight said.

Krulick addressed me. "Are you saying you think that has something to do with Mr. Benet's death?"

"I don't know," I admitted.

Slight moved restlessly. "You finished with us?"

Canales looked over Slight's shoulder, and suddenly I recalled who was back there. The lug wrench tightened my ribs another notch.

"Are we finished, Frances?" Canales asked her.

She didn't move, but she finally spoke, in a voice as deceptively neutral as her gray suit and her white car. "Mr. Harlan, you and Mr. Everett must have been extraordinarily devoted to Mr. Benet to work for him all those years, take care of him when he was sick, even move up here with him. I'd think you'd both be interested in seeing his killer apprehended."

Slight gazed at her for a long moment, a look that she held without blinking, and without any apparent effort. "Yeah, well, don't think I'm not," he finally said. "Now if you will excuse us, I promised Ms. Cain I would ride her around the ranch, give her a few lessons in raisin' beef cattle. Okay with you?"

She glanced over at Canales as if to say: your game.

Canales nodded, and Krulick said, "We'll wait for Everett."

"Up to you," Slight said. "Come on then, Jenny."

I noticed what Slight didn't—that Canales's eyebrows rose at the familiar way in which Slight addressed me, and that the detective continued to stare after us as we walked side by side to the barn.

"He thinks we're Bonnie and Clyde," I whispered.

"Nah, you're better lookin' than Faye Dunaway."

I stubbed my toe on a rock and stumbled into the barn.

"But a damn sight clumsier," he added.

17

It was after two o'clock by the time we rode out of the big barn, I on a small gray mare by the name of Molly, Slight on a big palomino he called Buck.

"For obvious reasons," he said, by way of explaining his horse's name. "You know what a gelding is, Jenny?"

"Yes," I said quickly. "You don't eat those, too, do you?"

"Nope." He grinned and gave Molly a swat to get her moving faster. I hung on for dear life. The horse felt fine under me, it was the saddle that hurt, digging into certain tender places that leather didn't usually reach. I hadn't ridden a horse since my mother took me on pony rides at the zoo.

"I'm not going to last long, Slight."

"We won't be riding long, Jenny."

What he meant, it turned out, was that we weren't actually on horseback all that much, because we were constantly mounting and dismounting our horses—one or the other of us—to open and close gates, or to get off and sit on a fence while Slight lectured me on the economics of ranching. I learned that he and Carl could run a place this size alone, with only part-time hired hands. I heard all about breeding seasons and salt licks, bromegrass and stickleburr, winter feed and equipment prices, weather patterns and pasture burnings, weanings and brandings, pregnancy testing and spraying for flies and ticks, making money and losing it. Mostly losing it, it seemed to me. The more I heard, the more I marveled at Cat Benet's choice of the Port Frederick Civic Foundation to own this place, and the more I realized how very difficult it was going to be for me to oversee 13,000 acres from 1,500 miles away.

Finally, we tied the horses to one last fence and perched ourselves on top of it. By now, we had covered so much ground—literally and conversationally—that we'd put a lot of distance between ourselves and cops and KBI agents. The ride had bounced my ribs—and every other bone—loose. There was a large pond—Slight called it a tank—over a small rise just in front of us.

"Tell me about yourself, Slight," I said, "to which you will reply, 'Not much to tell.' "

He laughed. "Well, you're wrong there. There's a lot to tell, and there'd be a lot more if I hadn't been dead drunk and unconscious a good part of it. Liquor's a terrible thing, Jenny. Look what it did to Cat's liver, look how it's destroyin' Carl. Well, what the hell, I can't complain. A lot of it was fun, and I seem to be survivin' it."

"So is this the story of you or of demon rum?"

"All right! Are all easterners as persistent as you are? Hell, I was born in Midland, Texas, one mother, one father, three sisters. Worked oil rigs, ran a goat farm for a while, a short while, thank God, but mostly I've spent my life lookin' down a horse's neck at the back of a cow. Strangely enough, it is a view to which I am partial, and I think I'll probably keep doin' it until I get so old they just let me tumble off Buck into an open grave. *Adiós*, Quentin."

On impulse, I blurted, "Slight, can I trust you?"

He looked at me in a startled way.

"Because I'm going to have to," I said. "How in the world am I ever going to know if you're running this place as it should be run? There's no way I'm going to turn into an agricultural expert in one easy lesson. No way. And there's not a soul in Port Frederick who knows a cow's tail more about this business than I do right now, this minute, sitting in this darned pasture with you. I'm going to have to take your word on everything. Everything! What kind of way is that to run a business? It's crazy. With all respect, I think your pal Cat Benet was nuts."

"There are books—"

"Books!"

"There's an International Stockman's School—"

"Right."

He smiled. "I got no good reason to run this place into the ground, Jenny. It's my livelihood now, mine and Carl's for the rest of our lives, I guess. I've got every reason to make it work. For all of us."

"So I can trust you?"

His smile turned into a wolfish grin. "I didn't say that."

I jumped down from the fence on which we'd been sitting and looked up at him. "Say it."

His look turned skeptical. "Say what?"

"Say, yes, Jenny, you can trust me."

An airplane buzzed overhead, causing both of us to look up. It was a single-engine type that looked a lot like the one that had delivered me the day before.

"Descending," Slight noted, both of his hands shading his eyes as he peered upward. "Must be going into Rock Creek Airport." He lowered himself down off the fence and then reached back with his right hand and dug around in his right back pocket until he came out with a bone-handled pocketknife. He opened the knife. Then he opened the palm of his left hand and used the knife to knick the tip of his middle finger so that blood trickled down into his palm.

"What are you *doing!*"

He raised his bloody hand toward me and with his other hand, pointed the knife in my direction.

"Open up your hand, Jenny."

I stepped back from him. *"What?"*

"You want a pledge? Let's make it a blood pledge, like the Indians."

"You're crazy!"

Slight leaned closer to me and reached out for my left hand. I stumbled back from him and then ran until I was several feet away. "You come near me with that thing and I'll kick it out of your hand, you hear me?"

He flicked the knife so that it whizzed through the air, passing me en route. It landed, point first and sticking straight up and vibrating, in the ground behind my left shoulder. I looked back to find that Slight was sucking his stuck finger and chuckling to himself.

"*You crazy son of a bitch!*"

He squinted at me, grinning. "God," he chortled, "Cat would have loved this."

I walked over to where the knife still quivered in the ground and pulled it out. Then I folded the blade back into its handle. I grasped it in my right hand and lifted my arm high in the air—

"*No! Don't you do that—*"

He ran toward me just as I rared back and threw his knife into the middle of the cattle pond.

"*Goddamit, that's my favorite knife!*"

He raced to the pond, stopped on the rise above it, and stood staring down at the ripples where his knife had drowned.

"God," I said behind him, "Cat would have loved this."

When he heard that, he turned around and grinned. Then he started to laugh. I walked toward him, but he quickly moved away from the water, clearly afraid that I might push him into it. He circled me, until he could get me between him and the pond, and then he moved in closer, until our chests were nearly touching, and he looked down at me, opening his blue eyes wide.

"You can trust me, Jenny . . . but can I trust you?"

"Come a couple of inches closer," I suggested, raising my right knee. "And we'll see."

He jumped back, and this time I was laughing, too.

We rode back to the barn then, with Slight in high good humor and with me in agony, because the insides of my thighs felt as if I'd been riding an iron horse. The two sedans were gone from the gravel drive. I knew we'd been out in the fields a long time, but when I looked at my watch, I was shocked to discover it was nearly five o'clock. Saturday night. That left me only one more day to learn everything I could about the ranch and the men who would run it for the foundation. I needed more time with them. As we unsaddled, I said, "If you'll take me back to the motel, I'll check out. And then, if the offer's still good, I'll take that spare bedroom upstairs."

"You sure you want to?"

"You'd rather I didn't?"

"Well, you're settled in at the motel, and all—"

"But it would save you time—"

"I got lots of time." He shook his head, as if reminding himself of something, perhaps of the fact that I was now his boss. "Oh, hell, of course we want you to stay here. Hell, it's your house."

I walked toward his truck, thinking that was a highly unsatisfying answer. Maybe he was angry that I'd turned the tables on him, back there in the pasture. Heaven knows, I'd seen grown men go into terminal funks just because they lost their pocketknives. Maybe that had been an awful thing to do. Well, tough. If he was going to keep dishing it out to me, he was going to have to keep taking it, as well.

But on the drive back he was so amiable and gabby, I decided he wasn't angry at all; that, in fact, he relished the thought of telling the knife tale to Carl, even though he, himself, was the butt of it. I liked him for that. I liked him for a lot of reasons. His wit. His intelligence. His unpredictability. The amazing blue of his eyes. The flat belly above his buckle. The way his muscles moved under his jeans when he shifted his legs to press the clutch or the brake. The way he remembered to roll down his window to let the smoke out when he lit a cigarette. I remembered all too vividly exactly how it had felt to stand so close to him in that pasture. I liked him for all too many reasons, I told myself.

Cool it, I told myself.

You're married. He's too old for you. He lives clear across the country, and you'll probably never see him again . . . well, now *there* was an argument that cut two ways. But there was one argument that brooked no opposition: There existed the possibility—a slim one, I hoped—that this man had killed his boss, either out of sympathy or to secure his lifetime job a little sooner. And it did seem to me that a woman who committed adultery would be adding insult to injury if the lover happened to be a murderer and the husband happened to be a cop. I turned my face to the side window so that I couldn't see Slight Harlan's blue jeans even in my peripheral vision, and I concentrated very hard on imagining twilight on Cape Cod Bay.

18

S light stayed in the truck while I went into the motel office to settle
my bill. I had to ring the silver bell on the counter to summon the
owner out of the rear to help me.

"I'm checking out of three," I told her.

"Now?" She was a scrawny woman in her sixties, with a pleasant
smile, knobby knuckles on her red, raw-looking hands, and gray hair
permed into stiff ringlets held in place by a gossamer-thin hairnet. "I
had you down for three nights, dear. Something wrong with the room?"

"No, I'm going to stay with friends. What do I owe you?"

"Well, I'll have to charge you for tonight—"

"I realize that."

"But listen, it doesn't seem fair to make you pay full price for what
you only half-used. How about if we split the difference?"

"That's more than fair."

She presented me a bill for an amount that, even with a full extra night added on, would not have covered one night at a motel back home. As I handed her my American Express card, I had the feeling she had some point of curiosity she needed to satisfy. I felt I owed her one, so I said, "What is it?"

"Can I ask you something?"

"Sure."

"Well." She delicately patted her hairnet, then she pressed her hand against the side of her neck as if she had a pain there. "Something happened here a while ago that's got me more het up the more I think about it. Last night, I checked that girl into six. She was driving a white Volkswagen convertible, cute little car. I seen you talkin' to her over to the Pizza Hut last night, so I thought maybe you'd know somethin' about this thing that just happened . . .

"A couple a hours ago, I seen these three people walking past this door, like they was going to a room, only they wasn't anybody I'd sold a room to. And they wasn't driving. I don't know how they got here. Or where they parked their car. And they was dressed funny, I mean, they was dressed *nice*. The young man had a nice suit on, and the two older ladies had on just real pretty dresses—oh, I just loved their dresses . . .

"Anyways, so I was wondering who they was going to visit, so I kinda peeked out the door, you know. Well, they walked up to room six, where I'd put that girl. And the young man, he knocked, and then the girl come to the door, and so they all went inside. And not very long after that, they all come out again. And the young man, he was carrying the girl's suitcase, and both the ladies, they had her by an elbow.

"Well, they all four of them got into the girl's little car with the man driving, and they stopped by here at the office. One of the ladies, she got out and come in and paid the girl's bill. She was real nice about it, I have to say that. And then they driven off north."

"Toward Kansas City?"

"Um hum." She rubbed the back of her neck. "Well, the thing is, I followed that lady to the door and I looked in that car, and I seen the girl was crying. Well, this upset me then, and I've been getting more upset every hour. What do you think? You think they kidnapped her or something? I guess that's what I'm afraid of. You think maybe she was in one of those religious cults, and that man was what they call one of those, those—"

"Deprogrammers?"

"Right, deprogrammers, and they was come to take her back? I mean, I'm a Christian and all, and I don't like them cults no better than anybody else does, but golly, they just come and took her away, just like that! I hated to see her cryin', a nice, pretty girl like that. So I wonder, you think maybe we ought to call the sheriff? Or not."

"Can you tell me a little more about what the three people looked like?"

She described a trio who sounded to me like Dwight Brady, Alice Lawrence, and her sister, Margaret Stewart. They had come to haul Lilly back, all right, before she endangered her inheritance.

To the worried motel owner, I said, "I know the girl. From the sound of it, that was her mother and her aunt who came after her, along with a lawyer. I don't think they want to hurt her. In a way, I think they probably just want to try to keep her from hurting herself."

"Oh," she murmured with a sad and knowing look. "I hear there's a lot of teenage suicide in the cities."

"No." I smiled at her. "She's not suicidal, at least not that way. But it's good of you to be concerned. If I had a daughter and she was staying at a motel away from home, I'd like to think somebody like you was watching out for her."

That seemed to satisfy—and gratify—her.

I signed the American Express bill and took the top slip.

"Thanks," I said.

"You, too." She smiled. "I feel a lot better now."

I walked back out to the truck, wondering how Lilly's family had known where to find her. I supposed they could have assumed she would drive down here. And Brady might have known, from making my reservations, that this was the only motel for miles around. Or would only his secretary know that? Still, he might have called here and asked for Lilly Ann, to confirm her presence.

I turned on my heel and opened the office door again.

"Excuse me . . . did the girl get any telephone calls?"

"No," the owner said. "And I'd know."

I smiled at her again and closed the door. Maybe the owner would know that, and maybe she wouldn't. She couldn't have been in the office every minute Lilly was there. Somebody had to wash and change the sheets on the beds, and I'd seen her raw, red hands. I'd also seen her pushing a laundry cart early that morning myself.

I hoisted myself back into the truck.

"Lilly's gone. Her family came and got her."

"Just as well," Slight said. He slid the gearshift into first and we bounced over to room number three. He waited outside again while I packed, but when I emerged in the doorway with my stuff, he hopped down to help me. This time when he threw my bags in the back, I didn't even flinch. We got back into the truck and he backed out of the parking lot.

"Slight, how do you think her family got here?"

"What do you mean?"

"Well, they all drove back in her car. Do you think they flew down?"

"We saw that plane go over."

"That's right! We did. But then how'd they get from the airport to the motel? Is it close enough to walk?"

"Well, it's a good fifteen miles, I'd say. Maybe they hitched a ride with somebody."

The idea of that trio sticking out their thumbs was a dubious one, and I said as much to him. "Could they have called somebody from the airport?"

"It ain't JFK, Jenny," he said. "There's no phone. But I remember flyin' into Cedar Key, Florida, one time. By the time we had all three wheels on the ground, there was a fellow waiting for us to sell us a ride into town. It could be, some enterprising kid in Rock Creek saw the plane comin' down and drove out to make a buck."

I finally shrugged off the question as unanswerable for the time being. Somehow, they'd known to come here for her. Somehow, they'd managed it. Now she was gone, and overall, I had to admit I was glad to be rid of her.

19

Slight stowed me and my baggage in the spare bedroom on the
second floor. "This was Cat's room," he told me. "It ain't
haunted, I don't think."

"I gather he liked practical jokes, though."

"Yeah." He smiled a little. "So, if you find a dead badger on your
pillow, you'll know it wasn't Carl nor me that put it there. You going to
be okay in here?"

I looked around me at the big, plainly furnished room: double bed
on a bare frame with no headboard, table, chest of drawers, two
windows, and a closet.

"Fine, thanks."

"Good. Oh, and I think those are fresh sheets. I'm pretty sure we've
changed 'em since Cat slept in 'em. You might want to sniff 'em,
though, see if they smell like old cowboy." He picked up a framed

photograph from the bedside table and said, "What's this doing in here?" I peeked over his shoulder and saw it was a picture of a little boy, maybe three years old, all duded up in jeans, cowboy shirt, boots, hat, and a big grin. A real cutie. A smaller snapshot of a handsome blond teenager, clearly the little boy several years later, was stuck in a lower corner of the cheap gold metal frame.

"Who's that, Slight?"

He hesitated before he said, "Cat's nephew, Laddy. I'm going to check on those heifers again, you want to come?"

But I had heard the tires of the Cadillac crackling over the gravel drive and so I said, "Not this time." Slight nodded, then left me alone in the room, taking the photographs with him. I sat down on the bed. The mattress sank several inches under my weight, not a good omen for the coming night's sleep. What I really wanted at that moment, however, was not slumber so much as a long, hot bath to wash the prairie off my skin and to ease my aching muscles. But I also wanted to use the opportunity of Slight's absence to try to get to know my other new employee better. When I heard Slight drive off in his truck, then heard the back door slam, I walked downstairs to the kitchen.

Carl Everett stood at the counter, taking bacon out of a grocery sack.

"May I help?"

He jerked around toward me. "Uh, no. Thanks." The phone rang, and he grabbed it. "Yeah? Slight's not here. Yeah." He hung it up, went back to his unloading.

I leaned against a wall, watching him put things away, and thinking: How am I going to get this silent man to talk to me? My presence there clearly discombobulated him—he dropped the jar of instant coffee on the floor and then shut his hand in a cabinet when he went to put the coffee away. With every new clumsiness, he flushed an ever-deeper pink. To try to set this man down at a table, and try to get him to look me in the eye and talk to me, would seem an act of cruel and unusual punishment.

"May I ask a favor, Carl?"

The six-pack of beer cans he held broke open, spilling the first two cans onto the floor, but he nodded as he stooped to pick them up.

"I've driven through the pastures with Slight, but I haven't really looked at all the buildings yet. Would you show me around?"

"Okay," he said, flushing. Before he put the six-pack into the refrigerator, he took one of the beers out. He was starting to pull the tab on it when he looked up at me, startled. "Now, you mean?"

"If you have time."

He looked at the can in his hand. "Uh, I guess. What do you want to look at?"

"Oh." I strained to keep impatience out of my voice. "The bunkhouse, the other outbuildings."

He nodded and moved to the screen door. It was only when he'd stood there a moment, holding it open, that I realized he was holding it for me. I stepped past him and then outside into the coolness of the twilight on the prairie. The setting sun transformed the landscape into a pale and eerie painting viewed through a lavender scrim.

"I've never seen a place where the light changes color so often, and so beautifully."

If Carl heard me, he didn't respond.

We walked to the bunkhouse without speaking. Finally, I broke the silence by asking a question that wouldn't have been allowed on any legal employment-application form.

"You ever been married, Carl?"

He nodded.

"What about Slight?"

He took a drink before he shook his head. But then he nodded.

"Yes or no?"

"Well," he said after clearing his throat, "I don't exactly recall."

We had, by the close of this crackling conversation, reached the front door of the bunkhouse. Carl pushed it open, leaving me to enter first. I went on in and found that the structure was one long room containing a straight-backed chair and an old square table with a record player and a pile of long-playing records on top of it. There were two big trash bins overflowing with beer cans and liquor bottles and styrofoam cups. Even more than the house, this place smelled like a brewery, and one where they didn't take any great care with sanitation. *This* was where Slight had originally given me a choice of staying? One of his wry jokes, clearly. My only real choice was the main house.

Carl came in slowly behind me.

I strolled over to the table and, trying to act casual, sneaked a look at the record covers: Glenn Miller, Benny Goodman, Guy Lombardo. They were the big bands of the thirties and forties, playing "Stardust" and "Chattanooga Choo Choo" and "One More for My Baby and One More for the Road." So this was where Carl came to do his drinking, and this was what he did while he drank. I had myself a melancholy alcoholic for a lifetime, salary-guaranteed employee.

I walked away from the table—it felt like walking away from a desk with private papers on it—and went over to stare out one of the dirty windows. After a moment, I turned around. Carl waited just inside the doorway, the beer can in his hand, watching me.

"Did you see those detectives today, Carl?"

He sniffed, swallowed, shifted from one foot to another, switched his beer can to the opposite hand, sniffed again. "Yep."

"Did they ask a lot of questions?"

"Uh, not too many, I guess."

"What'd they ask, Carl?"

He shrugged his massive shoulders. "Nothin' much."

"Carl, who do you think killed Mr. Benet?"

He flushed the same deep-purple shade that he turned whenever Slight needled him. "Some damn fool."

"Yeah." If Detectives Canales and Krulick weren't any better at questioning him than I was, they had wasted a good part of their afternoon. I wondered if they'd finally given up, as I was about to do. "Well, thank you, Carl. You don't have to show me the other buildings. It's okay. I'll take a look on my own."

He remained standing there.

"In a few minutes," I said.

He walked out of the bunkhouse.

I leaned my head against the windowsill. Then, in lieu of immediately taking that bath, I placed a Benny Goodman record on the player. I sat down in the single chair, rested my head on the rim of it, and as twilight deepened into night, I listened to that sweet, soaring clarinet play "Time

After Time" and Sophisticated Lady" and finally, "Rhapsody in Blue." I
played that side of the record through again, and then I played
"Rhapsody in Blue" two more times. The final lovely clarinet solo was
winding to its haunting conclusion when I heard a deep voice speak to
me from the doorway.

"May I have this dance?"

I opened my eyes. Slight Harlan stood there, cigarette in one hand,
cowboy hat in the other. In the darkness, I couldn't make out the
expression on his face.

I reached over to lift the needle back to its rest, then I switched off the
machine.

"No." But it came out softly. I cleared my throat and tried again.
"No. I'm going in."

He didn't move back to allow me to walk by him, and so I had to
brush heavily against him on my way out the door. I felt as if my body
were metal to his magnet, and I had literally to pull away from him.
Once past him, I looked back. He was still there, gazing down the two
steps at me.

"No," I said more clearly.

I turned and started back to the house.

His footfalls sounded behind me. I wasn't sure I could step away
from him again, not while I still ached from pulling away from him the
first time.

But when he caught up with me, he didn't touch me.

"I can take care of Carl, Jenny."

I didn't look at him. "My guess is that you and Cat have been taking
care of Carl for quite some time."

For once, he was without words.

We were nearly to the kitchen door when I said, "We could try to get
him into some kind of recovery program, Slight. There must be
something around here—"

"No."

"But—"

"No." We were approaching the kitchen steps. He said in a louder
voice, "So what's it going to be for supper tonight, Jenny? You want
Tater Tots and pork chops or black-eyed peas and corn bread. *Carl?*

You in there? You start supper yet? We still got that frozen peach pie we could heat up for dessert?" He opened the kitchen door for me.

"If your new jeans weren't tight when you bought 'em, they will be by the time you leave here, Jenny."

His grin looked hard and forced.

I went directly upstairs after supper, peeled off my clothes, fell onto the old mattress, and rolled into the valley in the middle of it. I pulled the covers up and then lay there like the dead, like a mummy enveloped in swaddling, too tired even to find a more comfortable position for my aching body. I dreamed I heard a jingling in my room that night, a crisp, high-pitched musical rattle, like wind chimes tingling in a breeze.

20

Sunday, I awoke warm and desirous of my husband, a feeling that lasted all of about ten seconds—when the rest of my body woke up. It didn't ache as much as it had the night before, it ached more. The smell of coffee was tugging me downstairs, but when I moved my legs to attempt to swing myself out of the valley in the middle of the mattress, my inner thighs screamed in protest. They felt as if somebody had flogged them black and blue—or forced them to straddle for too long a large, moving animal. I could only be grateful that Geof was fifteen hundred miles away from me. I sank back into the mattress again.

"Oh, groan."

Would I ever walk again?

"Ouch, ouch, damn and groan."

I gave up the idea of movement below the waist and spread out my arms on the pillows beside me. It didn't hurt to do that. Well, good, if I had to live in a wheelchair for the rest of my life, at least I would still have upper-body mobility. The problem was, when I spread out my arms like that, one of my hands came to rest on something cold, hard, and sharp. I didn't recall there being any such thing on the pillow when I went to sleep.

I willed myself to remain calm, then I turned my head to look.

"Very funny," I said to Slight and Carl when I crept downstairs to breakfast a little later, after a long, hot bath. "Real cute."

Carl looked at me strangely, and Slight said, "What?"

"I had a ghost in my room last night, fellows," I informed them dryly. "He must have slept with his head at the foot of the bed and his boots on the pillow, because he left these next to me."

I tossed onto the table a pair of silver spurs.

"You're kidding," Slight said.

I sat down—slowly and carefully—and reached for the box of cornflakes.

"Guess it was Cat," I continued, "since he dearly loved his practical jokes. You think it was Cat?"

"Come on," Slight said, grinning at me. He passed a quart of milk my way. "You didn't find these in your bed. They were in the closet with his old boots."

I glanced at Carl, who was concentrating on his cereal.

"I guess Slight's saying he didn't do it, Carl. I guess it must have been you, then."

But when he raised his head, he looked confused and, I could have sworn, frightened. He looked at Slight and muttered, "That's not funny. You shouldn't ought to do that. It ain't funny at all."

Slight spread his arms wide and pulled a look of wounded innocence. But that only made Carl throw his napkin down and get up and stalk out. I was startled to see that he looked truly upset.

"Slight," I chided him, "a joke's a joke, but don't you think maybe this was too soon after Cat's death to be funny? In the final accounting, I don't know that St. Peter will record this as your most sensitive moment . . ."

I trailed off. He wasn't listening to me. Slight had picked up one of the spurs and was rolling them with his fingertips, gazing at them with a pensive and sad expression. I looked away from him. Suddenly, not feeling very hungry anymore, I got up and quietly cleared the breakfast dishes from the table. On my second trip back into the dining room, to pick up the milk and sugar, I saw that Slight was gone, and that he'd taken the pair of silver spurs with him.

Left alone, I used the solitude to wash the dishes and then to use the telephone. The stone house held on to the cool of the night; the natural light that filtered through the windows was pleasant to sit in, and there was just enough of it in the living room to enable me to use the phone without turning on a lamp. It being Sunday, I dialed Dwight Brady at his home number.

"Hello, Jenny," Dwight said in his flat, midwestern voice. "How are you getting along down there?"

"All right. How's Lilly Ann, Dwight?"

After a moment's hesitation he said, "Fine, as far as I know."

"That was you, wasn't it, along with Alice and Margaret who came and got her yesterday?"

"Well, yes, it was."

"Are they clients of yours now?"

"I suppose you might say so. They requested my help in this small matter, since I was familiar with that area."

"How did you know where she was?"

"You might say I deduced it."

"How—"

"Did she go onto the ranch, Jenny?"

"No."

"She is an impetuous young woman," he said in tones of the strongest disapproval.

"That is redundant, Dwight."

"What is?"

"Young and impetuous." Why did I get into these stupid conversations with him? This one was going nowhere. "I'm curious, Dwight, how did the three of you get from the Rock Creek Airport to the motel?"

"Mr. Everett picked us up."

"And how did he know to do that?"

"I called and requested it."

"I'm going to need a ride out of here myself if I'm going to make that flight in the morning."

"I'll send the plane tonight if you like."

"No, make it early tomorrow. Really early, like five-thirty, all right?"

"Fine."

"Thank you."

"You're welcome."

"Good-bye, Dwight."

"Good-bye."

That Dwight, I thought as I replaced the receiver, such a chatterbox, such a gossip. I was getting ready to redial, to reconfirm my airline reservations, when Slight called my name from the kitchen.

"Jenny."

I started. From where I sat, he was just visible at the kitchen sink. I heard water running in a heavy, noisy stream.

"Why don't you call him back, Jenny? Get him to have that pilot come back for you this afternoon. I'll drive you over to the runway anytime you say."

I eased myself out of the chair and walked toward him. I had come downstairs in my stocking feet to avoid having to cram my sore arches into the new cowboy boots again. Now I noticed only small twinges of pain as I walked the bare boards of the floors.

"Trying to get rid of me, Slight?" I said in the dining room. I moved a few steps closer, then I finally got a good look at him. What I saw caused me to run the remaining distance between us. "Oh, my God, Slight, what happened to you? Here, let me do that—"

He was covered with blood.

"I'm okay—"

There was blood in his hair, on his face, covering the front of his shirt, his shirtsleeves, his blue jeans, even the tops of his boots. I felt ill and panicked at the very sight of him, but I grabbed the towel that he was holding and I started frantically wiping him off, looking for the wounds that had produced this appalling flood, this cataract of blood.

"I'm not hurt, Jenny."

But when he stuck his hands under the water running from the tap, the flow turned red and soon the sink bubbled with blood as well as with water. With his wet, washed hands he began to unbutton his shirt. I dabbed at the blood on his head, still looking for wounds. I couldn't believe that he could be covered with so much blood and not be mortally wounded somewhere.

"We lost a calf. Had to pull her from her mama, and we got there too late. Calf was dead by the time we got her out, suffocated, I guess. Nice little heifer, too. And the mama lost so much blood, we're probably going to lose her. Shit. I mean that, Jenny. Cowshit and blood, that's all this goddamn business is some days. Let go of me, you're going to ruin that pretty new shirt of yours."

"Shut up," I said.

I helped him pull his bloody shirt off, then I tossed it into the sink. The blood had soaked through the material, coating his skin beneath. I ran the dish towel under the water until it was good and wet, wrung it, then began to wipe the blood from his chest and shoulders. Slight worked at his boots, kicking at the heel of one with the toe of the other until he pried them off and stood in his stocking feet. He unclasped his belt buckle, unzipped his bloody jeans, took them off, and tossed them into the sink on top of his shirt. Meanwhile, I washed him down, rinsing the towel, wringing it, washing him down again, and every now and then taking a swipe at the horrid mess on the floor, as well. As the blood came off, I uncovered a red, swollen welt on the front of his left shoulder and another one at the edge of his jaw.

"Did the cow kick you, Slight?"

"What?"

I touched the welts gently, but he winced anyway.

"You've been struck."

"Yeah." He broke away from me to plunge both of his hands under the water and then to splash his face. "She got me good a couple of times."

Standing close to him as I was, looking at his bare, bent back, I suddenly became acutely aware that he was stripped down to his underwear. Jockey shorts. Thick cotton socks. The back of his neck was deeply and permanently tanned, as were his hands and his face, but the rest of his hard, lean body was pale. The contrast might have been repulsive; the paler skin might have looked pasty on another man. But Slight's natural complexion was a deeper color than mine would have been after a week in the sun, so the contrast wasn't as great as it might have been on a lighter-skinned man, and it certainly wasn't unattractive. The hair on his chest was curly and almost entirely dark brown, with a few gray hairs. There was only the slightest hint of age in the loosening of his skin under his upper arm muscles, around his waist, and under his jaw. His clothes didn't hide an old man's body, but one that looked nearly as young as my husband's, even though I felt that Slight could be as much as twenty years older than Geof. I clenched my hands into fists to keep them from touching the ridge of his backbone where it emerged from the elastic of his shorts. But my hands felt as if they had a life of their own; they ached to run my fingernails lightly up that ridge, to massage the muscles bunched in those shoulders as he bent over the sink, to slide around that tight waist . . .

He straightened and grabbed blindly for the towel I held. After I handed it to him, I opened my hands at my sides and spread and stretched my fingers, trying to release the tension in them.

"How old are you, Slight?"

He rubbed his face vigorously, and then his hands, before he said, with a glance at me, "Old enough to know better, and young enough not to care."

"Come on, really."

"I thought age was supposed to be irrelevant, Jenny."

"I suppose it is if you haven't got much of it."

He smiled and draped the towel over the faucet.

"How old are you, Jenny?"

"Older than some, younger than others."

"Touché." He looked me over. "Thanks. I'm sorry about your new clothes. Maybe you'd better hit the road before we've got you down to skivvies and socks, like me."

I looked down at myself and discovered that I was speckled with blood. When I looked up, I discovered that he was starting to peel off his socks. Oh, shit, were his shorts coming off next, right there in front of me?

"I think I'll go change clothes," I said quickly.

I turned heel and fled the kitchen, fully expecting to hear the sound of his laughter following me. When it didn't, I had this very clear thought: *What's wrong?* Was he simply upset about losing the calf, or was there more to it than that, and was he really trying to get rid of me?

The phone rang as I climbed the stairs, but he let the machine pick it up.

As I changed clothes in the spare bedroom, I chided myself for being paranoid, not to mention self-centered. I was in the way here. This was a working ranch, after all. The men couldn't devote whole days at a time to giving personal tours to dudes from back east, even if the dude was an owner. It was time for me to leave, and yet I was reluctant to go for reasons having nothing to do with Slight: I wanted to see the light change over the prairie one more afternoon and evening, I wanted to lean out of my bedroom window to listen for a coyote howling under the moon. I wouldn't mind a walk down by the stream, or even another horseback ride if my legs would agree to go with me.

I suddenly stood still, loose sock dangling from my hand.

"*I'll be damned,*" I said out loud.

I liked it here. Who'd have thought it?

I finished changing my clothes, then I ran downstairs to tell Slight that I would be leaving, but not until the next day.

But he wasn't there. Gone again. Where he'd obtained fresh clothes without going upstairs, I couldn't imagine, but he'd done it. He'd left me a note, however: "Jenny, would you feed the calf this afternoon? There's a bottle already mixed in the fridge. Thanks." I laid the note down and ran to the kitchen door and opened it, just in time to see him ride out of the barn on big, golden Buck. They took off at a fast trot, but by the time they hit the dirt road, they were galloping, as if both horse and man had nervous energy they needed to get out of their systems.

I stepped onto the back porch to watch them go.

Well. Now I could take that walk by the stream, although a run would be better for shaking loose the tension that burned in me. Then I'd come back and rustle up (*Stop that,* I thought when I heard myself) some lunch for anybody who happened to be around. Maybe by then my rear end wouldn't object too strenuously to another ride on Molly. I smiled at the lone prairie and breathed in deeply of the cool, clean air of "my" ranch.

21

Neither of the men came back to the house for lunch, so I ate a bologna sandwich and a Coke by myself. Then I grabbed the huge plastic feeding bottle, which had the most enormous nipple I had ever seen, out of the fridge and headed for the barn to feed the orphaned bull calf. The liquid in the bottle looked white and foamy, like regular milk, but I guessed it was a formula of some kind, so I shook it as I walked. I was more nervous about this assignment than I ever was before a foundation board meeting, but I was looking forward to it, too. The little calf was so sweet. Maybe he wouldn't kick me. Or bite me. Or pee on me.

But before I reached the barn, I heard the sound of tires on gravel and turned to see Sheriff Pat Taylor pulling up in a red Wagoneer.

"Hi!" she called through her open window.

I waved with my free hand and waited for her.

She came striding up with both thumbs hooked into her gun belt. "That your official sheriff's car?" I inquired.

"Nope." She grinned. "I've got to run car pool today, carry some of the football team over to Newton for a game, and I don't like to use the taxpayers' money to do it. How you doin'? I had a visit from a couple of Kansas City cops yesterday, askin' about you all."

She didn't say "y'all," she said "you all."

"I told 'em I'd never had any trouble with anybody out here," she continued. "They seemed a mite disappointed to hear it. But I told them I'd get back to them about this shooting accident, if it turned out to be something else. Want to show me where it happened?"

"I wish I could, but I'm embarrassed to tell you I have no idea where we were at the time. I'm still at the stage where all the pastures look alike." I pointed to the corrals beside the barn. "That's Carl Everett over there, he could tell you."

"Thanks, I'll ask him."

She strode off, leaving me with the feeling that Hood County, Kansas, was in honest, if overworked, hands when it came to law enforcement.

With the afternoon sun behind it, the stone barn cast an enormous shadow in my direction. Off to the side of it, Carl had stopped whatever he was doing with a few cattle and was watching the sheriff's approach. I waved halfheartedly, but he either didn't see me or he ignored me. I walked up the graveled grade to the gaping mouth of the barn and peered into its dim, cool, vast interior. It seemed a monster craw into which hors d'oeuvres the size of Clydesdales and oxen teams might disappear forever. I felt dwarfed by it, not only in size, but in spirit, as well.

A tangerine cat slipped in ahead of me.

This barn was too big for mere mortals and our puny pets, I thought. The horse stalls were empty, except for Molly and for a big roan horse that must have been Carl's. And the one that held the calf, of course. There were huge round bales of hay scattered about. Straw covered the floor like a loosely woven carpet of hemp. Spiderwebs glistened in the stray snatches of sunlight that filtered down through cracks in the wooden roof four stories up and through chinks in the stones of the walls. I heard a light, quick rustling, as of cat's feet through straw, or maybe rat's feet. One of the horses snuffled, but all else was silent as I walked in.

I was afraid to open the stall where the calf was, for fear he'd push past me and escape, so I awkwardly climbed over and dropped down beside him. That startled him enough to jerk him to his feet. He backed away from me, into a far corner of the stall.

"Here . . . here," I whispered.

What do you say to call a bull? There's no equivalent for "Here, kitty, kitty."

"Food," I said, and held out the bottle.

He bunched himself farther into the corner.

It occurred to me that I was bigger than he was, and that thought injected me with enough false courage that I headed toward him.

He bolted from that corner to another.

"Milk!" I said. "Um, good!"

I moved toward him again. He started to bolt away again. I lunged, grabbed him around his smelly, furry neck, and stuck the goddamned bottle into his mouth. My, isn't this fun, I thought. And just then, he got the idea. His muscles relaxed, his hindquarters dropped to the straw, then his forelegs buckled under, and he began to suck contentedly on the monster nipple.

I stroked the curly white hair on the top of his hard skull, between his ears.

Well, maybe it was fun, after all.

"Nice little bull," I crooned. "Don't let those nasty men get anywhere near you with a knife, baby."

We stayed there happily, he and I, as he slurped and birds twittered in the rafters, until he'd emptied the bottle down to a layer of foam. When I pulled the bottle away, he tried to grab it back, but I stood up quickly. He gazed up at me with his lovely, sweet, brown eyes and licked his white lips with his big, pink, moist tongue.

I moved my left boot forward in the straw and felt a sudden, quick, heavy weight pass over it.

By the time I reacted and looked down, the snake that had slithered across the instep of my boot was gliding off into a hole at the back side of the stall. But what I could see of it was very dark, very long, and very thick.

The shriek that rose instinctively in my throat didn't make it out of my mouth, but I felt its vibration through my body anyway. *Don't move.* My imagination bit with snake's fangs through the thick hide of my boots. I felt the imaginary venom streak up my veins to my heart. *Don't move. Wait. Wait. Wait.* Only when I felt sure it was gone did I scramble over the walls of that stall, run out of the barn as if a stampede of snakes was slithering after me, and stumble over the gravel down to the corrals. The sheriff was gone, probably to investigate the pasture, but Carl was still there, closing a calf into a small pen. I forced myself to slow down to a walk.

"*Carl?*"

He turned my way, nodded his recognition.

"Carl, there's a snake in the barn. It ran over my boot."

He nodded again calmly. "What kind of snake?"

"*Kind? Kind? A big kind!*"

Slight would have mocked me for that, but Carl merely nodded again and finished locking the calf in the pen.

"I'll take a look," he said.

But he walked off toward the house first. When he emerged, he held a gun. He disappeared into the barn. It wasn't long before I heard a shot, then a second one. The horses went crazy, whinnying and kicking at the boards of their stalls. I heard Carl yell at them, and they quieted down. Soon, he appeared in the doorway, with the gun in his right hand and trailing something long and dark from his left. Feeling relieved but queasy, I walked over to take a look.

He threw the thing at my feet.

I jumped back as if it had, indeed, bitten me.

"Timber rattler," he said.

It took me an unbelieving moment to comprehend that the meaning of that phrase was "rattlesnake." The creature at my feet had no head left, but I could certainly make out the "rattle," which looked like horny rings tapering to a button on the end. The snake looked huge to me, maybe four feet long even without its head, and as thick as the calf of my leg.

He kicked at it, and it rolled closer to me.

"Awful smell," I managed to say.

"Yeah, they do stink."

"Thank you, Carl."

He gave me a quizzical look, as if my gratitude puzzled him. Sure, I thought hysterically, no big deal, kill a rattlesnake every day. Why we did it all the time in Port Frederick, when we weren't shooting coyotes and prairie dogs. My knees and ankles were so weak that the stiffness of my boots was the only thing standing between me and a dead faint. I had seen dead bodies before. I had seen blood, just that morning, in fact. I had watched herpetologists on public television extoll the "beauty" and "mythological significance" and the "environmental value" of snakes. But this dead rattler with its head shot off and its horrible tumors at the end of its tail was more than this town girl could take.

I bolted, like a spooked calf, for the house.

In the second-floor bathroom, I made a wet compress out of a washcloth and took it with me to the spare bedroom, and then I lay down on the bed and put the compress on my forehead and folded my hands over my stomach and closed my eyes.

You're a pansy.

Right.

Somebody knocked on the closed bedroom door. I sat up so fast I made myself even dizzier. "Yes? Come in."

Carl opened the door, poked his grizzled head in, and nodded at me. One of his big hands appeared and he laid an object on top of the dresser beside the door.

"Thought you might like to take home a souvenir."

He retreated, closing the door behind him.

I didn't have to get out of bed to guess what it was that lay there—the rattle from the dead snake. I leaned over the side of the bed and vomited into a metal wastebasket.

22

I woke up an hour later, surprised I had slept.

The house was quiet as only houses in the country can be. I judged the time to be near two o'clock, because the sun was peeking in the windows on the west side. By now Carl might be drunkenly dozing in the bunkhouse. Slight, well, who could know where Slight was at any moment; he could be downstairs reading one of those cattle magazines that littered the floor of the living room, or outside riding, in town, out of town, on the road . . .

I rolled over lazily onto my side.

The sour odor that greeted my nostrils forced me out of bed. I carried the metal wastebasket past the mutilation on the dresser and into the bathroom. I emptied the basket into the toilet, then washed it out under the spigot of the big white claw-footed bathtub. After that, I scrubbed the tub. Then I washed my face and my hair under the silver spigot in the deep porcelain sink, scrubbing until the fragrance of shampoo washed out the odor of rattlesnake and fear.

When I finished, my hair lay in a wet, tangled mass on my shoulders. I combed it out, braided it, then went looking for an office. Where there are headquarters there should be an office, I reasoned, and where there is an office there should be rubber bands for my wet hair.

I walked down the hall, past a bedroom: Slight's. That was evident from yesterday's shirt hung on a bedpost. I glanced into the bedroom across the hall. The beer can on the bedside table made it easy for me to identify this room as Carl's. There was a photograph in a gold frame behind the beer can, and I stepped in far enough to get a look at it: It was the little cowboy again. Cat Benet's nephew, I thought Slight had said, "Chad" or "Laddy," something like that. I was touched by this unexpected sign of sentiment in Carl, although on second thought, I guessed it wasn't so unexpected in a man who got drunk to the strains of "Rhapsody in Blue."

I found the office at the end of the hall.

It, unlike the rest of the house, was furnished with contemporary pieces—the sort of expensive, nondescript desk, credenza, chair, and cabinet suite that can be purchased at any office-furnishings store. Still, modest as it was, it was the only place I'd seen thus far where Cat Benet had spent money on anything other than land, livestock, and machinery. He certainly hadn't lavished it anywhere else in his home.

For a moment I felt like an intruder, until it struck me that the business that was conducted in this office was my business now. Slight would have to send the books to our accountant, but why not get started now on my own? Invoices are invoices and ledgers are ledgers, I reasoned, no matter if the product in question is animate or inanimate. If I could read profit and loss statements for banks and museums, I could probably read one for a ranch.

In the long, top desk drawer, I located my rubber bands and used them to make pigtails.

Now with both hands free, I toured the contents of the office.

The bottom file drawer was stacked front to back with annual reports from American foundations, Port Frederick's among them. Suddenly I realized that maybe here in this office I would finally come across the reason that Cat Benet had picked us, out of all the possible foundations in the world, to leave his ranch to.

Our own annual report for the previous year—which I had written —gave me no clues, so I started reading the others. I examined their comparative net worths, I studied the names on their boards of directors, I noted their geographic locations, I perused their statements of purpose, I noted how their funds were accrued, invested, and dispersed.

What I discovered was that most of them had larger net worths and more prominent boards of directors than ours. Several of them listed farm or ranch land among their assets, indicating they had some expertise in managing same. At least half of them dispensed their funds nationally, rather than being limited, as we were, to local disbursement. And of all of them, we were the one located farthest away from Hood County, Kansas. Given these choices, I would have picked any foundation but ours. But Cat Benet hadn't done that. He had selected—after considerable research, if this pile of annual reports was any indication —the foundation that would know the least about his business and the one that was the farthest away from it.

Now why would an astute businessman do that?

Because he wasn't so astute?

Or could it have been because he *wanted* ignorance? And he *didn't* want interference? Now there were thoughts to give one pause, and I did pause, feeling stunned, as if somebody had figuratively whacked me on the head with the ol' two-by-four. Because those ideas would imply he had something to hide, maybe something relating to the land or cattle, since those were the areas of our greatest ignorance. And from 1,500 miles away, we probably would never interfere much with the operation, relying instead on Slight and Carl.

It was a chilling thought: Was the Port Frederick Civic Foundation being made an unwitting accomplice to some sort of fraud?

I don't like being used, or being made a fool.

I used the phone on the desk to call Roy Leland.

"If there is fraud," Roy said, "the members of Benet's families may hold the key, because they're the ones he barred from the place."

"That's right. Maybe there's something here that he didn't want them to see, something that would arouse their suspicions."

"You think it could be connected to his murder?"

"I think that's quite possible, but *what?*"

"Ask 'em."

"Who?"

"Whoever's on that list, Jenny."

"You want me to call them?"

"Go see 'em."

"Roy, they're spread all across the country."

"They have airplanes out there, don't they? I won't allow the foundation to be made party to a fraud by that screwball Benet. The sooner you see these people the better, Jennifer."

That's what I was afraid he'd say.

"There may not *be* any fraud, Roy."

"Well, there sure as hell is something screwy going on."

I sighed to myself: *Bon voyage, Geoffrey, my love.*

"All right, Roy, but you'll have to see that Geof gets the word when he docks in Provincetown tomorrow."

"That's no problem. Just tell me where he'll be, and I'll have somebody there."

Trying not to sound martyred, I told him, "And Roy? Don't ruin his trip entirely. Just tell him Benet died and I'm having to work on the bequest."

Downstairs, a screen door slammed.

"*Carl?*" It was Slight, hollering in the front room. "*Jenny? Children?*" I smiled, in spite of myself. "*Daddy's home!*"

I said, "Roy? I've got to go."

"Any more dead cows?"

"Snakes."

"What?"

"A rattlesnake slid over my boot, but Carl Everett shot it."

"Your boot?"

"No, the snake."

"Hell, save it, have some more boots made out of it."

"What a good idea," I said faintly. "Good-bye, Roy."

As I hung up, I heard Slight clump into the kitchen, and soon he was making pan-rattling noises. I walked quietly back down the hall to my bedroom, retrieved Dwight Brady's letter from my briefcase, then tiptoed back to the office and called him. While I waited for somebody to pick up the ringing phone in Kansas City, I twirled my chair around so that I could put my feet up on the windowsill behind the desk. When Dwight came to the phone, I told him I had a question about the will.

"I'm curious," I said, "who *are* these people?"

"How were they related to Benet, you mean?"

"Yes."

"Well, the ones in Illinois are Benet's second wife and their children, who were adopted by her second husband. The ones in California are his third wife and her son by another husband. The two in Texas are Cat's sister and nephew, and the one in New Mexico was his fourth wife. Of course, you know the Kansas City contingent."

"He left something to all those people?"

"Yes, trusts, sizable ones."

"Even to his ex-wives?"

"Yes." Dwight's dry tone suddenly took on the note of wonderment that we all seemed to get in our voices when discussing Benet's marital history. "You might be interested to know, Jenny, that this is in *addition* to the settlements he made on his wives when they divorced him, as well as the child support payments he continued until all of his children were twenty-one, even including the two children who were adopted by their stepfather!" The dry tone returned. "Mr. Benet was a generous man."

Or one with a guilty conscience?

As I thanked Dwight and hung up, I whirled the chair back around until it faced the door—where Slight Harlan stood, leaning casually against the frame, gazing in at me.

When I had caught my breath, I said, "I don't get it, Slight."

"What don't you get, Jenny?"

"Who ever heard of leaving trust funds to your ex-wives? And yet Cat, who felt warmly enough about *his* ex-wives to leave them each a lot of money, barred them from this ranch."

"Don't you recognize a bribe when you hear one?"

I stared at him. "Bribe?"

"What are the terms for everybody getting their money?"

"That they won't contest the will and they won't come here."

He raised his eyebrows. "Do you get it now?"

"He wanted us to have the ranch, and you guys to run it with absolutely no interference from anybody. Have I got it? Is that it?"

He nodded, smiled, and walked away.

I continued staring at the space he had vacated.

There it was again: no interference. And if he wanted ignorance, he was getting it from me, all right: I felt as dumb as a post.

23

Before going downstairs, I returned to my bedroom and steeled myself to pick up the snake's rattle. It felt like it looked—horny and rough, and smelled bad enough to make me want to throw up again. When I gave it an experimental shake, I didn't hear anything, but the movement released more of the awful odor. Holding the evil thing as far out from myself as possible, I carried it with me to the kitchen.

Slight looked at my pigtails this time and said, "Well, if it isn't Little Mary Milkmaid." He grinned. "So how does your garden grow?"

"With silver bells and cockleshells." I laid the "souvenir" on the kitchen counter, then wiped my hand off on my jeans. He raised his eyebrows at the ugly thing, then at me. "And rattles all in a row."

"Heard about that," he said.

"It was horrible. What's this?" A glint of broken metal on the kitchen counter had caught my eye. When I got closer, I saw that it was the picture frame holding the photographs of Cat Benet's nephew, only now the glass was broken—a couple of large wedges were missing— and the frame was split at two corners, so the whole thing was held together mostly by the backing. It looked to me as if Slight had been trying to slide the photographs out.

"*Crotalus horridus horridus.*"

"What?" I jerked around, turning my back on the photographs.

"Latin name for it. A timber rattler's one of the most aggressive creatures on the face of the earth. They're as irritable as some women I've known, present company excluded, of course." He picked up the rattle and gave it a shake. "Did you know you can't make these things rattle? Can't shake 'em fast enough."

"I didn't even hear it," I said.

"They sound like somebody hissing through his teeth."

"I'll remember that."

He frowned at the thing, then set it down.

"I'm leaving," I told him. "Tonight, if we can get that pilot to come back for me. I've had enough of the hazards of the country, Slight. I'm going back to the city where it's safe."

I didn't say which city.

"I'll fly you," he said.

"You'll what?"

"I'm a pilot." He squinted that amused smile at me. "Go get your things together, and I'll fly you."

So astonished was I by that piece of unexpected information that I completely forgot about the broken picture frame on the counter behind me.

It was dark by the time we took off.

The metal shed at the end of the runway on the ranch held a four-seater airplane, a Beech Debonair Slight called it, that he said Cat sold to him when Cat got too sick to fly it himself. All three men, I learned, had pilot's licenses, although Slight was a little vague about whether or not he and Carl had kept theirs current.

The little plane had dual controls, which made me smile to myself: as if I could use the extra yoke that was right in front of my chest or those big silver rudder pedals at my feet! Fat chance. I'd crash before I figured out what to do with them. There was a fat little blue notebook stuffed up under the left rudder pedal, I saw, undoubtedly to keep tinhorns like me from stomping on it and throwing us into a spin.

I was nervous at the start of this flight, but not nearly so much as I'd been flying out to the ranch. Heck, I was an old hand at this now, and besides, it wasn't even raining.

"Copilot ready?"

"Check," I yelled over the roar of the engine and the *whap, whap* of the propellers.

"Door locked?"

"Check."

"Seat belt on?"

"Check."

"Barf bag ready?"

"Oh, shut up."

We taxied straight onto the dirt runway, heading into a light south wind. I suspected that what we were doing was illegal, as there were no lights on this field, but by the time I had that thought, we were already in the air.

Slight glanced over at me. "Whoopee."

I smiled at him.

He climbed straight ahead. Then he started a long, easy turn, still climbing, to the east. We got partway into it when suddenly the plane skidded under us, refusing to turn any farther left. It was the funniest feeling, like sliding across ice. Unnerving as it was, it was kind of fun, and I grinned at him.

"What was that?" I yelled over the noise.

But Slight, who looked surprised, didn't answer.

He pulled us out of the skid and we flew straight ahead, continuing to climb. At 3,500 feet, he attempted another left turn. Again, we skidded, and this time, before he pulled us out of it, the back of the plane dipped down and the nose came up. I felt a sickening looseness, but Slight brought us out of it, straightened us out, and got us going straight ahead again. I tried to keep the panic out of my voice. *"What's going on?"*

"I'm taking 'er on up," he yelled.

Clearly, for some reason, this plane wouldn't turn left. I didn't know how frightened to be, didn't have any context into which to place this terror. Logic tried to override fear: Couldn't we just circle the field, making right turns, until we were lined up with the runway to land again?

Slight glanced over at me.

He looked worried.

My instincts immediately told me to shut up—for God's sake don't distract him. And I no longer worried about how frightened I *should* be. I just plain was.

The altimeter inched up toward 7,500 feet.

Suddenly I was horribly aware of the fact that I had put my life in the hands of this near-stranger. Just because he claimed to be a pilot didn't mean he was a good one. At the moment, he looked nearly as panicked as I felt. I had to fight my own urge to grab the wheel and wrest control of the plane from him. Helpless to do anything, I looked back at him with a gaze of complete and completely false confidence: *I believe in you,* that gaze was meant to say, *you can do it.*

We were now flying over a little town whose lights twinkled innocently below us. Rock Creek? I thought of families sitting down to supper in those dining rooms below us, of babies in their cribs, and mothers bending over them and dogs howling up at us from backyards, and I thought that none of them knew what danger they were in at that moment, and I willed us far away from them.

Slight's left hand shifted on the yoke.

Oh, Lord, he was going to try another left turn.

I watched his hands delicately twist the wheel to the left, barely, barely. I braced myself for the terror to come. He turned it a little farther and we started to skid again. A gust of wind came up under the right wing, tipping us left as we continued to skid. Slight tried to compensate, but suddenly we were nose up again, and then some sort of warning siren was screaming at us. I didn't know much about flying, but I knew enough to recognize that we were going into a stall and what follows a stall is a dive and what follows a dive is a crash. Sure enough, from our nose-up position, we suddenly plunged nose down. I was pressed back against my seat; my gaze was locked on the floor of the plane.

"*No left rudder!*" Slight yelled.

Well, at least I'd know what killed me.

And then it hit me: ohmigod.

I kicked my left foot forward, battling the pressure of the dive, until I managed to knock the little plastic notebook loose from under the left pedal in front of me.

Immediately Slight regained left-rudder control.

After another couple of heart-stopping moments, he brought us smoothly out of the dive.

When we were flying level again, I reached down for the notebook. It was about seven by five inches and maybe two inches thick, a spiral-bound owner's and operator's manual of some kind. I held it up for Slight to see. I pointed to it and then down to the rudder pedal.

His eyes widened, and his mouth dropped open.

Then he attempted another left turn.

This time it worked.

We burst into speech at the same time.

"I'm sorry—"

"Thank you—"

"Are you—"

"I'm fine, you—"

Slight laughed shakily, then reached for the notebook and looked at it and then at me.

"It was stuck up under that left pedal," I said.

He nodded and gave it back to me. "I usually keep it in that pocket in front of your seat. It must have dropped out and slid down there. I don't know what to say, Jenny. I'm sorry as hell."

"Well, we survived."

"Barely," he said.

I stuck the deadly notebook back in the seat pocket where it belonged and leaned back in the seat. For the rest of the trip I was silent and Slight didn't talk, either, except to the air controllers. After landing on a jet runway at Kansas City International Airport, Slight taxied to a general aviation gate at the terminal.

He switched off the engine, and the cockpit went dark and quiet. Slight reached over with his right hand and grasped my left one. I squeezed back, hard. He unsnapped his seat belt, and I undid mine. I pulled him toward me until I could get my arms around him, then he put his arms around me and we just held on to each other for a while.

"Thanks for not killing me," I murmured.

"No, you saved us," he said, then he lifted my hair off my neck and kissed the lobe of my right ear. "But I'll take the credit, if you like."

I pushed away from him. "And I'll take the blame for this. I'm sorry, Slight." And I was, oh, I was. "But I'd better go."

"Yeah," he said.

He carried my suit bag to the terminal for me.

We stood at the door looking at each other.

"I'll miss you . . . ma'am."

"It's been . . . exciting."

He laughed a little. "You won't forget me, back in Port Frederick?"

"Probably not," I admitted, "but I'm going to try."

He smiled at that and opened the door for me.

I stole a last glimpse of him through the glass as he trotted back to his airplane. That man and I were as intimately and permanently linked as two people could be who had faced sudden death together. *Cape Cod Bay,* I said to myself, *Cape Cod Bay Cape Cod Bay Cape Cod Bay.* I quickly turned so he wouldn't catch me looking and walked over to a ticket counter where I canceled my morning return flights to Port Frederick, then made new reservations on the red-eye that night to Chicago. Then I called Dwight Brady one last time to tell him that he didn't need to send the plane, that I'd already arrived at KCI and would fly out tonight.

I just didn't say "out" where.

"How are the police coming with their investigation?"

"They've been after me to tell them why Benet would leave a fortune in land and cattle to total strangers," Dwight said, and my heart, which had never completely gotten back under control anyway, started thudding unpleasantly again. "They can't seem to believe that I don't *know* why. Canales seems to have the idea that you and Quentin Harlan cooked up some scheme together."

"That's just great," I said bitterly.

"They're going to want to talk to you again," he warned me before he hung up.

Catch me if you can.

I hoisted my bags, walked out of the terminal, and hailed a yellow cab.

PART III

Happy Trails to You

24

Did it always rain in Kansas City? Or only when I was there? I had no more than stepped out of the cab in front of the Kansas City Medical Center when the first drop fell. I remembered then the sudden gust of wind that had nearly tipped the Debonair into kingdom come, and I thought: So there was a storm coming, and I'd been too intent on surviving to notice. I spared a thought for Slight, flying home in rain and lightning, but that was the only other thought of him I allowed myself.

Once again, I struggled through the hospital's revolving doors with my belongings. Again, I passed the reception desk and traversed the long corridor to the swinging doors. Again, I thought how practically anyone could walk through here without being questioned, especially if that someone were wearing white or green, or using crutches. Or a wheelchair.

Instead of making a right turn to room 1080, this time I stopped at the nurses' station. I was lucky and located a nurse who had assisted the day Cat Benet died. She was at dinner in the cafeteria, I was told by another nurse, so that's where I went looking for her.

Kelly Eames, she was, an RN who looked about half my age. Kelly was eating by herself—egg salad on whole wheat, a small bag of barbecued potato chips, and a Diet Pepsi—at a table by a window. She had the clear, soft skin of a child and the body of a fifties movie star. Her name tag hung halfway down her left breast, like a sign on a mountain for advanced skiers. When I introduced myself, I described myself, vaguely, as someone who was "taking care of some of his business interests."

"Hi," she greeted me in a friendly way. "Sit?"

I did, in the chair opposite her.

"I'm sure sorry about Mr. Benet," she said.

"Were you one of his regular nurses, Kelly?"

"Um hum," she said, her mouth full of egg salad. After she swallowed, she smiled a tender and apologetic smile at me. "I liked him a lot. I'm real sorry he got killed the way he did."

For a moment I was confused, wondering if she meant she would have preferred him to be stabbed, instead of smothered. Then my brain kicked in again.

"Why'd you like him?"

She looked surprised. "He was nice! And he was funny. Even when he was real sick, he'd laugh and crack jokes on us. Mr. Benet was one of those patients, you know, that you don't mind going in to see, even when it's going to be bad news when you get there."

"Bad news?"

"Oh, you know, tubes and shots and pain and agony, and all that. There's patients who cry about it and there's the ones who get mad and there's the depressed ones and there's the ones who cop a feel and there's the fake nice ones and the fake brave ones, and he was one of the real brave ones. If he was feeling too sick to laugh, he'd just lie there quiet and try to smile at you. But most of the time, he could manage a joke or a smile. He never said anything mean to any of us, except if somebody screwed up his pills or jabbed him too hard, then he'd be pretty sharp about it. Heck, I don't blame him. And those friends of his really expected us to do right by him. Himself, he expected you to know what you were doing around him, I could see that. There was a couple of people around here didn't like him for that. I mean, after he snapped at them for screwing up his IV or something. But all the rest of the time, to the rest of us, he was always very nice. I felt real bad when I heard he got killed. I've known a few patients, let me tell you, I wouldn't mind killing myself. I shouldn't say it, but it's true, real nasty so-and-sos, but he wasn't like that—"

"What friends, Kelly?"

"What? Oh, there were a couple of old cowboys used to come by once a week or so, one of them was big and never said much, and the other one was cute and talked a lot. But boy, I want to tell you, if Mr. Benet ever needed anything, they *both* could talk and plenty loud. They'd be hollering down the corridor *"Where's Mr. Benet's pain shot?"* or *"We need a nurse in here,"* or whatever it was. A lot of people here didn't like that, but I understood. His friends, they were only looking out for him. There wasn't anybody else to do it, and we're busy, too busy, really, so I think it was good that they were looking out for his best interests."

"Was he rational, Kelly?"

"Oh, yeah."

"Always?"

"Mostly. He was real alert."

"So he probably could have read things—maybe even complicated things like contracts—and understood them? If he had signed a contract, or his will, say, he would have known what he was signing?"

"Oh, sure, unless the pain was too bad, or he'd just had a shot or some awful treatment and he was too out of it. But when the pain would die down and he wasn't drugged up, he could talk, you know, and read and function pretty well. He liked to watch *General Hospital,* isn't that funny? A lot of our patients do. It probably made him feel better to stay busy, you know?"

"Any other visitors?"

"Just that lawyer."

"Were the cowboys here the morning he died, Kelly?"

She shrugged. "I didn't see them."

"Did he have any other visitors that day?"

"Besides you and that lawyer, you mean?"

So she was observant.

"Yes, besides us."

"I doubt it." She shook her head to make it definite. "There never was anybody else come to see him. Just that lawyer and those cowboys. Lord, that cute one was an awful flirt, worse than Mr. Benet himself, and that's saying something. I'll say one thing for them, though, they never made any boob jokes around me, and that made them good guys in my book."

I felt ashamed of my own private joke about her ski slope of a chest. I also felt that it was just as well that she hadn't been able to read Slight Harlan's mind.

"I heard he was a rich rancher," Kelly said. "And that he'd been married seven or eight times. Do you know if that's true?"

"I don't know what's true," I admitted.

But she wasn't really listening. Romance had her imagination in thrall. "All those wives and all that money," Kelly said dreamily. "He must have been some kind of man in his day. You know, you're not the first one to show up here asking about him. I'm beginning to think it's like a pilgrimage or something, all these ex-wives wanting to come see the place where he died—"

"*Who* did you say was here?"

"One of his other ex-wives." She leaned dangerously over her egg salad and whispered, "I hope you don't mind me saying this, but you might want to avoid that waiting room on the first floor, 'cause she's still in there. She showed up this morning, and she hasn't left yet! You and her, I guess you've got something in common"—but Kelly looked doubtful as she said that—"but she looks the hot-tempered type to me, red hair and all, you know, and I don't know if you'd want to mess with her."

What kind of type did *I* look? I wondered. Not hot-tempered, evidently. Cool and collected, as befitted my Swedish genes? Geof would get a good laugh out of that, if I ever got a chance to tell him.

"Which wife was she, do you know?"

She shook her head. "Which one were you?"

"I'm not an ex-wife."

"Oh," she said significantly.

"No! I wasn't married to him."

"Wow," she said, "so you don't get any of the money, 'cause you don't have any legal status, right? Were you common law, maybe?" She snapped her fingers. "You ought to get that lawyer, what's his name out in Hollywood, Marvin Michelsburg or something, and get him to get you some of that palimony, I think they call it, you know?"

"Good idea," I said. "Thanks, Kelly. And thanks for taking such good care of . . . Cat."

I received that tender smile again. "Sure."

I walked away thinking that I had not clarified matters much: I'd been trying to establish whether the bequest was Cat Benet's idea—free, clear, and rational—or somebody else's, like Slight's and/or Carl's. In other words, if somebody was hiding something, which somebody was it who was doing the hiding? I had not really come any closer to finding out. Anybody could have slipped a will under his nose for him to sign while he was drugged; on the other hand, he could have signed it when he was completely lucid. Who was responsible for the strange document that bound the foundation to impossible terms? I still didn't know.

I did know that I was enjoying being around women again. Not only did they *talk* but sometimes they even told you something.

25

There were several people in the waiting room where Canales had interviewed Brady and me, but only one of them was a woman with red hair. Real red hair. That's "real" as in natural and very. Tangled heaps and masses of it springing out as curls around her heart-shaped face and as ringlets from the ponytail fatly massed at the nape of her neck. This woman, too, had breasts like missile nose cones, but hers stuck out more than Nurse Kelly's and were loosely contained in a white T-shirt with a hot-pink flamingo on the front of it. The bird, whose beak curved around the woman's left breast, had been drawn in profile; its thin mouth curved up in a lewd and evil grin, its beady green eye staring aggressively over my shoulder, as if casing the joint for somebody more likely looking. The sleeves of this woman's T-shirt were rolled up onto her shoulders, revealing shapely, muscular, tanned upper arms. A pink fur jacket (I suspected mink) was slung over her

shoulders. She had tucked the T-shirt into blue jeans so tight it was a
wonder some nurse hadn't called a Code Blue on her for circulatory
failure. Completing the ensemble were: sling-back heels held on to each
of her plump and tiny feet by thin, pink vinyl straps; lots of pink plastic
bracelets and rings; and huge, very dark pink plastic sunglasses with
lenses shaped like hearts. The nose beneath the glasses was small and
cute, the lips below the nose were sensuous and cute, although now
they drooped with sadness, weariness, or sulkiness—it was hard to tell
without seeing her eyes. The redhead looked so darned wild, so
incredibly brassy, so unbelievably out of context, so adorable and
funny, that I loved her on sight.

"Mrs. Benet?" I inquired.

The heart-shaped sunglasses focused on my face.

"Sort of," she said in a deep drawl. "Who's askin'?"

I sat down beside her on the waiting-room sofa. The other people in
the room were trying very hard to appear disinterested in this fabulous
creature. I figured her for about thirty-five, or as the possessor of the
name of a great plastic surgeon.

"My name is Jenny Cain. I'm the director of a charitable foundation
to which Mr. Benet bequeathed the Crossbones Ranch. One of the
nurses here told me you were married to him. She didn't tell me your
name—"

"Marvalene."

Of course, I thought, of course it's Marvalene, how could it be
anything else?

"Podhurst," she added. "But in my heart"—and here she placed
both of her plump and tiny hands between her breasts, which was a
little like burying a couple of turtle doves in pillows—"I'm still Mrs.
Charles Benet IV." Her beautiful little lips trembled. Tears ran from
under the sunglasses, over her plump cheeks. "That's why when you
asked was I Mrs. Benet, I said sort of. I changed my name back to my
maiden name when we got divorced, but only 'cause I was pissed at Cat.
God, was I pissed! But I wasn't angry in my heart. In my heart, I loved
that rotten, no good, lousy son of a bitch and I always will, damn his
copper-plated balls for leavin' me like this. Oh, my lordy," she said with
a sob, "do you know this means I ain't never going to get to ball my

little old lover again? I mean, it is true that I haven't in years, us bein'
divorced and all and him bein' for a time married to my former best
friend, but it was always possible that we might get together and do the
deed again sometime. And now we can't ever. Except in my dreams. I
don't think I can stand it, honey, I think I might as well pack it with
cotton and stick a Band-Aid on it, 'cause it ain't gonna be no use to me
no more."

"Are you, by any chance, from Texas?"

She lifted her glasses, revealing sexy, slightly slanted, little green,
water-clogged eyes. "How'd ya know *that?*"

"A lucky guess."

"Did you know him?" She said it pleadingly, as if she wanted me to
say yes. "I hope you'll tell me you knew him. I cain't find anybody in
this damn old hospital who knew anything about him but his arse and
his arteries. I want to talk to somebody who *knew* him."

"Why'd you come here, Marvalene?"

She puckered up, as if she might cry. "Where else'm I going to *go?* I
get this phone call from this lawyer saying my little old sweet
Catty-fart's dead, and there isn't nobody to call, there isn't no funeral to
go to, there wasn't no house to drop by, hell, I don't even know where
this last damn ranch *is* he bought—why he bought it outside of Texas I
can not imagine—so there wasn't anywhere for me to go to express my
grief, you might say. I could *kill* that damn Slight Harlan and that old
drunk Carl Everett for failin' to notify me of the fact of my former
darlin's deceasement. There I am, livin' in San Diego where I don't yet
know a living soul save my little old sweet lady neighbor and my boy,
Daniel, who's in the Navy, and here's my little old sweet Catty-Balls
dead in Kansas City, Missouri, and I don't even have a grave to weep my
lovin' tears on, and so I come to the last place he was. I have come
here." She jabbed one long, hot-pink fingernail into the sofa. "I figure
they have seen a few grievin' people in their lives and they can just put
up with little old weepin' me. And they can tell me he ain't a patient no
more, and I'll tell them he used to be, and if anybody'd *told* me he was
here, if anybody'd had the sheer pol*ite*ness to *tell* me my little old sweet
booby was dyin', why I would have come and done my cryin' *then,* but
nobody did, so here I am, and I'm going to stay right here in this little

old waitin' room and cry my eyes out until there ain't no tears left in 'em and then I guess I'll go home to San Diego, and you can quote me on *that.*"

"I'm not a reporter," I said.

"Why, honey, I didn't think you was." She leaned closer to peer at me. It struck me that Marvalene's sunglasses might be prescription ones. "You're awful damn pretty, and I'll bet that's natural blond hair you got, too. You sure you didn't know Cat? He'd of been about ready for a clean-cut-looking girl like you, right after me and Freddie Sue, that's who he married after me, which we used to be best friends, the lyin' bitch, I still miss her, I really do. We were friends. Still can be, I guess, now that Cat's gone. Oh, God, I'm gonna miss that scrawny little rich fucker. I already miss him like hell. You really did know him, didn't you?"

"I'm sorry, but I really didn't."

"Aw, shit." Marvalene put the glasses back on and slumped against the sofa. "I need a shoulder to cry on, and the man with the biggest damn shoulders in the whole Southwest is dead, damn him, and my best friend is not a friend to me no longer, at least not for a while probably yet, and you probably think I'm crazy—"

"I don't, Marvalene."

"You should of known him, Jenny, honey. Then you'd know I wasn't crazy, except crazy about him."

"Then why'd you divorce him?"

"Well." She rubbed her dainty chin. The other conversations in the room had trickled down to nothing, although some of the other people were at least keeping up the pretense of staring at magazines or at a wall. "It was sort of a accident. I kind of didn't mean to."

I wanted to be sympathetic, but I was starting to grin, I couldn't help it.

"Well," she repeated, pronouncing it wahll. Then she sighed regretfully. "I just got pissed at him being gone so much, runnin' those damn ranches, that I thought, well, what's the use bein' married to a man who's gone all the time? I'll swear Cat didn't even drop by the house as often as the UPS man did with packages from Neiman-Marcus. Hell, I thought I might as well be *married* to the UPS man, if all I wanted was a drop-in husband. Although I suppose it woulda been more practical to marry Stanley Marcus. Well, anyways, so I was in a royal piss one day and I called him and said I'm divorcin' you and taking all your money, and he laughed and said, you can take the money, Marva, honey, but you'll have to pay some *in*terest on it, and that really branded my ass with a hot iron, 'cause he thought I was only jokin' him, so I did it. Me and my impulsive nature, as my mother delights in sayin'. While he was riding the damn range, I lassoed a lawyer and got me a quickie divorce."

She pronounced it *dee*-vorce.

"When did he marry your best friend?"

"A year later. I went to the wedding."

"You did?"

"Sure, what the hell, I like a good party."

"Weren't you mad at them?"

"Mostly at myself. Wasn't Freddie Sue's fault I left him, that was my fault. And I couldn't hardly blame her for fallin' in love with him, so would any woman with a workin' glandular system. Nah, I was mad at myself, 'cause it could have been me in bed with him that night, 'stead of her. Now *that* killed me."

"Marvalene," I said in a whisper, "hasn't anybody told you he was murdered?"

"He was *what?*" She lifted her glasses to stare fully at me. "Well, now. Finally, somebody's makin' sense around here. You know any good place we could go to get us some supper, Jenny, honey? I'm sick to death of that cafeteria puke."

26

Marvalene Podhurst attracted as much attention at the fern restaurant we found near the hospital as she had in the waiting room, the only difference being that the restaurant patrons ogled openly, being insensitive to her bereaved condition. I gathered, from their stares, that hers was not a fashion sense common to Kansas City. By Marvalene's side, I was invisible. If I ever wanted to rob a bank, I would take her along; none of the witnesses would remember me; I probably wouldn't even register on the security cameras.

The hostess wisely placed us at an inconspicuous table where businessmen were less likely to trip or to drip salad dressing on their ties when they saw Marvalene. Before the waiter arrived, I told her what happened to her former husband.

I stopped talking when the waiter appeared.

Marvalene filled the silence by saying, "I don't understand what it is you do, Jenny, honey."

"Sometimes I don't, either," I confessed, and then we both ordered. Greek salads with pita bread for both of us. Two iced teas with lemon, no sugar. These common interests seemed to please us both. "I run a charitable trust to which Cat Benet, in his dubious wisdom, left the Crossbones Ranch. I am not a rancher. I live on the East Coast. I never met, nor did I ever previously hear of, Cat Benet. Why did he do this to me, Marvalene?"

The waiter returned with our drinks.

She unwrapped her straw and then sucked thoughtfully on one end of it.

"You met him one time, right?"

"No, honestly, I'd never even heard of him."

"No kidding? That's amazing. I thought everybody'd heard of old Catty. Well, I don't know what to tell you. He was no fool, except maybe about women. He was awful good with cattle and land; it's awful hard for me to imagine him leavin' any of it to people who don't know nothing about either one of 'em. What's Slight say about it?"

"It's one of the few subjects on which Slight has very little to say."

"I don't suppose Carl says nothin' but 'Pass the beer'?"

"Right."

"You got me, honey. Now you tell me, why didn't they tell me he was sick? I mean, if they didn't tell me, believe me, they didn't tell anybody. Cat and me, we wrote to each other more or less regular, well, I guess I mean I wrote and he called—ain't that usually the way with a man? That bastard never said anything about having cancer or liver disease or anything that was eatin' away at him. I could just plain kill him for being so stupid brave about it. And if you're saying that somebody killed him, I'll skin and fillet the son of a bitch who did it."

"That's more or less what Slight says."

"Yeah, I'll bet him and Carl are grievin'."

"I think so," I said hesitantly.

"Oh, they might not show it, but there's too many good and hard years gone down between 'em for them not to miss him almost as powerful as I do." Marvalene smiled, then chuckled. It was a rippling, infectious sound that probably gave every man within earshot an erection. A similar thought may have crossed her mind, because she said, "Good and hard. Hah. That was my sweet little old Catty, too." I saw the man at the next table tighten his lips, making it difficult for him to insert his grilled cheese sandwich into his mouth. Marvalene was oblivious—or nearly so—to the flurry of reaction she caused merely by existing. Her smile faded and her lower lip trembled again. I reached over to pat her hand. "God, I hate it that his boots ain't going to walk this green earth anymore. He was some powerful cowboy, Jenny. You woulda loved him." The lips turned up into a smile again. She winked at me and squeezed my hand. "I have a definite feeling you woulda definitely *loved* him."

She laughed and released my hand.

I laughed, too, nearly convinced she was right.

"So, Marvalene"—I spread my napkin on my lap—"did somebody hate him enough to do it?"

The waiter, who had been staring at her as he approached our table with the food, suddenly shifted his glance to me. He set our food down quickly and left without asking if we needed anything else.

Marvalene picked up her fork and tucked in.

"I loved him. Freddie Sue probably loved him. Slight loved him. Old drunk Carl loved him, I suppose. His first wife's dead, been gone a long time, so it doesn't matter how she felt about him. I didn't know the other one. Not to mention all the girlfriends in between."

"What about his children? Is your son Cat's boy?"

"Nope." She stabbed a black olive. "Cat, he was one of those men had himself convinced his kids were better off without him. You know the type. They make fine lovers, but you'd best not marry 'em, I guess, and you wouldn't want 'em as dads. He gave 'em money, I never knew how much, and he had me send them birthday cards, so I expect he had the other wives doing the same job, but I don't know that he ever dropped in on them after he left their mothers. Or got kicked out, which is more likely. So I don't know how any of his kids *could* love him, not knowing him very well, but I could sure understand it if they hated him. My boy hates his daddy for desertin' him, no matter how many excuses I try to make for the lousy son of a bitch, which is really not fair to his mother, her bein' a nice lady, and all."

"Who? Who's a nice lady?"

"Oh, my first mother-in-law. Sorry, I know I don't always make sense all the time. Anyway, so his kids might hate him. Cat wouldn't have understood that, but then that's also the kind of man he was. Selfish, when it suited him, which I have to admit to you that it suited him quite a bit of the time, which is a good part of the reason why I divorced him and why once I quit cryin' over the good and rowdy times we had together, why I'm still gonna be glad I did. Divorce him."

I swallowed a forkful of lettuce and feta cheese.

"You ever know him to do anything dishonest, Marvalene?"

"Like what?"

I laughed a little. "You mean he did?"

"The man never paid a parking ticket, I suppose that's dishonest, and I 'spect he slid out from under every speeding ticket he ever got. But I happen to know he settled fairly with all of his wives and he paid his child support, too."

"How long are you going to hang around here?"

She shrugged and started to answer me. But then she suddenly put down her fork and grabbed for her sunglasses and put them on. She sniffed loudly and put up one of her hands, palm out, toward me. I knew what she was saying: Upset. Crying. Can't talk now.

I let her be. We finished our salads in the loud silence that the consumption of raw vegetables always produces. Her salad was salted more than mine, from the big tears that plopped onto it. She pulled herself together well enough to eat banana cream pie for dessert.

"I always eat when I'm sad," she told me.

"Would you like to talk to Cat's lawyer?" I asked her.

After a moment's thought, she said she certainly would. I smiled contentedly to myself as I handed her the business card that Dwight Brady had given me. The idea of putting him and Marvalene Podhurst together in the same room vastly improved my day.

After supper, we walked to a bank of pay phones in the foyer. I used one to call a taxi. She used one to dial Brady's home phone number.

"I'll get this lawyer fella to put me on a plane or put me up for the night after I get through with him." Her eyes were covered by the dark sunglasses, but her lips curved up. "If you're ever out San Diego way, you give me a call, you hear me?"

"Thanks."

She nodded just as she said into the receiver, "Dwight Brady? Dwight, honey, this here's Marvalene Podhurst . . ."

My taxi returned me to the airport, where I took the red-eye flight to Chicago. It took all of the courage I had to get onto a second airplane that night, and I clutched the armrests for a good half of the trip.

To distract myself from thinking either of crashing or of Slight, I read bits and pieces of the family history that Margaret Stewart had handed to me on my way out of their house. *The Barons of Branchwater*, by Dr. F. S. Gomez, Ph.D., traced the Benet family from the early 1700s in France. I skimmed, looking for interesting black sheep, but all I found were pure women and noble cowboys. I discovered no clues at all as to what killed the man who symbolized the end of a dynasty spanning three centuries.

27

I slept late in a hotel room near O'Hare International Airport. When I finally pried my eyes apart, it was to look out on a perfect autumn day with a sun like a medallion polished to a blinding sparkle and framed in blue velvet. Guessing the temperature to be in the crisp fifties, I dressed in my light wool business suit and my water-stained red leather heels. After breakfast in the hotel coffee shop, I rented a compact car.

Then I drove to Winnetka to meet the Railings: Anna, the second wife, and Mark and Suanna, her children.

I'd been to Chicago previously on business, but never to the northern suburbs along Lake Michigan. They were beautiful, once you got off the toll roads. I felt more comfortable here than I had in Kansas City, possibly because the architecture looked more like home, or at least like a midwestern version of New England.

In downtown Winnetka, I parked on a street called Green Bay where there was a railroad track to my left and a store named Scotland Yard Books, Ltd. to my right. At that moment, I wouldn't have minded consulting a real CID man—or woman—from Scotland Yard. As it was, I had to manage with my wits and a map of Winnetka.

They led me to a three-story brick house that could surely have brought a half-million dollars in mint condition. This mint had been chewed a bit. The decay of this house was a blight on the otherwise immaculate neighborhood.

I parked under a bare pin oak tree in front of the house and puzzled over the decay.

The man who answered the doorbell looked about sixty years old. "Yes?"

The word was like a swat, quick, hard, hissing through the air to land on the pestiferous fly buzzing at his door.

"Mr. Railing?"

"Yes."

Never had an affirmative sounded so negative.

"I would like to speak to Mrs. Railing."

In fact, I suddenly wanted to speak to anyone but him.

"She's sick." His almost imperceptible glance upward suggested her existence on the second floor. He was tall, thin, and nearly colorless in the way of some Nordic men, with skin the ivory color of the face powder my mother used to wear. His gray-blond hair was parted way down by his left ear, and he'd combed it into long, thin, greasy commas that ended in sharp points beside his other ear. He wore reading glasses of the type you can buy in any dime store; the little half-lenses looked incongruous perched low on his nose in the center of his large face. He stared down at me, over them. "She can't come down."

"I'm sorry to hear she's ill," I stalled.

A mistake. A hint of sardonic humor appeared in his eyes, which were just slightly more blue than your average glass of tap water, and he said, "You're twenty-five years too late in saying so. She's in a wheelchair, with multiple sclerosis. What do you want with her?"

"I'm looking for an Anna Railing who was married to a man named Charles Benet."

The sudden tightening of his facial muscles and the further hardening of the ice in his eyes told me I'd definitely found the right people.

"Come in," he said harshly.

I entered his home feeling like a fly who'd gotten through the screen, only to have the nasty feeling that somebody was waiting inside with a swatter. I glanced up at the ceiling, trying to sense her through it. When I looked back at him, I caught him doing the same thing.

He led me into what was literally a parlor. It was an exceedingly dark room with heavy, brocade, floor-to-ceiling draperies that were drawn together, admitting not a glint of sun, and Victorian-style furniture upholstered in faded patterns of dark flowers. Several threadbare oriental-style carpets lay upon the walnut-colored wood-plank floors. It was decorated for the nineteenth century and might even have been beautiful when the fabrics were new and the drapes framed the light of day. I suspected the carpets and furniture would appear valuable to a knowing eye; they were probably the sort of down-at-the-heels antiques that dealers snatch at estate sales to resell later at exorbitant prices. The room looked and smelled like one into which neither fresh air nor fresh thoughts had penetrated, much less circulated, in years.

I sat down in a long-backed, upholstered chair in front of a bookcase. Railing didn't sit but remained standing about seven feet from me, with his feet slightly apart, his hands in his front pants pockets, and those glasses still on his nose. He wore a white short-sleeved shirt buttoned to the neck, a thin, brown tie with tiny yellow lions rampant, a thin, black belt, trousers the color of peanut butter, and brown shoes with black laces. There was blond hair curling out of the backs of his wrists. He was put together with such exceedingly fastidious bad taste that I was willing to bet he wished he could shave those hairs off. He must have hated them, those ungovernable sprouts of masculinity that betrayed him as human and hormonal. They irresistibly caused me to wonder if wild loops of blond hair also matted his chest—repellent thought.

"Who are you?" he demanded.

I told him. Then I waited for his predictable next question. He didn't fail me.

"What do you want?"

I told him what I thought he'd like to hear, even embellishing it.

"I am looking for evidence that Charles Benet may have committed fraud. I am hoping your wife can provide me with information that may help me to establish a case against him."

I was right. He tried not to give it away, but he couldn't help but betray his pleasure—the corners of his mouth lifted, a closed-in expression of smug triumph flashed in his eyes, and he relaxed, in the manner of one child when another one gets blamed. He liked this news I had brought him. He would help me any way he could. I disliked him intensely.

"I'm going to get a drink," he said suddenly. Not quite grudgingly he added, "You want one?"

"Sure," I lied. "Whatever you're having."

He walked out of the room.

I felt as if I'd been left alone in a funeral home. Surely, I might find a casket hidden among the somber shadows here. To shake off a contradictory feeling of nerves and lassitude, I got up and strolled around the room while I waited for him to return. The walls were desecrated by several enormous and grim still lifes depicting scenes after the hunt: limp rabbits, boars' heads, dead foxes, shotguns laid down beside spent cartridges.

But next to the ornate gold-leafed frame of one of those paintings I found a modern convenience: a room monitor, one of those wall gizmos that invalids use to call for help. It was turned to OFF. On impulse, I switched it to ON then sat down in a chair close to the monitor.

"Scotch," he announced when he handed it to me.

I set it down on the filigreed metal end table beside me.

"Now." He nearly smiled as he gazed over the top of his drink at me. "What'd the bastard do?"

"Cat Benet?" I raised my voice to a volume that might be picked up by the monitor. "What did *Cat Benet* do to cause me to suspect him of fraud? Well, before he died he—"

"*Dead? Benet's dead?*"

His excitement, his widening eyes and smile, informed me this was news to him, and that astonished me. Did that mean *she* didn't know, either? I hoped I hadn't caused a heart attack upstairs.

"Yes," I said, thoroughly unnerved by the gleam of pleasure in Railing's eyes. "He died a few days ago in a hospital in Kansas City." Riding solely on intuition, I plunged on. "He was murdered."

His pale blue eyes opened wider and his smile grew almost gay. If this wasn't a surprise to him, then he was a superb actor.

"In his will, he left my . . . company . . . a valuable piece of property in Kansas, and I'm afraid there may be some sort of fraud attached to the bequest. *I was hoping to talk to your wife,* to learn more about Benet and his business practices, to see if she might be able to tell me something about his character."

"Character?" Railing laughed explosively. "The man had no character. He was a scoundrel and a cheat who married my poor wife and then deserted her and the children. I adopted and raised Mark and Suanna as my own." Self-righteous pride oozed from him. "I'm surprised somebody didn't kill him years ago. There must have been dozens of men who hated him, with good reason." The ice in his blue eyes was melted now by the internal fire of his hate. Interesting, I thought, that he spoke of *men* who hated Benet, when you'd have thought it might be the women who felt wronged by him. "He went through life taking what he wanted whenever he wanted it, with no regard for anybody else. I have never forgiven him for what he did to my wife and children, never."

"Mr. Railing, do you know of any specific instances in which he cheated people?"

"He cheated my wife by marrying her and then leaving her!" he thundered. "He cheated my children by having them and then leaving them!"

"What about business deals? Do you know of anybody he cheated in business?"

"I don't have to, to know the man."

"Was he ever arrested—"

"I don't doubt it."

"But you don't know for sure?"

"I don't have to know it for sure—"

"—to know the man, yes, I see. Then I don't suppose you know if he was ever imprisoned on any charge, or if any lawsuits were ever filed against him?"

"A man like that? Of course he was sued!"

"Of course," I murmured. "I would still like to see your wife. Could I make an appointment to—"

"She doesn't see people, she's too ill."

He set his glass down with a thud on a table where there were many rings left by many other wet glasses.

"Then I'd like to call her."

"She doesn't take calls."

"Then I'd like to meet your children."

"They don't live here."

I took a deep breath and got up.

"Well, I'll go then." I added wickedly, "I'm sorry to be the one to break this sad news."

He was suddenly at my side, grabbing my arms in his big hands and shaking me. "If you find out who killed him, I want to know. I want to know it, you'll call and tell me. I want to know right away. I want to write the man a letter. I want to congratulate him. I want to go where he is and shake his hand!"

"*Let go of me.*"

He released me and wrapped himself in his own embrace, rubbing his upper arms as if he were cold, or gleeful. He followed me back to the front door like that, madly rubbing his arms and grinning all the way. Made his day, I had, maybe his life. Oh, it's grand to perk somebody up like that. Just grand. As I walked near the monitor, I said, "If there's anything more you think of to tell me, give me a call. I'll be staying"—I raised my voice—"*at the Best Western by the airport. Ask for Jennifer Cain.*"

When I reached my rental car, I looked back at the house. Downstairs, he was closing the front door. Upstairs, the lower corner of a curtain was raised, at about the height that a woman in a wheelchair might be able to lift it. I stared at that spot until the curtain dropped. Would she call me?

* * *

The answer to that was no.

I thought about staying in my room all that night in case she called, but I'm not good at waiting around for other people to do things. So I called some college friends who lived in Chicago and arranged to meet them for pizza in the city that evening.

It was two in the morning when I returned to the Best Western. I was sober but fuzzy with exhaustion and with the excitement of seeing old friends. As I put the key in the door of my room, I was preoccupied, recalling old jokes, remembering other old friends, smiling to myself. I was totally unprepared for the slamming of the car doors and the footsteps pounding toward my back.

28

I whirled to face my attackers, room key held weapon-high, mouth open and ready to scream. And then I saw them.

Whatever I had been expecting, they weren't it.

Two people, a man and a woman in their thirties. The only "weapon" in her hands was a bulky purse; his hands were empty.

Still . . .

"*Stop right there*," I said.

They did, though she immediately began to edge closer to me again.

"*Stop that.*" I brandished my key at her.

The man hissed at me: "*Shh!*" He stared about, with a wary, frightened expression, at the line of motel rooms, then stared reprovingly at me. "You'll wake people up!"

Thoughtful muggers. This was very odd.

"Yes, that's the idea."

I pointed my key threateningly at him. He put his hands up to his face and stepped back as if I'd actually scared him with my puny weapon: *Stand back, or I'll carve a new lock in you.* Granted, these two weren't very scary, but my knees still felt like soufflés on the verge of falling, and my heart was a Ping-Pong ball in play.

The woman spoke past me to the man, "She thinks we're going to mug her, Mark. Tell her who we are."

"B-but how do we know it's her?"

"She's got *her* room, doesn't she?" The woman sounded exasperated with him. "Who else could she be but *her?*"

I looked back and forth from him to her during this confusing and ungrammatical volley of pronouns.

"Her who?" I said.

They both looked at me.

"Jennifer Cain," he whispered.

I didn't acknowledge it.

"Tell her who *we* are," the woman demanded of him.

"Great idea," I said. "And do it right now."

"I'm M-M-Mark R-R-Railing." He moved his right hand abruptly, prompting me to jerk back in fear, but he was only gesturing toward the woman. "Th-th-this is m-my s-s-sister, S-S-Suannnna."

"Take a deep breath," she commanded.

I did, and then I realized she meant him.

"My sister," he said again, and sighed.

I lowered my key a little bit. "Anna's kids?"

He nodded. She edged closer to me, and I raised my key again.

"Number one, prove it," I said. "Number two, it's after two in the morning, and what do you want that couldn't wait until after breakfast?"

"We were afraid you'd leave town," she said.

"W-we have to talk to you."

"Who was your natural father?" I demanded.

He looked puzzled, but she understood and said promptly, "Charles Whitepaw Benet the fourth."

"What was his profession?"

"Cattle rancher."

"When did he divorce your mother?"

"Nineteen fifty-six."

I lowered the key. "Answer number two."

"M-Mother asked us to," he said.

I opened the door to my room. "All right, come in." But I turned on all the lights and propped the door open.

They were twins, alike in their dark, graying hair, in their pudgy Tweedledum and Tweedledee bodies, and their blue eyes, but very different in temperament. She wasn't so bad, really, although she seemed gruff and pushy compared to her shy, stuttering brother. Mark Railing stuttered less as he relaxed more. There was something both endearing and annoying about this timid, middle-aged son of Cat Benet, and his twin sister.

They settled into chairs on either side of a round table by the window; I sat on the bed, facing them.

"We've been sitting in Mark's car all night waiting for you," Suanna Railing told me.

"*Why?*"

She leaned forward. "Did you tell Father about the trusts that our . . . Dad . . . left us?"

"No."

She heaved an enormous sigh and fell back into her chair. "Thank God."

"What's going on?" I demanded.

They looked at each other, seemed to come to some sort of tacit agreement.

"W-we don't want h-h-him to know."

"Why not?"

"We want to use the money to help Mother," Suanna interjected. I was ashamed that I found it such a relief when she did the talking instead of him. "We want to take her to the Mayo Clinic and we want to get her a new wheelchair and we want her to travel and we want to fix up the bedroom, make it pretty for her, and put in a chairlift for the stairway, and . . ." She sighed, a sound that somehow combined sadness and frustration with excitement and hope. "But if he finds out where the money came from, he'll refuse to let us do it, or he'll take it away from her. He'd never let us get by with spending a cent of . . . Dad's . . . money on Mother."

I asked, "Where are you going to tell him you got it?"

Mark: "W-w-won a lottery."

Suanna: "Made it in the stock market."

Mark: "F-found it somewhere."

Suanna: "Got raises at our jobs."

"You haven't entirely thought this through?" I asked gently.

He shook his head in the solemn way he had, and she sighed again. I had a feeling he was a great head shaker and she was a sigher of the first order. Did they get these traits from their presumably long-suffering mother? Had she sat upstairs in her wheelchair for years, sighing in boredom, shaking her head in despair?

"Where'd all the other money go?" I asked them.

"What other money?" Suanna said.

I looked at her for a moment before I said, "The settlement your father made with your mother. And the child support for you."

They stared at me.

"That money," I said.

They were still staring at me.

"Look, I don't know for sure it's true," I said quickly, "but I was told that your father settled financially with each of his wives, and that he continued paying support until you were twenty-one."

"We don't know anything abbout this," Mark said.

"When M-M-Mother married F-Father, she told us we'd have to live on what he provided, which wasn't much. He's a r-retired accountant; he worked for a smmall company and he didn't make much m-money."

"Oh, yes, he did! If this is true, he made all of *our* money! Yours and mine, and probably what was left of mother's, that's what he made!"

"B-but where is it, Su?"

"I don't know where it is! Maybe he's got it in a secret Swiss account and when Mother dies, he's going to abscond with all of it!"

"B-but he could have done that years ago, Su."

"Then maybe he gambled it all away."

"F-F-Father? Gamble?"

"I don't know, Mark!"

"Please don't jump to these conclusions just because of what I've said," I pleaded. "Please investigate, ask your mother—"

"We will," she promised. It had the sound of a vow.

"Su? D-do you think Mother *knew?*"

His sister shrugged, but it was more a gesture of helplessness than of doubt. "If Father didn't want us to have the money, what could she have done about it, Mark?"

His fists clenched, and his face red, he said without stuttering, "Lots!"

But this time it was her turn to say, skeptically, "Mother?"

"Did your mother ever talk to you about your natural father?" I asked them.

"S-she didn't d-dare," Mark said. "He . . . *he* . . . wouldn't allow it."

"He hated our . . . Dad," Suanna explained. "Because our . . . Dad . . . cruelly cut us off without a penny . . ." She trailed off, hearing from her own mouth the big lie of their childhoods, the monstrous lie that had ruled and possibly ruined their lives. As she sat speechless, her brother took up the tale. He stuttered less now, his indignation seeming to give him a new power that slid the words more easily from his tongue.

"About a week aggo, Su and I got letters from our . . . D-dad. He said he was sick and he wanted us to know that he hoped we'd be happy in our lives, and he was leaving us each a trust fund. We thought he was trying to make it up to us, for neglecting us. We told Mother about it and made her promise not to tell F-Father. Then when the lawyer called from Kansas City to say D-Dad had died, luckily F-Father was out and M-Mother took the call. She told us, and not him. So when you showed up at the house today, she called Su and told her and Su told me and we came to plead with you not to tell F-Father about our in-in-inheritance."

"But why not?" I asked. "At that time, did you suspect him of anything?"

They glanced at each other, glances full of fury.

"Only of selfishness and stubbornness," Suanna said. "We were afraid he wouldn't let us spend any of the money on Mother, once he knew where it came from. Do you think we should go to the police?"

"Go to your mother first," I advised. "Then to a lawyer. He'll tell you what sort of case you have. But please . . ."

They both stared at me, hearing the intensity in my voice.

"Please don't spend all of your inheritance trying to get revenge on your stepfather. If the money's gone, it's gone. If you spend all of this new money on lawyers and lawsuits, you'll be letting him steal that from you, too."

I couldn't tell if I'd gotten through to them, and I couldn't blame them if they didn't want to hear it. They'd spent their lives in false and miserable penury; by now, they might have lost any talent they had for happiness. I thought: Cat Benet, you have some of this to answer for—did you think the money would be enough, did you think that all you had to do was instruct your accountant to mail checks and everybody would live happily ever after?

His pudgy, unhappy children left my motel room soon after that, promising to keep in touch. I gave them the names and addresses of their half sisters in Kansas City and of the boy named Ladd Benet in Fort Worth, but I didn't really expect them to do anything with the information. None of this had the makings of a great family reunion.

When I finally got to bed, it was with questions whirling in my brain, colliding with each other: Just how deep and obsessive was the hate that Railing bore for Cat Benet? Enough to demand some final, ultimate, irrevocable outlet? Had he somehow learned of the trusts that would come to his adopted children upon the death of their natural father? What was the source of his hate? How much did the woman in the upstairs bedroom know about what her second husband had done with the money? Why had she allowed him to cheat not only herself but worse, her children? Just how crippled and helpless was she, really?

I wished I could meet her.

And I did, in my dreams that night. She wore a white diaphanous gown and she floated over the prairie like a cloud, never coming to earth.

I woke up a few hours later, convinced the best thing for me to do was leave town.

29

Over a late Tuesday morning breakfast of pecan waffles, bacon, scrambled eggs, and coffee, I glanced through the appendixes of *The Barons of Branchwater* and discovered something very interesting. There at the back of the book was a family tree—one of those foldout jobs because the author had traced the Benets back so many generations they wouldn't all fit onto one page. And there, branching off from Cat Benet's mother and father was a second twig: *Judith.* And out of Judith came: *Ladd,* the nephew in the broken picture frame.

It was Judy who intrigued me—Cat's sister, born almost a generation later than he. Of whom I had thus far heard scarcely a word. Who was not mentioned anywhere else in the book, although it was true that no one of her generation was, because the narration stopped at the marriage of their parents, which meant, of course, that the biography didn't tell me all that much about Cat, either, except to place him in his lineage. But what about Judith?

After breakfast, I returned to my room and called my office.

"Mr. Dwight Brady is trying to reach you," my assistant said.

"Did he say why?"

"No, but he's called twice already."

When I screwed up my courage and called him in Kansas City, he told me it was a false alarm. Lilly Ann Lawrence had slipped away again, and they had been frantically looking for her when she came home protesting her innocence and claiming to have spent the night at a friend's house.

The man had no idea how much of a false alarm it really was, and how rapidly my heart was beating as a result of it. I had half-expected him to tell me there was a warrant out for my arrest.

"Why call me?" I asked him.

"To see if you thought she'd try the ranch again."

"I don't know her that well, Dwight."

"Consider yourself fortunate."

That made me want to rush immediately to her defense, but I clamped my tongue on it. Stay out of it, I warned myself. Their business. Not yours, not unless she actually steps on the property. Still, my tongue got loose long enough to say, intending sarcasm, "I guess you'll just have to hire a private investigator to follow her around, Dwight."

"That's not a bad idea."

"Yes, it is," I said firmly.

I got off the phone feeling extremely annoyed with Mr. Cat Benet, cowpoke and philanthropist. So annoyed that I had to express it to somebody.

I called the ranch, only to get the telephone answering machine. As I was leaving my message, Slight's voice cut in.

"Good morning," he said.

I felt so relieved that he'd flown safely through the rainstorm that I sounded like an irritated parent when I said, "Don't you ever just pick up the phone and answer it?"

"I like to know who I'm talkin' to."

"Before you talk to them. Right. I have a question for you, Slight. Is Judy Benet still living in Fort Worth?"

There was a silence, and then he said cautiously, "Cat's sister? I don't know the answer to that."

"Well, hell, what *do* you know?"

"I know three more heifers delivered last night."

"Poor things. Slight, did Cat handle his child support payments himself?"

"I doubt it," he drawled. "He had secretaries and accountants through the years, you know. Had to, operation the size of his, at least the size it used to be. Small as it is now, comparatively speaking I mean, it don't take more 'n' Carl and me and a part-time tax man to handle things. But back then, yeah, I expect he had somebody else doin' that stuff for him. Why, Jenny?"

"His children in Winnetka never got their money."

I thought I could feel shock waves coming through the phone lines from Kansas. When he finally responded, it was with a low, skeptical "Whaaat?"

"Mark and Suanna, his children by Anna."

"I remember," Slight said huffily.

"Then you probably know Anna remarried, to a man named Railing. It looks as if he took whatever was left of her money, as well as the children's money, and they never saw a penny of it."

I could hear heavy breathing. "How do you know?"

"Mark and Suanna told me."

"*Told* you? What are you up to? Where *are* you?"

"Sitting by the bed, calling you. They don't know what he did with the money, Slight, but now that they know he cheated them, I hope they'll be able to find out."

"The checks were made out to her," he said heavily.

"Anna?"

"Yeah."

"How do you know that?"

"I just do."

"You're sure?"

"Pretty sure."

"Then she may have endorsed them and turned them over to Railing. How could Cat have let this happen, Slight? How could he just send that money up there and never check to see if it got where it was supposed to go? Why didn't he write to his children? Didn't he ever try to see them? He was their *father,* for heaven's sake. What was the matter with him?"

"Anna asked him not to." Slight's voice was full of defensiveness for his late boss. "When she remarried, she wrote to him and said, leave us alone, we've got a new life now, you stay out of it. The new husband offered to adopt the children and I guess Cat thought that might be best for them, so he went along with it. But he kept sending the checks, Jenny. Legally, he didn't have to, 'cause they weren't his kids any longer. But he did keep sending the money—"

"For all the damn good it did them!"

"He didn't know Railing was a crook! You've got to understand—"

"I do understand. He had children and he abandoned them. Slight, they're pitiful. They're fat, scared, shy people. Their mother's an invalid who apparently never leaves her room. Mark stutters worse than any adult I've ever heard. Was all of this necessary so that Cat Benet could have his precious freedom? Was it?" I heard myself nearly yelling at him and stopped. "Oh, Christ, Slight, I don't mean to yell at you, it's not your fault. I'm sorry, it's just that—"

"Anna's an invalid?"

"Multiple sclerosis."

"Oh, God Almighty."

"Mark and Suanna want to buy her a better wheelchair," I said bitterly.

"She was beautiful," he murmured. "She didn't have much of a sense of humor, poor woman, but she was pretty as a beauty queen. Is the daughter pretty?"

"No."

He sighed. "Lord, I feel sorry about all this."

"I do, too," I said tiredly. "And I'm sorry to take it out on you, Slight."

"Who better?" he asked lightly. "When you comin' back to us, Jenny?"

"I thought you wanted to be rid of me."

"Carl and me? Never. We miss you. Molly misses you."

"I'll bet. What's the livestock market doing this week?"

"If I told you, would it mean anything to you?"

I laughed. "Probably not."

"Hogs are up," he said.

"I'm so glad."

"But pork bellies are down."

"Where else would they be?"

"And soybeans are steady."

"As so few things are in this world."

"I do wish you'd come back," he drawled. "One day."

"You think it's safe for you to say that because you don't think I'm going to do it," I said, and he chuckled. "But you'd better keep your boots shined, Quentin, because you never know when I might show up. I just might surprise you."

"I hate surprises."

"The hell you do," I said, and hung up without telling him where I was or where I was going next.

30

I reserved a ticket on a flight to Fort Worth, but it wouldn't leave until that evening, so I used the rest of the morning to find a Laundromat and wash my clothes. What I also needed was a dry cleaner for my suit, but there wasn't time for that. No, what I really needed was a couple of cooler outfits for the warmer climate of the South. Now there was a lovely excuse, if I ever heard one, to drive back into Chicago to visit Marshall Field's Department Store.

So I did just that, after checking out of the motel. I spent—in more ways than one—the afternoon shopping in the vast and famous old store downtown. It was unaccustomed luxury to one who was used to picking up quick bargains at her brother-in-law's discount emporium back home in "Poor Fred." I bought a hot-pink T-shirt dress, belted at the waist, a cool khaki suit for traveling and business, and a pair of white slacks with an African-print tunic overblouse. And a brightly flowered cotton dress in case I went to dinner someplace nice. And a pair of leather sandals. And a summer purse. And a T. J. MacGregor mystery novel from the book department. And a box of Marshall Field's famous candy. And a pair of khaki shorts for Geof. And I had a beautiful brass fireplace screen shipped back to our new house, for the fireplace in our bedroom. And then I had them mail a catalog home, too, just in case I'd missed something.

I ate a late lunch at the store. While I chewed an egg salad sandwich and sipped a vanilla milk shake, I mulled over my retrograde shopping spree in this old-fashioned emporium. An observer might have thought I should have spent my free afternoon in scholarly pursuit at the Museum of Natural History. Such an observer would obviously not be a native of Poor Fred, where it's a whole lot easier to find nature than to find better dresses.

It was, I mused, for afternoons like this that ladies and their children and nurses once boarded trains bound to Chicago or Kansas City from the ranches and farms and small towns of the Midwest. If Lilly Ann Lawrence had come along a few generations earlier, she might have been one of those children. When her glamorous trip was completed, she would have gone home to a ranch, just the sort of place where the girl romantically thought she'd like to be now. Was she a throwback, caught out of time, out of step with her own generation? Or was she just a rebellious teenager with no better ideas about how to stage a revolution from her parents' values?

I was feeling mellow enough to be foolish.

After lunch, I found a pay phone and called the Lawrence home in Kansas City. Without identifying myself, I asked for Lilly, half-hoping she wouldn't be there.

"Hello?" the girl answered, in a low, dull voice.

"This is Jenny Cain," I told her. "I have an idea. You said you want to get to know your grandfather. Well, I think I know how you can do that, without getting yourself into trouble or debt. Since you have money to burn, I suggest you catch the first flight out of Kansas City to Fort Worth. Take a cab to the downtown Holiday Inn and ask for me. If I haven't checked in yet, tell them you're sharing my room and get them to give you a key. I'll add your name to my reservation."

"I don't get it," she said, but her voice sounded more lively, less dull.

"You might get to meet some people who knew him, and maybe they'll tell us more about him. You might even get to see one of the old ranches. I can't promise anything will come of this, but do you want to take the chance?"

"Yes!"

"Will you meet me in Fort Worth tonight?"

"If I can! If I can get on a plane!"

"Do me one favor, Lilly Ann."

"What?"

"Tell your folks where you're going, all right?"

"All right." She tried to sound grudging, but her heart wasn't in it anymore. "I'll see you soon!"

I hung up and turned around to stare at the counters and aisles of the department store. "You did this to me," I silently accused Marshall Field's. "It's not enough that you lure me in here and run my credit card to the limit. No, you have to get me in a sentimental frame of mind so I'll do something as quixotic as take an overgrown adolescent girl under my stupid wing. Well, enough is enough. I will *not* order anything from your catalog for Christmas!"

On my way out of the store, I happened to pass by the toy department where they happened to have perfectly marvelous jigsaw puzzles on sale. My niece and nephew loved jigsaw puzzles. All right, just one. Well, two. One for each of them, and maybe those two little ones over there for their Christmas stockings.

"Thank you for shopping at Marshall Fields," the clerk in the toy department said graciously.

"How do I get out of here?" I pleaded.

"Go past cosmetics—"

"No! Isn't there a closer exit?"

I managed to escape without buying anything else, although I did get sprayed with a sample of some new perfume whose French name sounded like "Buy Me." Leaving the store was a shock, like walking back into the real world, where I had real big problems. I looked back, once, wistfully at the store and thought, Thanks, it was a great escape for a little while.

I drove directly to the airport, where I turned in my rental car. In half an hour, I was aboard a nonstop flight to Dallas/Fort Worth.

The room at the Fort Worth Holiday Inn was dark when I entered it. I started to flip the light switch, but then I saw that Lilly was asleep in the bed near the window, so I slipped into the bathroom and turned on that light instead. The girl didn't stir during the small commotion I made in opening closet doors, sliding zippers, hanging things up. I began to move about the room with less hesitancy once I remembered what it was like to be young enough to sleep like the dead. That thought unnerved me for a moment, however, and I walked over and took a good look at her.

Good. Whew. Breathing.

I undressed, showered, got ready for bed.

After I pulled back the covers on my own queen-size bed and slid in, I sat up against a pillow for a while, considering the sleeping girl. Her long, straight blond hair was spread out wildly around her on her pillow. She was sleeping on her left side, curled up tightly except for her right arm, which was flung onto the pillow over her head. Interesting body language, I thought, the fetal curl of a child, the bold, free arm of the independent adult. She wore a pink T-shirt to sleep in.

It was clear to me that I had been crazy to invite her. She'd only be in the way—her own distinctly aggravating way at that. Just what did I think I was going to do with Ms. Lilly Ann Lawrence now that I had her down here?

31

I took her to lunch with Miss Rose Sachet at the Century Club in
downtown Fort Worth. The legendary Miss Rose was the director
of a Texas foundation that was so fat you could practically hear a burp
when you opened the pages of its annual report. I knew her from having
attended national conventions where she was always a star, in part
because of her encyclopedic knowledge about Texas and foundations,
but also because of her unusual appearance and personality. It was Miss
Rose's membership that admitted us to the penthouse restaurant in the
skyscraper bank building, but only after I'd given her firmly to
understand she was my guest.

"Your guest?" she said when I phoned her at her office that morning.
"Or a guest of your foundation?"

"My guest."

"Thank you," she drawled, a note of approbation in her deep, smoker's voice. Miss Sachet was known as a believer in the theory that funds given to charity ought to go for charity and not to buy fancy lunches for herself. I was of the same school. We got along fine.

"I have another guest with me," I warned her when I called. Lilly Ann was in the shower at that moment. "She's a girl who appears to own only boots, blue jeans, and cowgirl shirts. Will the Century Club let her in dressed like that?"

"This is Fort Worth, my dear."

I took that as assent.

I didn't tell her the identity of my guest, saving that for a surprise at lunch.

"So you're Cat's grandbaby," Miss Rose drawled, looking surprised and pleased. She was seventy years old, and nearly as wide as she was tall, which was only about five feet. Despite her name, there wasn't anything flowery about the old lady, except maybe for an edge of sweetness about her, the opposite of the way some smiling people have a hard edge to them. In her case, it was like finding a bit of lace trim around a solid block of mesquite. Miss Sachet was reputed to be as tough as that Texas brushwood; I knew from experience that her conversation could be every bit as biting and pungent as the smoke from its burning. But for now she offered her lace-edged smile to the girl. "Well, I don't suppose that means much in Kansas City, but down here that makes you near royalty, child."

Lilly drew back her head and turned her face a bit to the side, looking as skeptical and suspicious as a turtle. I bit back an impulse to laugh and to tell her not to worry, that didn't mean she had to dress up.

Miss Rose hadn't missed the girl's reaction, either, and now she sent me a shrewd glance. I nearly missed seeing it, because my gaze kept being distracted by the view. We were about thirty-five stories up, surrounded by floor-to-ceiling windows. Miss Rose had already pointed out to us the old stockyards, an airport, a river, the courthouse, and other landmarks. Outside was a cloudless sky, as clear and bright as water reflected in glass. The city sat on land so flat I felt as if I were sitting atop a map spread on a table. To the east was Dallas, Miss Rose told Lilly Ann, a city better known but nowhere near as well loved as

Fort Worth, she claimed. To the west, Lubbock and Texas Tech. To the north, the Red River of Oklahoma. To the south, Austin, with its lakes and live oak trees and the University of Texas, and "away on down from there, San Antone and Houston and Galveston, and on across the Rio Grand-ee, Old Mexico."

She was a one-woman chamber of commerce for her state, about which it was known that she did not brook criticism gladly. I sat there, looking out at that arid, monotonous, merciless landscape and felt trapped at the center of the earth. I thought longingly of my cool cottage in the woods, of my ocean slapping at my feet, of our azaleas that bloomed so profusely without much watering. It was only a moment of acute homesickness, and maybe a touch of fear, and I hoped it would pass quickly. I said nothing to Lilly Ann or Miss Rose about it, especially not to Rose, since a longing for my own home might imply criticism of hers.

Our tablecloth was white linen. We had selected food from a three-table buffet that offered black beans and rice in one brass chafing dish and fried okra in another. Lilly'd had to ask what the "fried green stuff" was, which was just as well, since I didn't recognize it, either, thinking maybe it was chopped broccoli stalks. When Lilly learned it was okra, she made a face and passed it by. I had put some on my plate and was now discovering that I liked it. It went down well with the roast baron of beef, mashed sweet potatoes, corn bread, and jalapeño peppers on the side. We both helped ourselves to the fried chicken nuggets. Miss Rose was drinking Wild Turkey and soda, Lilly had a glass of beer, and I had iced tea. Never could hold my liquor at high altitudes.

Miss Rose listened as I told her about the bequest and about Benet's death, and then she said, "Why'd he pick y'all?"

"Beats me, Miss Rose."

She had a smoker's chuckle, full of phelgm, ending in a cough. "If that don't sound just like him," she drawled once she recovered from her coughing jag. "Cat Benet was pullin' surprises on people ever since his poor mama expected a nice sweet little girl child and got Cat-Boy instead. He was born on April Fools' Day, which ought to of told the world ever'thaing it ever need to know 'bout Cat Benet."

"Could you be more specific, Miss Rose?"

She snorted, a sound not unlike the one Molly had made when I pulled her reins in a direction she didn't want to go. "Hah. Charles W. Benet the fourth. Four generations of ranchers, not all that many by our standards, but enough to take his family back to the days when Texas was a territory and the land was up for grabs. Enough to get 'em mineral rights, especially if his great-grandma was a full-blood Osage girl. Those first and last names are French, but anybody tell you what the W stands for?"

"I don't remember."

"Whitepaw. There's a funny mix of blood there, wild and cultured, tamed and untamed. Lot of aggression in that blood, don't you see? A lot of pride, too, 'cause you got aristocracies on both sides, French and Osage. It's a name that tells a story, if you've an ear to hear it."

"I'm listening."

"There's a book you want to read. I 'spect you don't know this, no reason you should, but most of the big Texas ranching families have their own personal family biographies. Like other families have photo albums, I s'pose. Of course, the King family does, the XIT people do, the Halsells, all the big ones and some of the little ones, and so do the Benets. It's called—"

"*The Barons of Branchwater,*" I said.

"Good for you." Her weather-beaten face suddenly took on a shrewd look. "Of course, the best way to know a cattleman is to stand on his land and look at his animals. You'll know the man by the condition of his property and his cows."

"What's that mean?" Lilly said.

I felt embarrassed over the girl's rudeness. She had awakened that morning seeming edgy and defensive, and those were still the predominant notes in her voice. Every suggestion I made, from having breakfast at the hotel to walking to the club, was met with ill-humored consent. You'd have thought she was twelve years old and I was dragging her along to church on Sunday, instead of being an eighteen-year-old woman, here of her own choice. She had toyed with her food at breakfast while I tried to amuse her with stories from the family biography, which she had never read. For all the response I got, I might as well have been reciting my annual report to her. Now I was hoping the steak and fries on her plate would cure her cranky attitude.

"What does it *mean?*" Miss Rose repeated the silly question, which seemed to me to have such an obvious answer. The girl was being purposely obtuse. "How well did you know your grandpappy, child?"

"I didn't know him at all," Lilly said bitterly.

Miss Rose's eyebrows shot up at that, but then she gave a couple of nods that made her look like a wise old gnome. "I could tell you what it means, but I'd rather show you." She turned to me. "You have time for a drive this afternoon?" When she saw the questioning look on my face, she added, glancing back at Lilly, "I could take you out to the old Benet place, La Segunda. It's the ranch your grandpappy grew up on, Lilly. Your great-aunt Judy Benet still lives there and her boy, Laddy. She kept the Benet name for both of them, for reasons that would be obvious to you if you ever lived in Texas. It is not a name a person would like to relinquish." Miss Rose frowned. "Though I don't rightly know how happy they'll be to see us . . ."

I don't think Lilly even heard that. For the first time that day, she smiled. It was a small one, but a smile nevertheless, and one that had about it a glow of hope as well as a shadow of nervousness, or maybe even fear. Again, Rose glanced at me. I moved my shoulders in a small shrug and wondered why the worry lines suddenly looked deeper between the old lady's eyes.

I said, "Judy's still living?"

Rose smiled at that and uttered a laugh like a bark. "I should say she is."

Our waitress presented the dessert tray, from which Lilly selected an éclair, I picked a napoleon, and Rose chose a delicate pink petit four. As we ate and drank coffee, Miss Rose accepted the greetings of other diners who stopped by our table to pay homage to her. "How you doin', Miss Sachet?" the men inquired. They wore cowboy-cut suits with wide lapels and flared trousers (to accommodate their boots), and they held their hats respectfully in their hands as they addressed her. And, "So good to see you lookin' so well, Miss Rose," said the women in their big gold jewelry and their beautiful silk dresses. They greeted her with warm smiles and sweet drawls and deference, and they were all properly introduced to Lilly and to me.

"Cat's grandbaby!" they exclaimed, wide-eyed.

It amused me to see that Lilly's nods of acknowledgment gradually turned regal as she caught on to the respect that tinged their astonishment. Cat Benet's granddaughter. As Miss Rose had told her, it seemed to mean something down here. It seemed to make her somebody down here, somebody special, even in her blue jeans and boots and cowgirl shirt and ponytail. By the time we finished lunch, the girl's spine had straightened from its sulky slouch, her head and neck sat on her shoulders like a princess's. She looked like a young woman who might sit a horse beautifully, or a throne.

On our way out of the restaurant, we passed by the buffet table, and Lilly picked a fried chicken nugget out of the chafing dish and popped it in her mouth.

"These are great," she said.

"Really," I agreed.

"Yep," Miss Rose said, "some of the best calf fries I ever tasted."

32

On the long drive south out of Fort Worth, I asked Rose why Judy lived at La Segunda.

"I thought Mr. Benet sold all of his ranches except the Crossbones," I said.

"La Segunda wasn't his to sell," was the tart reply. "It's Judy's, turned over to her by their mother and daddy when she turned twenty-one and they moved to a luxury apartment in Dallas. It was even named after her, the second child. Her folks always had in their minds to give her that ranch. Cat got most everything else, being first and a boy and all. They figured Judy'd marry rich, La Segunda would be a mighty fine dowry, and she wouldn't want for more. That was a big mistake on their part, I regret to say. Judy has wanted more ever since she was old enough to figure out how much more there was to want. Well, maybe anybody would. When her folks saw she wasn't goin' to marry rich, at least not in their lifetimes, their advice to her was, sell the ranch, put the money in a trust, and go live in Palm Beach with young Ladd for the rest of your life. But Judy ain't the Palm Beach type. So she hung on to the place and got lucky like a lot of us did, 'cause she hit oil back when that meant somethin'. Lived pretty high, like a lot of us, for a good many years. Skiin' every winter, cruises, fancy dress balls, shoppin' trips to Europe couple times a year, real good schools for Laddy. I don't know how's she managing now the bottom's dropped out of oil and cattle ain't sellin' for practically no more than you can raise 'em for. I'm curious about her myself, kinda glad to be havin' an excuse to drive on out to see ol' Judy."

Miss Rose was driving her own Lincoln, a massive old black number in mint condition that took the long roads as smoothly and powerfully as a panther on the pampas. I sat in the passenger's seat up front with her, Lilly sat behind me, staring out the window, not partaking in the conversation. She had plenty to think about and plenty of time for it. Miss Rose's head barely cleared the back of her seat; she'd had blocks of wood attached to the gas pedal to enable her stubby legs to reach them. She drove stiff-armed, with her hands at nine and three o'clock on the wheel. Every time she turned, I figured we were going into a ditch, but somehow we never did. Clearly, they had never heard of speed limits down here—she passed ninety-five the minute we hit the highway, and cars were still passing us with a toot and a wave. For the first time, I understood why western states howl at national speed limits set by eastern legislators. Out here, there was so much distance to cover and so much of it was sooo monotonous. At fifty-five miles an hour, or even seventy, a person could die of boredom.

"If this is Judy's place," I said as we drove over a cattle guard onto the ranch, "why do you say we'll learn about Cat from seeing it?"

"Because this is where he grew up. It formed him and left its mark on him. This is where he learned ranching, and he learned it by doing whatever needed doing here. He was almost a whole generation older than Judy, and so he ran this place for several years before she was old enough to take charge. You might say Cat trained under his dad and Judy trained under Cat."

From the backseat, Lilly said, "What happened to Grandfather when his sister took over the ranch?"

"Got more or less kicked off," Rose answered. "His folks said, time for you to run our other places, time for Judy to run this one. We're leavin' for Dallas, and you're packin' your bags, too."

"Wasn't that hard on him?" I asked. "Being dumped from his childhood home and the ranch he'd managed?"

"Cat knew it was comin'," Miss Rose said unsympathetically. "He had plenty of time to saddle his horse. The Benets never mollycoddled their kids, neither Cat nor Judy. Gave 'em plenty of responsibility early on, expected 'em to cinch their own saddles."

I twisted around to look at Lilly. She had her right elbow on the armrest and was leaning forward, chin on fist, nose to the glass, staring out.

"So, Lilly," I said. "What can you tell about him so far?"

She shrugged as if she weren't going to answer, but then she muttered a few words into her fist. It was hard to hear her.

"There's not much out there," I thought she said, and she was sure right about that. The land looked empty, almost barren, to me. Evidently there was a car or truck traveling ahead of us on the empty private road, however. I could see its dark funnel of dust rising on the horizon. I expected to hear disappointment in the girl's voice, but I wasn't sure I did. There was a stillness about Miss Rose at that moment as she, too, strained to hear what the girl said. Lilly paused between her muttered phrases, as if she was observing and then thinking before committing herself to an opinion. "Hard ground. Hard to grow anything on it. Must take a lot of acres to feed a cow. They must have a hard time keeping the brush down. It's so dry and brown. It's not pretty, like Kansas."

"So?"

"So maybe he was a hard man," his granddaughter muttered. "Or maybe he was a persistent man. Or maybe he was always looking for something softer and easier and prettier. Maybe that's why he got married so often. Maybe getting kicked out of his childhood home made him feel he didn't belong anywhere. So maybe he could never stay anywhere for very long." There was an especially long pause this time before she spoke again. "I wonder if he felt cheated."

"Like you?"

Miss Rose glanced at me without moving her head.

When Lilly didn't answer, I turned around to face forward in my seat again. I assumed she was still staring out the window, chin in hand, looking for herself as we sped along the dirt roads of her family's past, trailing a cloud of dust.

We were drawing nearer to the vehicle in front of us, which was raising an unbelievable amount of dust.

"Far," Miss Rose said.

It didn't look so far away to me.

"Big far," she said.

"Far?" I said. "Oh, *fire!*"

She pointed to the dark cloud on the horizon and now I saw that it was much too tall and wide to have been raised by any moving vehicle.

"Funny time to be burnin' pastures," she commented. A little farther down the road she said, "That ain't grass burnin', that's woodsmoke. I think ol' Judy's got her barn afar."

Miss Rose punched that Lincoln into overdrive, and we flew up the rocky dirt road to the ranch headquarters doing sixty miles an hour, spraying rocks the size of doorknobs to every side of us. They banged against the belly of the car and nicked its sides and windows, until I felt sure we'd either bust an oil pan or get brained by one coming through the glass. I clutched the handhold above my door. I heard the click of Lilly's seat belt.

When we were close enough to see flames as well as blue-black smoke, we realized it wasn't a barn that was burning, it was a house, a big one.

There were a woman and a young man sitting on the ground about a hundred yards away, watching it burn. The woman had a shotgun lying across her lap. At the sound of our approach, she jumped to her feet and leveled that shotgun at our windshield.

Miss Rose laid her left palm on the horn.

The young man also jumped up. He tried to wrestle the gun from the woman, but she butted him in the stomach with it and he bent double, then fell back onto the ground.

Miss Rose continued to lay on the horn. We sounded like a freight train roaring into a crossing.

I slid down in the front seat, trying to brace my feet against the floor, trying to remove my head as a target.

"*Miss Sachet!*" Lilly screamed. "*Stop!*"

The old woman took her palm off the horn, but only to give herself a free hand to lower the automatic window on her side. Still barreling like a bat out of hell toward the burning house and the woman with the shotgun, Miss Rose leaned her head out of the window and bellowed, "*Y'all cut that out now! Judy! Put that damned shotgun down! It's Miss Rose, you hear me?*"

We slid to a surprisingly smooth stop right beside the woman. The man was rolling about in the dirt, clutching his abdomen.

"Miss Rose?"

The woman, tall and slender and deeply tanned, slowly lowered the gun and stepped close to the car. Her long, dark hair was wild and uncombed, and she wore no makeup, but she was beautiful in a tough way nonetheless. When she saw who was behind the wheel, she grinned and said, "I could of shot you, Miss Rose, you know that? What do you want to come driving up here like that for, like a Mafia moll in a big black Lincoln?" She glanced back. "And look what you made me do to poor Laddy there."

I could now hear that the young man was alternately moaning, cussing, and crying "Mother!" in an aggrieved voice.

"I'm sorry, honey," she drawled to him. "But that was a dumb thing you tried to do. Now get up, honey, and say a polite hello to Miss Rose, who has driven all this way to see us get burned out." Judy, for this is who I assumed this pistol-packin' mama was, peered into the car, first looking me over, then Lilly. To her son, who was struggling, red-faced, to his feet, she said, "And look here, Laddy, she's brought company, too." Judy looked toward the burning house and sighed. "Ain't goin' to be any tea served in my house today, ladies, but come on out here. You can sit a spell with us.

"At least the ground ain't burnin'."

33

"You just goin' to let it burn down, Judy?"

Miss Rose's polite inquiry was tinged faintly with reproof. We had arranged ourselves in a semicircle in the dirt, facing the burning house, with me on the far left next to Lilly Ann, who sat next to Miss Rose, who sat next to Judy Benet, with Ladd Benet beside her. Neither my name or Lilly Ann's had elicited any reaction from either of them, and Miss Rose hadn't mentioned our connections to them. It was almost as if she were waiting for Judy and "Laddy" to catch on to it themselves. Miss Rose usually had good reasons for doing things her way, so I played along, and Lilly seemed shy about announcing her kinship. But if Judy Benet and her son had ever heard of us, you couldn't have told it.

"Laddy" was a handsome, blocky, sandy-haired boy, a little older than Lilly. He was the boy in the photographs, all right. At the moment, he looked pale from the blow his mother had struck him, and he kept touching his ribs, then wincing and looking martyred.

"I think you broke one of my ribs, Mother."

She ignored him in order to answer Miss Rose. "Can't hardly do anything else about it, Miss Rose. The fire burned out the wires, so naturally the pump don't work. Got no telephone left to call a fireman, got no vehicles in workin' order, got no horse I'd want to run that far and that fast. No need to worry about it spreadin', either, because there isn't anything between it and anything else except this here dirt. If I could get the marshmallows out of my kitchen, we could roast 'em, and that's about all we could do. Lord knows, Laddy and I are hungry enough we'd be happy for a wiener to roast right about now."

Miss Rose, who sat on the ground with her legs drawn up beside her instead of cross-legged like the rest of us, gazed at the burning structure.

"Too late for us to go for help for you," she observed.

"Yep," Judy agreed. "Been too late for hours now."

"When did it start in to burning, Judy?"

She looked at her son, who grunted.

"Early this mornin'," she said.

Miss Rose's eyebrows arched at that.

"Lot of hardwood in that old house," Judy said. "Mama must of built the only oak house in the county. It'll take a good long time to burn down. You know all that old walnut furniture Mama and Daddy left me?"

Miss Rose nodded.

"Imagine how long that's going to take to burn."

"Shame," Miss Rose intoned.

"Well, it is," Judy agreed.

I ventured to ask, "What happened to your phone and your vehicles?"

She looked past Miss Rose to me. "Well, the phone's in the house, you see, which doesn't do us a whole hell of a lot of good sitting out here. I should have put an extension in the barn, but I never did do it. Now I suppose I'm sorry. And the vehicles, well, I don't know what happened to them. All I can tell you is they won't any of them start.

Laddy?" She turned to her still-whimpering son. "Tell Miss Rose here what happened to my Bronco and your old Ford pickup."

"What happened is the battery ran down in the Bronco because you left the lights on, Mother."

"No, I didn't."

"Yes, you did, Mother! I ran out to start it and the battery was dead and you had the light switch pulled all the way out."

"Dirty lie," his mother said.

"And my truck had a flat tire."

"You couldn't fix it, Laddy?" Miss Rose asked him.

"Couldn't find the jack," he told her.

"Why didn't you charge the Bronco off the truck?" Miss Rose asked him.

"Because." He grunted again and placed his right hand over his rib cage. "The truck had a dead battery, too."

"Hah," his mother said.

"I didn't leave *my* lights on, Mother."

"Says you."

"I *didn't,* Mother!"

"I suppose you weren't smokin', either, when you went to sleep on the couch watchin' Johnny Carson last night?"

"I wasn't, Mother! Have I had a cigarette all morning? No, I have not. I don't smoke anymore, Mother. I haven't smoked for forty-eight hours, at least. You're the one who probably left a butt burning in your ashtray last night."

"I never do that." Judy turned toward Miss Rose and shook her head. "Really, I never do that." She sighed. "Lord, I would kill for a cigarette though. Any of you ladies got a smoke on you?"

Miss Rose opened her purse and took out a pack of Winstons and handed it to Judy. She sighed with pleasure and immediately lit two of them, one for herself and the second for Miss Rose.

"I'll take one," Laddy said.

"Thought you stopped smokin', boy."

"The stress of livin' with you is makin' me start up again."

She flipped him the pack.

"Where did the fire start?" I inquired.

Mother and son looked at each other.

"Your room?" he asked.

She shook her head, although it might have been to deny a truth. "Kitchen, I think."

"What woke you up?" I asked.

"Laddy woke me up," Judy said in a tone of complaint.

"Well, what was I supposed to do, let you burn to a pork rind?" he asked her. "All the thanks I get. I woke up because I heard a truck driving off."

Lilly, Miss Rose, and I all stared at him, but his mother didn't seem to pay that startling statement any mind at all.

"You were dreamin'," she said dismissively.

"I was not, Mother."

The house was by now burned almost completely away, with only a few flames shooting up now and then as a board split open to reveal its heart of fire. We were sitting to the north, upwind, so the ashes flew away from us like dead leaves in a hot breeze.

"Shit," Judy suddenly exclaimed. "I just remembered I had a brand-new pair of blue jeans in there." She started to laugh, and soon she was laughing so hard she was crying. "Hot pants. They're hot pants now. What the hell—Cat always accused me of havin' hot pants. Too bad he can't see how right he was!"

Judy Benet lay on her back, kicked her legs in the air, and whooped with laughter.

34

For the rest of that afternoon, we lolled on the rock-hard ground staring at that dying fire as if we were all gathered in their den watching logs burn in a fireplace. The wind changed once, so we had to scurry to the west to escape the bitter smoke and biting sparks. Then it shifted again, and we resumed our original positions, though we had to sweep some ashes away with our hands before we sat down again. Once Laddy strolled off behind a far tree to relieve himself, and once I had to hide behind the car. The other women seemed to have bladders of sponge.

Along about twilight, when the smoke turned the sky red, Laddy got up, moved closer to the house, and started throwing rocks into the ashes. Sparks shot up into the air with a red crackle every time he hit something of any consequence.

"Bathroom!" his mother cried when the third rock hit inside the fire.

And then with the next one, "Livin' room! Aim for the kitchen next time, Laddy, see if you can hit the refrigerator. Got 'er! Go for the hall closet, Sweetpea. Bingo!"

Beside me, Lilly began picking up rocks and tossing them from hand to hand, then setting them down again. She was fidgeting to join him. The fact that she didn't was probably a credit to her upbringing. I guessed it was not the done thing in Kansas City to throw stones at somebody's burning house. Actually, it wasn't in "Poor Fred," either. But it did look like fun.

"You do any more of that," his mother said after an especially colorful and noisy hit, "and there ain't goin' to be anything to save. I was hopin' maybe to wade in there tomorrow and salvage one or two things. A pot. A pan."

"A toilet lid," Laddy called back, and threw another rock.

Crack. Hiss. Whoosh.

His mother laughed. "I suppose that's right. Nothin' worth savin' anymore. Well, ladies, I'm hungry as a cow on a long march to Montana, and I'm tired and I got to pee. I'm afraid I can't offer y'all any supper, except maybe extremely well baked beans. If you'll drive us into town, Miss Rose, we'll report this little campfire and I'll buy y'all supper."

"No, you won't," Laddy called over his shoulder between throws. "You didn't think to grab your purse before you ran out of the house, remember?"

"Damn, that's right, I can't buy you supper." Judy raised her voice. "Since I now remember that Laddy didn't think to grab his wallet before he ran out of the house!"

Lilly, being the youngest and most agile, was the first to clamber to her feet. Judy, whom she resembled slightly, gazed up at her and smiled.

"You remind me of myself when I was younger, child," she said. "Except you got your grandpa's blue eyes. Pretty bright blue eyes, just like my brother, Cat."

In the heartbeat of silence that followed that remark, Laddy turned around and stared from his mother to Lilly.

"She's related to us?" he asked his mother. The question had an oddly aggressive sound. "She's on Uncle Cat's side?"

"That's right?" his mother asked Lilly.

The girl nodded shyly.

"Think you're too good for us, don't you?" Laddy snarled. He transferred all but one of the rocks he held into his left hand.

"What?" Lilly said.

"So you're Alice's daughter." Judy's smile turned mean. "My own little great niece. And little Miss Alice and little Miss Margaret are my nieces, who never have called me, or ever written to me, or so much as sent their aunt Judy or their cousin Laddy a Christmas card. Who never even so much as said thank you for the cards and gifts I used to send them, until I said the hell with Cat's people all together. That's who you're from, isn't it?"

This time Lilly shrugged and nodded at the same time, clearly not sure what was safe to say. I got quickly to my feet, then turned around to help Miss Rose when I realized she wanted to stand up, too.

"I never heard of you before," Lilly ventured.

"Liar!" Laddy cocked back his arm and threw the rock, a big, pointed one. It whizzed past Lilly's head, landing with a thud several yards behind her.

"Hey!" I yelled.

The second rock grazed Lilly's left arm.

"You son of a bitch!" Lilly bent down quickly, picked up the rock, and threw it back at him, smack into his rib cage. Laddy collapsed with a curse.

"What's this all about?" I shouted.

"Judy!" Miss Rose drew herself up to her full five feet. Her voice rumbled in the barrel of her chest. "That will be enough of that. Get ahold of yourself, both of you. I'll drive. We're going to supper, all of us."

"Yes'm," Judy Benet said. She walked over to her son and kicked him lightly with the toe of her boot. "Get up, Laddy. And you be nice, now." Her voice was meek, but the expression in her eyes and in her son's face was anything but meek.

So I couldn't have been more surprised when we moved toward the Lincoln and I glanced over at Judy and saw that tears were flowing from her blue eyes.

"I'm just tired, that's all," she claimed as we climbed into the car, but she began to cry harder. "It's just all got to me, that's all. Losin' my house and everything in it, and y'all showin' up and Cat gettin' himself killed, it's just all finally got to me."

Lilly sat up front, rigid as a fence post, and stared straight ahead without speaking. Miss Rose hurtled us back down the private dirt road and then back onto the highway like a ball out of a cannon. I sat in the middle of the backseat between mother and son.

Judy Benet wept all the way to supper.

"I can't believe he's dead," she sobbed. "The goddamned son of a bitch. Wouldn't speak to me when he was living, cut me off without a kiss or a hug or a single word, and now he's up and died on me, without makin' any peace between us."

"Aw, Mom," Laddy muttered. He was holding on to his rib cage again. Whenever he shifted in his seat, he managed to give the back of Lilly's seat a vicious kick, strong enough to make her head bounce, though she never turned around, never acknowledged it.

"What's the matter with you?" I hissed at him.

He just glared at the back of Lilly's head.

"What's the matter with him," Judy cried, "is that I divorced his father, and he's hardly ever seen his daddy since, and my brother cut us off from the whole rest of the family when I did it. It'll turn a boy to sour, being shunned like that, that's what it'll do. And now there's that goddamned will, barrin' us from his daddy's place for the rest of his life, as if Laddy was some pariah, not some innocent boy who didn't cause it all. Cat's the one caused it all, him and his self-righteous . . . *shit*."

"Your daddy's place?" I said. "Who's your father, Laddy?"

"Carl is," Judy sobbed. "Carl's his daddy."

"*Carl Everett?*"

Lilly burst into bitter speech from the front seat. "I don't know what any of you are talking about! I've never even *heard* of either of you before!"

"You see?" Judy wailed. "It's like we're lepers!"

Laddy gave Lilly's seat another kick.

"Stop that!" I told him.

"I can't," his mother sobbed.

"Not you, him."

"Come on, Mom, stop cryin' now."

"I told you, I'm tired, that's all."

"Aw, Mom."

"Aw, shut up," I said.

And they did for the rest of the ride.

We ate supper at a picnic table behind a filling station miles from anywhere. There was a single tree—juniper, I think—to keep us company in the dark, and a yellow bug light hanging above the back door of the station.

Judy had gradually gotten herself back under control on the long ride out, but then she'd retreated into herself, saying as little as possible to anybody. Laddy maintained a sulky silence that reminded me of his cousin Lilly, and he stuck close to his mother's side.

But the food was wonderful, thick pork ribs barbecued over mesquite in a halved oil barrel inside the garage. That was all there was to eat, just the ribs and colas from a machine, but it was probably the best meal I ever had in my life.

We heard cars and trucks pull up to the gas pumps every now and then. Once in a while we heard heavy footsteps on gravel as drivers or their passengers walked around to the side to use the toilets. And all the while, the owner of the Pit Stop Gas & Barbecue Station laid more slabs on the fire, selling the ribs along with the gas and oil. The blended aroma of gasoline, barbecue sauce, mesquite, and motor oil was heavenly to this starving easterner. I ate the meat off seven fat ribs without stopping to use a napkin. Let 'er drip, I thought.

Lilly, Miss Rose, and I sat across from Judy and Laddy, and for a while all you could hear from us was the sound of chewing and tearing in the dark. It was primitive, barbaric, a rending of flesh, five carnivores working out their aggressions on a dead pig instead of on one another. That would come later, I supposed. In the meantime, this sublimation was probably a good thing from everybody's point of view but the pig's. So there was only the gnawing of teeth, the sucking of bottles, the licking of lips, the discreet burp, the sated sigh.

Judy belched once, politely, behind her hand, and made an attempt to be civil. "Did you ever know about this place, Miss Rose?"

"Heard about it, is all," was the reply from the short, squat figure beside me. I could barely see her, and she wasn't any more than three feet away. "Never been here before, though. It's mighty fine, Judy."

"Yes, indeedy," I murmured.

On the other side of me, in the dark, Lilly giggled.

Laddy belched loud and long and impolitely.

And somebody shot the bug light out.

The second shot killed Judy Benet, but not immediately, not before she had a chance to say to her weeping son, "Tell Slight I said for him to tell you the truth."

PART IV

Bury Me Not on the Lone Prairie

35

The Albuquerque, New Mexico, airport was a warm and brilliantly sunny place in the late afternoon of the late October day on which I landed there. The wings of the Boeing 727 wobbled as we came down, and the plane bounced rather than slid to a stop. I struggled through what seemed to be endless construction of the earth-toned, tiled airport and caught the shuttle north to Santa Fe. During the hour-long trip past arid, rolling Indian land, I had some time to think.

It was Thursday, the day after Judy Benet was murdered, almost a week following her brother's death, and the first time in twenty-four hours that I'd been alone and awake at the same time.

First, there had been the desperate battle to pump oxygen and life back into Judy Benet as she lay bleeding into the Texas dirt. Then there was the wild fight to keep Laddy from driving Miss Rose's Lincoln off into the night to track down and kill the phantom who murdered his mother. It was far more likely that Laddy would be killed, the rest of us felt, and so even the gas station owner helped us to restrain the boy until the local police showed up.

Then there were the questions and the fifteen-mile trip to the sheriff's office, and the papers to sign. Did we think it was an accident? Or did we think somebody killed her on purpose? How was this shooting related to her brother's murder? We didn't know. To her house's burning? We didn't know. Why hadn't she reported the fire before this? Laddy explained that part, emphasizing the truck he said he'd heard, making it sound like arson.

We promised to return to testify if they found the killer, if it came to trial, if they needed us as witnesses.

Witnesses who hadn't seen a thing.

The only thing to which I could testify for sure was that Laddy got the telephone number of the Crossbones Ranch from me, that he called his father, that he left the message of his mother's death on the answering machine, and that nobody called him back, at least not while I was there.

We left Laddy in the sheriff's office.

"I'll watch out for him," Miss Rose promised.

That was followed by the long, sad, weary return to Fort Worth, with Miss Rose still insisting on doing all the driving. She took us to the Holiday Inn then insisted on waiting while we packed, then personally drove us to the airport. We said good-bye to her there. I spent what little was left of the night making reservations for myself and getting Lilly onto a plane for Kansas City.

And now I was entering yet another city. Santa Fe. As different from Winnetka, even from Fort Worth, as Rock Creek was from Kansas City, and Kansas City was from Port Frederick. I'd experienced so many different cultures in one week that I felt like a guide on a nonstop tour of an anthropological museum. "Now, ladies and gentlemen, we have come to our Native American wing . . ."

During the shuttle ride from the Albuquerque airport, I thought about the talk I'd had with Lilly in the Dallas/Fort Worth airport terminal. After all that had happened, Lilly's guard was down, all the way down.

"I really liked her at first," she'd said.

We were sitting across from one another in one of those ubiquitous airport cafeterias. Lilly had a Dr Pepper and a plate of french fries; I had a pot of tea and a piece of cherry pie. The girl looked as if she might burst into tears at any moment. I felt terrible for having exposed her to the danger and the trauma.

"I did, too," I said.

"Even if she hated me." Her lips trembled.

"She couldn't hate you, she didn't know you. I mean, what I mean to say is—"

"It's Aunt Meg's fault."

I had stared at her then, figuring I had misheard her, figuring my brain had finally melted from exhaustion, and that all of the little gray cells were lying in a pool at the base of my cerebral cortex. "What, Lilly?"

"It's Aunt Meg's fault that Judy hated our family. My mother told me all about it one time, even though I'm not really supposed to know."

"Please tell me about it, Lilly."

"Well, there was a time when Mom and Dad were married and Aunt Meg and Uncle Ray, that was her husband, were married, and my grandpa and they all tried to get to know each other. They invited him to their weddings, which were, like, within a year of each other, and he actually went, and then he invited them down to one of his ranches in Texas, to go horseback riding and hunting and stuff."

"So what happened?"

"What happened was that when I was four years old, they left me with my nurse and they all went down there. Only Uncle Ray didn't want to go. But Aunt Meg made him go, 'cause she wanted to suck up to Grandpa 'cause of all the money—"

"Your mother says that?"

"Well, not in those words, I guess."

"I guess not." I smiled at her, but she didn't return it.

"I'm serious. That's really why she made Uncle Ray go, because she wanted to get in good with Grandpa so he'd be sure to give her lots of nice stuff. So they went down there and Grandpa had it all planned that Aunt Meg and Uncle Ray would ride out on a picnic with him, but

Uncle Ray hated horses, so he said he wouldn't go, and he wanted to go hunting with my dad and mom, instead. Well, Aunt Meg was furious. She said they couldn't disappoint Grandpa, so my dad had to take Uncle Ray's place and go on the picnic. And that's the time Dad fell off the horse and got paralyzed. And then when Uncle Ray got back and Aunt Meg told him what he'd done, he turned around and went back out into the fields, and that's when he had his accident and shot himself."

"That's tragic, Lilly, but what's it got to do with Judy?"

"I think she was there, and she probably thought they were all fools, and she hasn't wanted to have anything to do with any of us ever since."

"Hmm," I said.

"Really," she said solemnly.

"I guess your family didn't want to go back to the ranches after that?"

"No," she said mournfully.

"And they lost contact with your grandfather?"

"They sure did, before I ever met him!"

"Hmm."

We walked together to her gate.

"Bye," she said, suddenly shy.

"Lilly, I'm sorry."

"It's okay."

I put my arms around her and hugged her.

"Really, Jenny, it's okay."

I remembered that this was the girl who'd rather fight lions, but I patted her on the back anyway before I released her.

She walked away, turning briefly, once, to wave.

I slept sitting up in a chair at the airport for the next forty-five minutes until the nice young woman behind the ticket counter woke me for my flight to Albuquerque, New Mexico, then on to Santa Fe, the last known address of Freddie Sue Gomez, former and last wife of Cat Benet, and former best friend of Marvalene Podhurst.

36

Her address turned out to be a stylish adobe-style solar home on a dirt road in the foothills north of town on the road to Taos. The house blended so beautifully into the hill that at first glance I couldn't tell where the earth ended and the house began. She didn't have any grass in her yard, but then neither did her neighbors. I assumed the houses were simply plunked down in the middle of patches of dirt, rocks, wildflowers, and cactus, until I looked more carefully and realized that each "patch" had been landscaped painstakingly to merge with the scenery.

I parked my rental car in her gravel drive and walked beneath a trellised veranda to her carved and weathered front door.

Someday, I thought, as I waited to see if she answered my ring, my life will return to normal and I'll actually call ahead when I want to visit people, instead of just dropping in to surprise them.

There were hollow footsteps on tile within, and then the knob turned. I expected the door to open on a woman who'd be as flamboyant as her former best friend.

"Yes?"

She was shorter than I, slender, dark-haired, and plain, wearing huarache sandals, a full rust-colored skirt that fell to her ankles, a Mexican-style peasant blouse belted with turquoise and silver, and a squash-blossom necklace. The trifocals she wore gave her the appearance of an English professor who had been interrupted while grading essays.

"Dr. Gomez?"

"Yes?"

"Dr. Gomez, my name is Jenny Cain, and I really need to talk to you about Cat Benet. I don't know if you know that he was murdered, but I hope you can help me figure out who did it."

She grasped the door for support.

"Charles, murdered?"

Thinking she might fall, I reached out to support her, but she held up a hand against me and saying harshly, "Come in," made her own way through the tiled foyer, trailing her left hand along the wall to keep her balance, into the living room. She collapsed onto a sectional sofa, and I sat down at a right angle to her.

"I suppose it would be appropriate for me to cry," she said.

"If you feel like it," I said, feeling awkward myself.

"I don't have any idea of how I feel. At one time, I had a good friend named Marvalene who did my feeling for me. When something bad happened to me, she cried for me; when good things occurred, she rejoiced; if I was wronged, she was the one who was furious. I seem to have an internal thermostat that remains set at the same temperature at all times. However, I realize that my body seems to be doing odd things right now, collapsing on me, as it were, and I know I'd like a drink. Charles always said that was my problem, that I knew how to think, but I didn't know a damn about feelings, particularly his."

"He was a fine one to talk about other people's feelings," I ventured.

She bristled at that. "He was a fine one. Period. I want to know who you are, why you're here, how you know about me, and what exactly happened to Charles to make you say he was murdered. I knew he had died, of course, but this! I can hardly believe it. I would offer you a drink, but I don't yet know if you deserve my hospitality. Please start with who you are."

I told her everything I knew, ending with, "You are the F. S. Gomez, Ph.D., who wrote *The Barons of Branchwater,* aren't you?"

"I am." She pushed herself up from the sofa. "I'm having a margarita. In fact, I'm probably going to have several of them. What about you?"

"Make a pitcherful," I suggested.

She returned from the kitchen carrying a hammered silver tray on which there were a matching silver pitcher, a bowl of lime wedges, and two chalices. In a small, napkin-lined Indian basket, she'd put warm, deep-fried chips around a small bowl of salsa.

"Are you hungry?" she asked as she poured.

"Always."

"There." She finished filling the chalices, sat down again, and lifted hers. "I can think of no appropriate toast to offer on an occasion such as this."

I dropped a lime wedge into my drink, then lifted the chalice toward her: "To the truth?"

She touched hers to mine. "We can attempt it, but we historians know better than anyone else that truth is the most elusive quarry of all."

"Did you write the truth in *Barons?*"

"I wrote half of the truth, the good half, the flattering half. That is what the Longhorn Foundation paid me to do, and that is what I did. I don't apologize for that, not even to other historians. It was their family, after all, and the story belongs to them. They can remember it as they wish. History is the study of lies, anyway, because no witness ever recalls events with total accuracy, not even eyewitnesses. Every history book, no matter how ostensibly objective, is basically lies filtered through bias and a certain amount of relative ignorance. *Barons* differs only in the degree to which I knew and admitted those biases."

Her cynicism left me breathless; either that, or it was the tequila. If that was really what she thought of her profession, it was no wonder that she'd rather drink than feel.

"You met Cat while you worked on the book?"

"No, I met him while he was married to a woman who used to be a good friend of mine, Marvalene Podhurst. I got the job because he recommended me to the foundation. When he and Marvalene divorced, in 1980, I was doing my research and that required long interviews with Charles. One thing led to another, as I suppose it usually did with him, and we were married the following year. It only lasted three years, which was longer than it actually took for him to decide that I wasn't much fun, and for me to weary of his perpetual, adolescent search for perfect freedom and amusement."

"You say you interviewed him at length, and yet there's really nothing in the book about his generation of Benets."

"No, he insisted on stopping the story at the marriage of his parents. He said it was supposed to be a history and that history was about dead people and he wasn't dead yet." She took a quick drink from her chalice. "I told him he was being too modest, but he only laughed at that."

"Do you have a picture of him? I've met Carl and Slight, but I never met Cat, and I'm curious to know what he looked like."

"Of course." She only had to point over my shoulder, to show me what I wanted, and it was even more and better than I'd expected: a photograph, framed in hammered silver, of all three of the Muskateers, Slight, Carl and the third man—Cat Benet, a brown haired, slim-hipped fellow with a moustache. He was attired, as were the other two, in the full working cowboy regalia of boots, jeans, chaps, long sleeved shirt, gloves, kerchief and cowboy hat. I couldn't really detect in the photograph his apparently extraordinary appeal to women, but I had Marvalene's word for it, and now Freddie Sue's, that the man had fairly sizzled with sex appeal.

"He must have been something," I murmured.

"Yes, he was," she said into her drink.

The more Frederica Sue drank, the straighter she sat and the better she enunciated her words. It occurred to me that Slight Harlan would find this little professor vastly entertaining. As her phrasing got more academic, his would slip into drawling colloquialisms; as her posture improved, he'd slouch further down on his spine, squinting those blue eyes until she would barely be able to detect the twinkle in them. I was willing to bet she'd had the same effect on his boss; it may even have been her charm and her appeal for him. Some men did dearly love to pull the bobby pins from a straitlaced woman's hair.

"What *didn't* you put in the book, Freddie Sue?"

She finished her second drink, poured another.

"I didn't write," she said, "that the Benets who remained in France forever after snubbed the Benets who came west. I didn't write that the early ones nearly died of loneliness and starvation and poor hygiene in south Texas. Or how many babies died before they walked, and how many young wives died in childbirth. I didn't write about the times they got cheated, or the times they did the cheating. I didn't describe the increasing burdens that their wealth placed on their descendants, or the prison it created for the last of their line—"

"Cat?"

She nodded solemnly. "There were three centuries of expectations placed upon him at the moment of his birth, and yet he was a man who had so few expectations of life. He wanted friends. He wanted lovers. He liked hard work, but not too much of it. He wanted a good time and enough money to buy a bed and clothes and a truck and a horse and food and drinks for his friends."

Freddie Sue studied her own drink.

"He said I wouldn't know a feeling if it bit me," she said, "but I knew that he was a sad man. He reminded me of a little boy who had found everything he ever wanted under his Christmas tree, but who felt like crying anyhow. I would have liked to have made him happier."

"Did he make you happy?"

She had to think about that. "I don't know. I suppose not. Except for the sex, I can't say that I missed him when he was gone." She gulped the rest of that drink, poured another. "I have missed Marvalene, though."

"She misses you, too."

"Do you think I should call her?"

I tried to think of a way to say it that would convince her. "I think it would be the *appropriate* thing for you to do."

"All right then, I will."

"Call her now," I urged, because I had something important to talk over with Marvalene Podhurst, too. Frederica got right to her feet and walked to a phone across the room.

"Marva, you'll never guess who this is," she began, sounding nervous. I heard the reply: "FREDDIE SUE!"

Soon they were gabbing ninety miles a minute, and I found that even I was grinning, listening to the former best friends make friends again. Finally, Frederica said, "Yes, she's still here, and I think she wants to talk to you, hang on." She held out the phone to me, and I walked over to take it.

"Marvalene?"

"Jenny, you sweet thaing, this is just the nicest thaing you've ever done, braingin' me together with my best pal again. Freddie's the onliest person in the world knows how ah fee-yel 'bout losin' Catty. How you doin', doll baby?"

"Hangin' in there. When did you marry Cat, Marvalene?"

"July seventeenth, 1975."

I did some quick calculating in my head. "But you said you didn't know any of the members of his other families, didn't you?"

"Well—"

"And it had to be in 1975, when Lilly Ann Lawrence was four years old, that those awful accidents happened at one of the ranches, when Merle Lawrence fell off a horse and was paralyzed for life, and when his brother-in-law shot himself. Isn't that right?"

"Well, I guess it is, honey."

"Marvalene, were you there?"

She sighed, then confessed. "Well, the truth is, I was. Jenny, honey, I don't like to talk about that time. I don't even like to re*call* it. I would like to plain forget it, it was plain awful, just a awful time, and I do blame myself for the whole kit'n'caboodle, even if my sweet little ole Catty-Balls never did blame me. But wasn't it me who kept tellin' him he ought to invite those people down and get to know them, them girls bein' his daughters and all? And wasn't it me kept after him to ask 'em until I just plum wore him out and he couldn't hardly say no? And wasn't it me said a picnic would just be so much *fun?* Lord forgive me, that poor man's in a wheelchair and that other poor fella's dead, and even if the Lord forgives me, I am never, I am *never* goin' to forgive myself."

"Aw, Marvalene," I said, feeling pretty guilty at the moment myself. "Come on, it couldn't have been your fault, not really. I'm sorry I mentioned it if it's going to make you feel so bad."

"Why *did* you, honeybunch?"

"Well, Cat's granddaughter, Lilly, told me about that trip, and I just had a feeling that since she wasn't even there, she might have had the story wrong. She thought the other woman there was Cat's sister, Judy, but I got to thinking about when you'd probably married him, and I figured it might have been you, instead."

"He didn't have any sister, honey buns."

"Yes, he did, Marvalene, and she was shot and killed about twenty-four hours ago."

"Lordy, I don't hardly know what to say."

I had to laugh. "This has to be a first."

She was still laughing at that when I handed the phone back to her reinstated best friend. They talked for another hour. I got drunk on margaritas. Freddie Sue, who didn't show any effects of the alcohol except that her vocabulary got ever more abstruse, poured me into a guest room that night. She, very decently, allowed me to sleep it off in the morning, then she even drove me to the Albuquerque airport on Friday afternoon. Lord, was I ever sick of airplanes.

37

For once, the sun was shining in Kansas City.

"Mr. Brady will see you now, Ms. Cain."

His legal secretary reminded me of my assistant, Faye, back home, so I gave her a particularly warm smile. She looked surprised and offered to bring me coffee.

"Hello, Jenny."

Dwight Brady stood up behind his desk to greet me.

"What a nice coincidence," he said. "You've come just in time to meet one of the heirs. Jennifer Cain, may I present one of Mr. Benet's other daughters—"

"Suanna!" I cried.

"Jenny!" she exclaimed.

Brady sank back down in his chair.

"Jenny, you'll never believe what's happened!" I sat down in the chair next to her. The stiff, shy woman from Winnetka was transformed; this new woman had a new suit and a new hairdo and she was nearly bouncing with excitement about something. "We have found the money! Father didn't steal it! At least, not exactly. He put all of it in an ordinary bank account, where it couldn't earn interest, and he left it all there."

I stared. "*All* of it? *All* of this time?"

"Yes, isn't that amazing? I have just been telling Mr. Brady that there is not one cent missing."

"*Why*, Suanna?"

"Because he was insanely jealous of the fact that Mother had been married before to a rich, attractive man. He couldn't stand to let her have the independence the money would have given her." Suanna's voice suddenly deepened and thickened with emotion. "And given us. He is a sick, jealous, stupid man."

Brady asked, "How did you find out, Ms. Railing?"

"We didn't," Suanna said. "We were still busy getting ourselves a lawyer and planning our attack when Father confessed all of this."

"No!" I said. I could not imagine that was true.

"Yes, we don't know what happened, except that maybe he was in a weakened condition, and he may even have been affected by the medication."

Brady and I glanced at each other. He looked every bit as confused as I felt.

"*What* medication?" I asked.

"The drugs he's on for the pain."

"Suanna—"

"Oh! Of course, you don't know! Mother and Father's house was broken into the other night. The burglar didn't actually steal anything, but he beat up Father. The police think Father must have surprised him in the act, and that's why he was attacked. I suppose he's lucky he wasn't killed." The dubious expression on her face testified to the ambivalent feelings she had about *that* narrow escape. "Father's nose is broken, and his jaw is dislocated, and he has a lot of bruises. Oh, he is really a mess."

She said it with enormous, undisguised satisfaction.

I said, "And it was right after this happened that he . . . confessed, Suanna?"

"Yes, the very next day in the hospital. He *insisted* on telling Mark and me all about it! He acted as if he just *had* to get it off his chest, as if he just couldn't wait another minute to do it!"

I looked over at Brady. He held my gaze steadily.

"Suanna," I said, "was there only one burglar?"

"He wasn't sure about that, Jenny."

"And I don't suppose he can describe anyone?"

"No, they wore stocking masks."

"That's what your father said?"

"Yes."

Brady interrupted. "Do you want to initiate any legal action against your adoptive father, Ms. Railing?"

She sighed, and some of the exuberance seeped out of her. "Mark and I haven't decided what to do about that. We're kind of afraid of the effect"—she sneaked a glance at the lawyer—"that might have on Mother. Anyway, Father says he will let Mother divorce him, which is what she has wanted to do for so many years. And frankly, that may settle it for us. We can't erase the last sixteen years, but with Father gone, at least we can begin to try to enjoy the years to come."

"I wish you luck," I said, knowing they would need it.

"We're very grateful to you, Jenny."

"Why?" Brady asked sharply.

"Oh," Suanna started to say, "she—"

"Why are you here?" I asked her quickly.

"To talk to Mr. Brady about our inheritance." Suanna Railing smiled. "Mark and I decided that I didn't have to phone him. I can afford to fly down personally to see him. So I did. I think we've settled all of our business, haven't we, Mr. Brady?"

"I believe so," he said.

"So I'll let you talk to him now, Jenny."

She surprised me again by embracing me before she left his office. "I thought I'd call my stepsisters while I'm here in Kansas City, Jenny. I tried calling a number at the address you gave me for Ladd Benet in

Texas, but the operator told me that number had been disconnected. Do you know where I might be able to reach him now?"

I suggested that she contact him through Miss Rose Sachet in Fort Worth. Let Miss Rose tell her, I thought, that her cousin won't want to hear from her. I just didn't have the heart to do it when she was feeling so high and hopeful.

After Suanna left, Brady said to me, "It's a nice day. Let's take a walk."

38

It was a long walk, all the way from his office south of the Country Club Plaza to a Vietnam veterans' memorial on Broadway. Luckily, I was in flat-heeled shoes, so if he thought he'd torture the truth out of me—about where I'd been and what I'd been doing—by making me walk twenty blocks in stiletto heels, he should have first looked at my footwear.

For the first five blocks, he tried to worm out of me where I had been for the last week. I found numerous ways of saying, essentially, "nowhere." He quizzed me about Suanna Railing, about how I knew her, where I'd met her, what she had meant by thanking me. To all of that, I hedged, fudged, and equivocated. He finally gave up, and for the remainder of the walk we discussed the transfer of the Crossbones Ranch to the Port Frederick Civic Foundation.

When we reached the memorial, Brady sighed down onto a concrete bench and said, "I like to come here for some reason. I wasn't even in this war. But I guess this reminds me that I am not the only man in the world ever to make foolish mistakes. It reminds me that there are victims of worse things than divorce cases. It reminds me that there are a lot of men of my generation who might like to be alive to have what I call problems: too much work, too little time." He gestured toward the names of the Kansas City soldiers engraved on the monument wall. "*They* know what it means not to have enough time."

"Or maybe they know time is not the question."

Much of the memorial consisted of a series of fountains that poured into each other, like separate pieces of experience contributing to a general pool of feeling. I recalled what the psychiatrist had told the Hyatt waiter: wounds that aren't allowed to close can never heal. I hoped this memorial was a stitch in the closing of some wounds.

"Something's not right about this bequest, Dwight."

He sighed. "I know."

"Do you know what's going on?"

"No." He glanced at me. "Honestly, I don't."

"Do you know, really, why he left us the ranch?"

He had his legs apart, his hands clasped between them, and he was staring at the fountains. "I think they don't want anybody to know what's going on down there. And no, I don't know what that is. But I think that's the answer."

"Only part of it, I'm afraid."

"I knew it," he said in a low voice.

"Knew what?"

"Knew something was fishy. Here was this rich rancher who comes up from another state where he undoubtedly had plenty of attorneys working for him at one time or another. But who does he pick to do his will? Me, somebody who doesn't know anything about him, or even about ranching."

"Like me, like my foundation."

"Exactly. Only I was too greedy to question it."

"Well, it was a chance for a big client."

Brady shrugged, not forgiving himself, and for the first time I liked him a little.

"Did you like Mr. Benet, Dwight?"

"He was all right."

"How many times did you meet with him?"

"Ten, twelve."

"Was he clear about what he wanted?"

"Yes, very."

"How was he to work with?"

"Difficult at first, until I caught on to the fact that he was never impulsive. He would never commit himself to a decision without first thinking it over. I'd raise a point, he'd listen carefully, take notes, then he'd promise to have an answer for me the next time he saw me, and he'd have it, every time. Maybe that's what made him rich, that kind of calm deliberation. I'd say he was a careful, calculating man.

"He didn't seem wealthy, Jenny, he was common as an old shoe. Had me call him Cat, right from the first. It seemed to tickle him. There he was, richer than Croesus, and all the nurses and doctors and orderlies and lawyers were calling him by his nickname. You would have thought he was just some old ranch hand."

"Why did he want to meet me?"

Brady took his gaze off the pools to glance at me. "He said he wanted to size you up, to see if you could handle the job. I think he wanted to make sure you *couldn't* handle it."

"That's what I think, too."

Brady gazed into the pools cascading into each other. "As I said, Jenny, there are in this world even bigger fools than I, and I think it may turn out that Cat Benet was one of them."

39

After I left Brady's office, I drove to the Lawrence-Stewart mansion on Ward Parkway Boulevard.

Sister Margaret was upstairs in her living quarters, I was informed by Alice, and Merle Lawrence was watching television. When I asked Alice if she had a cup of coffee to spare, she seemed to understand that my real purpose was to talk to her privately.

"Mrs. Lawrence," I began.

"Please call me Alice."

"Alice, there's a homicide detective here in town who would dearly love to pin your father's murder on me. Would you help me? Would you please tell me the real story of what happened on that ranch down in Texas when your husband was injured and your brother-in-law died?"

A shadow of old pain passed through her eyes.

"I can't imagine why you want to know."

"I just do, please."

She shrugged. "There's nothing much to tell, really. Merle and I went on a picnic with my father. We rode horseback to reach the meadow where Father's wife had laid everything out for us. Father was, of course, a superb horseman. I think he grew rather bored plodding along beside us on our old nags, and so he began racing ahead of us, and then returning to our sides. Once or twice, he had to jump a fence to do it. He rode a beautiful big palomino; I can still remember how powerfully that horse gathered itself for each jump."

She licked her lips, then pressed them together as if she were blotting lipstick.

"Well, Merle was a young man, adventurous as any young man, and it must have looked glorious to him to see my father take those fences. So, against my protests, and Father's, he tried it, too. He made it over the first one, barely, but on the second one, the horse balked and stumbled. Merle fell between the animal and a fence post, and that is how and when it happened . . ."

"Your father's fault," I suggested.

"Oh, no," she said firmly. "It was not."

"How does your husband feel about that?"

"If you mean, has my husband nursed a grudge all these years against my father, and did it finally result in an act of murderous revenge, the answer is no."

I felt myself properly rebuked, if not convinced, until she added softly, "I would say that if Merle has nursed a grudge all these years, it has been against . . . me."

"You? Why?"

"Why not?" She shrugged, but I saw tears come to her blue eyes. "If a person is not capable of blaming himself, he must blame someone, mustn't he? It was *my* father, it was my father's ranch, it was my choice to visit there . . . you see, none of it adds up to a logical reason to blame me, but logic is not the issue here, anger is."

"Why not blame Margaret?"

"My sister?"

"Wasn't she the one who insisted that you all go?"

"Yes." Alice inhaled deeply. "But it is difficult to hurt my sister. She is impervious to criticism. Believe me, I know. No, I am the object of Merle's anger; my sister is merely the vehicle through which he expresses it."

What? And then I remembered that Merle and Margaret had been together when they greeted me, seeming much more of a couple than he and Alice. "A close family?" I had asked Dwight Brady. "Evidently," he had replied. Now I wondered how much of an understatement that was, but I couldn't bring myself to push her any closer to the truth. She'd hinted pretty plainly at it anyway: that Merle Lawrence lived out his bizarre, unjust revenge by residing as intimately in this house with his wife's sister as he did with his wife. No wonder Lilly Ann rebelled against the values of this house.

"Alice, did your brother-in-law commit suicide?"

"Of course," was her simple reply.

"So did Father."

I was startled, but Alice was totally undone by the sudden appearance of her sister in the kitchen doorway. Alice stood stock-still, seeming unable to know what to do or say next.

Margaret swept regally into the room, with only the tiniest of sardonic smiles on her lovely face to hint that she might perhaps have heard more of the conversation than merely the last few words. With a mocking gentleness she placed her hands on her sister's arms to move her out of the way of the coffeepot. Then, as Alice trembled and I stared, Margaret calmly poured herself a cupful. She dropped in three cubes of sugar, one, two, three, slowly and deliberately so they made plunking sounds going in. Then she stirred, her spoon going round and round, grating on the sides of the cup and on my nerves. All the while, she smiled her cat's smile. I was beginning to think of it as a *dead* cat's smile.

I broke her spell, with scorn.

"You think your father *smothered* himself?"

"Of course he didn't do it himself. He paid someone, some hospital flunky to do it, out of remorse for being such a rotten daddy. For having caused Ray's death. For ruining Merle's life. And because he was a coward." Her glance at her sister was malicious. "An impotent coward, just like Merle, isn't that right, Alice?"

217

Her sister stared down at the countertop.

Was that how Margaret and Merle had managed it? I wondered. Did he claim impotence with his wife, so that she had to live with only the suspicion that it wasn't true where her sister was concerned? Or was he truly impotent, and Margaret only taunted her sister with the possibility of its being a lie?

"What a convenient theory that is, Margaret," I said. "If it was suicide, then maybe he wasn't of sound mind, and that would be grounds for invalidating the will, wouldn't it? And then maybe you could get the ranch for the Longhorn Foundation, or maybe even for yourselves."

Alice looked up at me, and I was astonished to see greed and interest in her blue eyes. Margaret was a witch! The woman could twist truth in upon itself until it resembled the exact opposite of itself.

"Mirrors," I said to her.

"What?"

"I think you do it with mirrors."

She ignored me and turned to her sister. "Alice, dear, Lilly's gone again. This time she took a suitcase and left a note, the gist of which is, basically, screw you all. Both pairs of her boots are gone, I don't know how many shirts or pairs of blue jeans, and that awful fringed jacket you won't let me throw out. The girl left dressed for the country, dear. You have to get her back, and when you do, I'm going to tie her to the bedposts."

Alice didn't even react; she seemed not to care.

I slid off the stool on which I'd been sitting.

"I'll stop her," I said, "give me the phone."

I called the ranch and got the damned answering machine, but I had more success in calling Sheriff Pat Taylor in Rock Creek.

"Sure," the sheriff said, "I'll try to keep an eye out for her, but I've got to tell you I can't watch the highway every minute. You understand. Say, that was some rotten trick they pulled on you the other day, wasn't it?"

"What trick?" I said.

"That snake. I heard those shots, and I came roaring back up to the barn, and then Carl Everett showed me that dead rattlesnake. Heck, I guess it was dead, like about three weeks dead."

"Three weeks?"

"Yeah, you mean you didn't know? Well, listen, those fellows pulled an old, old trick on you. It's the one where they tie a line to a dead snake and then they hide and then they pull it across your path so it scares the peewaddin' out of you. Then they laugh like hell."

"So the joke was on me," I said.

But I was not laughing when I left the Lawrence-Stewart home and got back into my rental car. It was Slight Harlan who'd seen me shiver at the mention of snakes, and it was Slight who'd sent me into the barn with the bottle to feed the calf. I peeled out of the Lawrence-Stewart driveway in a tire-squealing humiliated rage that would have gotten me ticketed if there'd been a cop around. On the long drive, the rage turned to fear for Lilly Ann.

40

It took me three hours to drive to the Crossbones Ranch doing eighty-five all the way. When I started, the sky was clear; two hours down the highway, the wind picked up so that the car kept swerving to the left as if it wanted to return to Kansas City. Monstrous black cumulus clouds were building to the southwest and moving fast. By the time I drove past the Pizza Hut across from the Rock Creek Motor Inn, the rain had started to fall, the clouds overhead looked as if they were boiling, and the air had a greenish look to it. It reminded me of the way the movie sky had looked right before Dorothy got whisked off to Oz. "Oh, Auntie Em!" I thought. As a coast dweller, I'd battened down for hurricanes before, but the mere idea of Kansas tornadoes turned my knees to yogurt.

I drove onto the state road that led to the ranch, directly into the face of the storm, then struggled on westward the three miles it took to reach the beginning of the fence line. The rain flattened itself against the glass as if God were tossing buckets of water directly onto my windshield. I turned on the headlights but still could see only the yellow line directly ahead of me on the left and a drainage ditch on the right. I didn't know I'd missed the padlocked front gate until I passed it, but that was all right, since Lilly couldn't get in that way anyway. I looked for her car along the road that bordered the fence.

Two miles farther on, I came upon a white Volkswagen convertible parked down in a wide gulley between the road and the fence. The water rushing down the gulley was already up to the middle of the VW's wheel covers.

I couldn't see anybody in the car.

I parked off the highway on the grass for a moment, taking a chance on getting stuck in the mud, but more afraid of the chance of getting rear-ended by a car or truck that wouldn't see me if I stopped on the road. I let the windshield wipers run and stared through the rain.

"Where'd you go, Lilly?"

I had to find her, storm or no, tornado, hurricane, cyclone, or blizzard. None of Cat Benet's ex-wives had killed him, of that I was sure, and the only family member with whom he'd had a real feud was his sister, Judy, and she was also dead. I didn't believe that Clyde Railing had killed Cat—he wouldn't even have known the rancher was sick or where to find him, and besides, he'd been attacked himself. But this I did know, or at least feel deeply—between gunshots, ghost spurs, rattlesnakes, and a near-miss in an airplane, Slight Harlan and Carl Everett had done their damnedest to scare me off the ranch. Both men were pilots, either could have flown that little plane to Kansas City, killed their boss, then flown back before morning. For that matter, either one of them could have flown to Texas, rented a car, killed Judy Benet, then flown back. If they wanted the Benets either dead or ousted, if they so desperately wanted this place to themselves, I had to consider that Lilly Ann was a Benet and she was here, and I'd better find her before either of them did.

I drove back onto the road, past her car, then I saw the gate that led into the pasture beyond it. I pulled up to the gate. "*Damn!*" The fucking thing was closed. I forced my car door open against the wind, which caught it and slammed it the minute I let go. By the time I'd managed to lift the barbed-wire noose that attached the gate to the fence, push the gate back, then run back and get into my car, I was drenched clear through and shaking with cold. I flipped the heater on to high.

I drove down the dirt road, longing for a truck instead of a rear-wheel-drive, automatic-transmission city car. I decided I'd go as far as I could until there was too much risk of getting stuck in the mud, a risk that increased with every minute as the rain fell harder. It was really dark now, though lightning strikes illuminated the landscape like spotlights, terrifying me with their crackling noise and naked brightness.

I drove on, spinning my wheels, wondering if this was a futile effort, because maybe she'd gone in a completely different direction.

Then a lightning strike illuminated the hills in front of me. Against the bottom of one of them, plain as daylight, stood a small tent, one corner of it rising and falling, flapping violently in the wind. As I watched, the wind pulled another stake out so that now a full half of the tent was flapping and it wouldn't be but a few minutes until the whole thing blew away. I could see the girl, frantically reaching for the flapping corners, trying to catch them, to peg them down again. I risked stepping on the gas harder and barreled on toward her.

With a crack and a roll of thunder, another lightning strike, closer this time, revealed another vehicle heading toward the tent from the opposite direction: a big, long car. Carl Everett's Caddy? It was weaving, its wheels spinning in the mud of the pasture, but it was definitely headed toward Lilly Ann's tent.

The Caddy and my own car got stuck at almost the same time. While I was spinning my wheels in the mud, alternately throwing the car into reverse and then into first, Carl got out of his car. I stopped long enough to watch him stand in the rain beside his car, then reach inside for what looked at this distance like a rifle. He turned toward the tent, his head down, the wind blowing his rain slicker back. He was weaving, not because of the force of the wind, I felt sure, but because he was drunk.

Did he know who she was, or was he going after her because he was drunk and thought she was a trespasser, even a poacher?

I laid on my horn to warn her, to distract him.

The wind and rain and a crack of thunder muffled the noise. I was terrified of confronting a drunken, rifle-toting Carl, but I couldn't let him hurt the girl. I threw open the car door and pushed out into the rain.

This time, a lightning strike illuminated Carl and me to each other. He looked up, must have seen a figure standing beside a car in his pasture, raised the rifle, and fired. Unharmed, I threw myself back into the car.

Carl fired again.

I started the car, rammed it into reverse, and spun wildly back up the road, managing to make it almost back to the gate before the car plunged backward off the road into the grass and got so stuck I couldn't move it in any direction. I left the car where it was, then ran through the open gate and down the highway, running, running through rain and terrifying lightning and thunder, running, running until I came to the open gate hidden by cottonwood trees.

I jumped the cattle guard, not wanting to take a chance of slipping on it and twisting an ankle. Then I plunged down the road, racing on toward the house, running over grass, mud, rocks, and piles of cow dung. Cattle were bunched together at the far fences, tails into the storm, and I felt as if they were watching me, the crazy woman, hurtling through their fields. I'd never seen such a storm as this, I'd never been in such a storm as this. The elements poured themselves down on me like vengeance out of a god's mouth. Anger. Spite. Jealousy. Drunkenness. *I am a jealous god, thou shalt have no other gods before me.* My feet pounded in time to commandments I didn't know I remembered so well: *Thou shalt not kill, Thou shalt not covet thy neighbor's wife or his oxen, Thou shalt honor thy mother and thy father, Thou shalt not commit adultery* . . .

"*Slight!*"

I screamed his name as I neared the house. I yelled it again as I wrenched open the front door, and again as I stood dripping in the doorway. I registered the presence of two men in the living room: Slight Harlan and the boy, Laddy Benet.

"*Slight!*" I was still screaming. I couldn't lower my voice, I couldn't stop it. *"Lilly's in the pasture west of the fence and Carl's out there with a rifle, he took some shots at me, Slight, you've got to help me, Carl could kill her, she's just a girl! Help me, help me, come on, come on!"*

Both men ran after me, not even stopping to put on rain slickers or jackets, and we raced back out into the storm in Slight's green pickup.

The gate on the west side of the road was still open, as I'd left it, and Slight plunged the truck on through. We half-slid down the slope of the hill toward the tent and the Cadillac.

In a flash of lightning, we saw them both, only now the girl was sitting inside Carl's car; even from a distance we could see her terror. Carl stood straddle-legged in front of his car, holding his rifle nose-high, aiming it straight at us. Slight accelerated toward them. For the second time in a week I found myself roaring toward someone holding a gun in our direction.

"He won't shoot," Slight yelled at us.

Carl shot one of the headlights out.

"Down," Slight yelled at us. *"Get down, kids!"*

Laddy and I obeyed, practically laying our heads on each other's lap to do it.

Slight skidded to a stop. He threw open the truck door and got out, hiding himself partially behind it, admitting the rain and the wind into the cab. He rolled down the window in front of him.

"You goddamned lunatic!" he shouted through it.

"Get back!" Carl's voice was so deep, so huge with drunken fury that we heard him plainly through the storm's racket. *"I'm takin' her! You goddamn sonsabitches took mine away from me, now I'm takin' her!"*

"Put the goddamned gun down, you goddamned moron!"

"Get back, you lying son of a bitch!"

While the two men yelled epithets at each other in the rain, the wind screamed around us, and Laddy whispered to me, "Can you get your hand under the seat? Feel if he keeps a gun under there."

I moved my left hand down to the gritty floor, which was getting soaked, and brushed it over whatever surface I could reach, and it did come in contact with hard metal. Carefully, I tugged it out by the barrel.

"Yes," I whispered to Laddy.

"Pass it to me."

I slid it across the floor until he grabbed it with his right hand. When I realized what he wanted to do, I cooperated by lifting my legs up on the seat so that he could slide himself along. He nudged Slight in the side with the gun.

Slight looked down.

"*No,*" Slight said.

"What d'ya mean *no?!*" Laddy cried.

"I won't shoot him."

"You got to," Laddy said. "Do it."

"Christ, he's your father," I exclaimed.

"No, he ain't," Laddy whispered.

"*Carl, no!*" Slight suddenly yelled, and I pushed myself far enough above the dashboard to see that Lilly, or something, had distracted Carl, who now had his rifle pointed inside of his own car. Now he swung back toward us. I ducked. He was wild, drunk, out of control. Slight bellowed, "*If you got to shoot somebody, shoot me, you crazy, drunk son of a bitch! Don't hurt the girl!*"

From where Laddy and I were crouched, we couldn't see out, but we both stiffened when we heard the single shot.

"*Carl, you bastard!*"

"Oh, my God," I cried. "No, no, not Lilly! Slight, did he shoot her? Slight, did he shoot her? Oh, no, please, please, no . . ."

Slight turned slowly toward us and reached out for the gun with an expression of infinite pain, weariness, and sadness. "Give it to me, son."

Laddy handed him the weapon.

Slight braced it on the bottom of the truck window frame. He braced himself in the mud and fired. I screamed. He fired again. Beside me, on top of me, Laddy Benet made a sound like a stifled sob and said a single word that sounded like, "Dad."

Slight Harlan crumpled to the mud.

Laddy kicked and crawled over and under me to reach the fallen man. I turned myself around and slid toward them. Laddy was kneeling in the rain, cradling Slight, whose eyes were closed.

"Lilly!"

The girl came running up, and she, too, fell to her knees beside man and boy. She looked up at me with the eyes of a mortally wounded fawn and she said, "I'm sorry, I'm sorry."

Carl had not shot the girl, he'd shot his old friend, who had then killed him in self-defense. Crying, I reached out a trembling hand to caress Slight's pale, cold cheek, then I bent down to softly kiss him. I am embarrassed to admit I said, "Oh, Slight."

Right under my lips, the bastard smiled.

H e's my father," Laddy told Lilly and me on our wild drive to deliver Slight to a hospital in Emporia. We had left Carl's body in the pasture, where the rain would surely wash away his blood, if not his guilt. "Slight's my real father."

It was from the hospital in Emporia that we called Sheriff Pat Taylor in Rock Creek. And it was the sheriff who decided, on the strength of our united testimony, that Slight had shot Carl out of self-defense and out of a need to protect Lilly Ann, and so there wasn't any reason to place a police guard on him that night. That was a big mistake, though we wouldn't know it until the next morning.

"When mother died," Laddy told us during that wild and extraordinary drive, "she told me to get Slight to tell me the truth, so I came up here and confronted him, and he admitted it. He said he and mother had an affair while she was married to Carl, and Mom got pregnant with me. They were all afraid of what Carl would do if he found out, so nobody told him. Not my real father, not my Uncle Cat, not mother, they all just agreed to pretend that Carl was my dad. Uncle Cat made Slight agree to stay away from Mom and me, and he was so mad at Mom that he never saw her again."

"But Carl found out, didn't he?" I asked.

Laddy nodded. "Yeah, in the hospital, Uncle Cat told Carl the truth. I guess he wanted to get it off his chest or something. It made Carl crazy to think he'd been cheated on to begin with, and that they'd all been lying to him ever since."

That might have been true, but I thought of the photographs of Laddy that I'd glimpsed on Carl's bedside table, and I thought: *He loved you, Laddy, or at least he loved the idea of you. He thought he had a son, then found out he'd been loving some other man's son all along.*

But I didn't say it out loud.

"So," Laddy continued, "Carl got drunk and decided to get even with everybody. First, Uncle Cat, then Mom . . ." The boy choked over that, but managed to go on. "He tried to kill Dad a couple of times, once when he missed and shot a heifer, or some damn thing instead, and another time when he sabotaged Dad's airplane."

"I was there both times," I said. But Laddy wasn't interested in that, he was only interested in saving the life of the bleeding man who lay with his eyes closed in the backseat of the truck, holding the hand I had draped over the back of the front seat. It was his right hand, on which the knuckles looked raw and swollen.

That was from beating up Mr. Railing, I suspected, from pummeling the man into a vow to tell Mark and Suanna the truth and to divorce Anna. I had never believed that story about a thief in the night in Winnetka; it was too pat, and far too coincidental. *You did it for your late boss,* I thought, gazing at Slight, *and to satisfy your own idea of justice.* I tried to condemn him for it, but couldn't; it *was* too damn satisfying.

Every time I tried to slip my hand away, his grasp tightened. By the time we reached the emergency room, my whole arm was asleep.

The irony was that by killing Laddy's mother, Carl Everett had given the boy back his father. Now the son rushed down the highway, driving as if he were saving his father's life, although the wound didn't look like a mortal one to me. In fact, I wondered why Slight didn't say so, to ease Lilly's sense of guilt, and to keep us all from being killed by his son's fervor. But then, maybe Slight was dealing with enough guilt and grief of his own to drown an elephant, I thought at the time; maybe that's what kept him so uncharacteristically silent on that long ride.

Laddy hovered around the attendants who placed Slight on a gurney. He tried to give orders to the doctors and nurses, who mostly ignored him. He pushed Lilly and me out of the way more than once in order to remain within touching distance of the uncharacteristically quiet man who never even spoke when the doctor probed his wound. It was only with the greatest effort that Lilly and I managed to drag Laddy away from Slight's private room in the hospital in Emporia after the anesthetic had knocked him out.

All of which made it seem so much worse when we trouped back to the hospital the next day, only to be told:

"*He's gone.*"

They didn't mean he was dead. Sometime during the night, Slight Harlan had slipped into his bloody clothes and disappeared from the hospital, from Emporia, from his son's life, from everybody's life, including mine.

42

Even Detective Luis Canales was satisfied with the answers Laddy gave him, which were the same ones that Slight had given to Laddy, and that Laddy had repeated to us in the car.

Of course, it helped that once they had Carl Everett pinned as the murderer, they were able to pick up circumstantial evidence to support the charge: someone who'd seen him fly the little plane into Kansas City the same night I arrived; the motel where he'd stayed that night while he got drunk and worked himself up to killing Cat; the motel where he'd stayed near La Segunda Ranch; and even some physical evidence that suggested he had set the fire there. It all pointed to Carl, and Carl was dead, and everybody was as satisfied as you can be in such circumstances.

Except me.

Oh, I believed he killed Cat and Judy, all right.

But I still didn't have the answers to those mysteries I'd gone to Kansas City to solve in the first place: Why did Cat Benet leave his ranch to the Port Frederick, Massachusetts, Civic Foundation, and why did he bar his relatives from the property?

I thought about it. For six months I worried it until it became such an obsession that Geof didn't want to hear about it anymore. He especially got tired of listening to me talk about Slight Harlan, and I couldn't blame him for that. But he also got tired of hearing me say, "Everyone talked about Cat Benet as if he was a wild and impulsive man, and yet Dwight Brady portrayed him as very deliberate, never making a snap decision, always thinking about matters before signing anything."

And, "They had this phone machine, Geof, and Slight never picked it up until he knew who was calling, but Carl, he'd pick it up on the first ring."

And, "First, he moves to Kansas where nobody knows him. Then he gets sick, but none of them tells anybody who might want to visit him in the hospital. Then he dies, but neither Slight nor Carl call Marvalene, or anybody else that I know of. And there wasn't to be a funeral. And the front gate was padlocked, and the relatives were barred. And yet he lets *us* in, perfect strangers, we get in."

"So maybe the cancer had spread to his brain, causing him to do irrational things," Geof said. "It's over, Jenny, let it go."

"I can't," I told him. "Because if I'm right, if I've guessed correctly, then that ranch doesn't belong to us, and it never did."

But I had suffered a miscarriage shortly after my return from Kansas, and Geof claimed that my obsession with the ranch was a sublimation of my feelings about that. It was that pregnancy, an accident, that had caused my bouts with nausea during my journeys. I accused Geof of refusing to acknowledge the validity of my suspicions as a way of sublimating his own denial of the death of a child he wanted. And so, alas, we spun psychological circles around each other, growing simultaneously more superficial and sophisticated, tossing jargon at each other, but never touching our hearts. We had wounds we didn't close that winter, and so they couldn't heal.

EPILOGUE

A Lone Cowhand

In my opinion, the Atlantic Ocean up north where we live is never warm enough for swimming. Even Geof puts on a wet suit until the end of June. So on the first of June, he was in the water, clad all in black rubber, but I was seated on the shore, watching him cavort like a dolphin.

"Who is that masked man?" I said to myself and smiled, though he wasn't watching and couldn't have seen the smile even if he were. I turned to my best friend, who sat in a full lotus next to me, and said, "Watch him for me, will you, Marsha, I'm going back to the house to see if the mail's come yet."

"Om um," she said.

I stood up, brushed myself off, and waved at him.

He happened to be glancing our way and waved back.

Then I picked my way over the rocks back up to our cottage, pausing to savor how gorgeous it looked when I approached from this direction. God, it was lovely. The yard was so green, the rhododendrons so pink, the roses so red. I felt as if, after a long, sterile winter, happiness was budding along with the spring flowers.

I got in my car and drove down our private road to the mailbox, opening it and reaching into it from inside my car. Three bills, two flyers, a letter from my stepmother in Palm Springs, and a letter-sized envelope with a typed address, a Utah postmark, and no return address.

Curious, expecting one of those computer-generated direct-mail pieces, I opened it:

Dear Jenny Cain from Massachusetts,

Well, there's nobody likes to tell a story like an old cowboy, so just sit back for a spell and let this one spin you a yarn. . . .

Once, in what seems like another century, there were these three cowboys, Cat, Carl, and Slight by name. Cat was the boss, or at least he had the money that paid the other two, so they let him pretend to be boss. Well, these cowboys had known each other a good many years, and drunk a good many beers together, and knew each other pretty damned well, when one night they maybe drank one too many whiskeys, and made one too many big plans, and decided to pull one too many jokes on the rest of the world.

"Lord, I'm sick of it all," Cat said that night.

"What are you sick of, boss?" Slight wanted to know.

"I'm sick of the responsibility, and the money, and the relatives waiting for me to die so they can get the rest of the money."

"Poor ole polecat," Slight mocked him.

Carl just kept on drinking.

"What if I could give them all their money now?" Cat said, looking sly. "What if I could get out from under all this load of responsibility before it puts me eight feet under the ground?"

"What are you dribblin' about?" Slight said.

Carl just kept on drinking.

"I'm talking about the fact that you're dying of cancer, and what good's that going to do any of us? It ought to be me that's dying. That'd make everybody happy, maybe including me."

"You're full of shit, boss," Slight observed, but he winced with pain when he pulled the tab off a fresh beer can.

"Possibly, but that wouldn't be anything new, would it? Carl, are you listening to me, or are you already dead?"

Carl grunted, and kept on drinking.

"Well, what if we moved someplace where nobody knew us, and nobody gave a shit about the legendary Barons of Bushwhack."

Slight chuckled into his beer can. "Montana?"

"Hell, no, think of their winters."

"Arizona?"

"Too much like west Texas."

"Where then?" Slight asked, still chuckling.

"Kansas," Cat said, and he let them digest that, and then he gave them a few more morsels to chew on. "They got good cattle country in the Flint Hills, good grass, there's at least a couple of weeks a year when the sun don't broil you and the cold don't freeze you, and it even rains now and then. You remember rain: it's that stuff we saw comin' down outside of Seattle that time."

Cat saw that Slight was beginning to get an inkling that he might be serious.

So he continued: "What if we bought us a new place, one last ranch, and I sold everything else off. And what if we put you in a hospital in another state and we called you . . . me."

Slight sat up straighter, but it hurt him to do it.

Carl stopped drinking long enough to stare at Cat.

"Say," Cat continued, "just say we set up a will that gave Quentin Harlan and Carl Everett lifetime employment on this new ranch. And say we set things up so nobody who knew us could get to us."

"Could a person do that?" Slight asked.

"I expect so," Cat told him.

"But you got relatives in Kansas City."

"They won't know a thing until—"

"It's over," Slight finished the thought, and coughed again.

Cat nodded. "And say I got me a lawyer who didn't know you from me, and say we found us an owner, like maybe some foundation, who didn't know squat about ranching, and who'd have to rely entirely on the wisdom of their lifetime employees. . . ."

"Quentin Harlan," Slight said slowly. "And Carlton Everett, town drunk."

"Fool," Carl said, and drank some more.

"So when you died," Cat summarized, leaning back in his chair in absolute drunken satisfaction at this brilliant plan of his, "we'd both be free."

"What about me?" Carl inquired.

"What do you care?" Cat asked him.

"Guess I don't." Carl shrugged. "Long as you take care of my boy, Laddy, like you said you would."

Cat and Slight eyed each other over their beers.

"He said he would, didn't he?" Slight said.

"I will," Cat assured both men.

And so they did it, those cowboys.

Cat thought he'd be free, you see, and live out the rest of his days easy, like the plain old cowboy he always thought he wanted to be.

But I'm not free, am I, Jenny?

I didn't count on Slight's having a fatal attack of guilt and telling Carl that Laddy wasn't really his boy, that he was really Slight's boy. And I didn't count on Carl's being so brain-rotted drunken crazy that he'd kill his former best friend and his former wife and try to kill me. And I didn't count on Laddy, my own nephew, coming to me and forcing me into the position of lying to him, claiming to be Slight Harlan, his real father. And I didn't count on meeting up with my own granddaughter, and loving her like my own.

Hell, she is my own. And that's why Carl, in his drunken rage, wanted to take her away from me. We had stolen his son, now he was taking my granddaughter. It still scares me, just to write it down."

I'm a fool, Jenny, and now I'm a "free" one.

So, what are you going to do with this letter, sweet woman from Massachusetts? If you can use it to prove I'm alive, you can get the ranch off your hands, and you'd like to do that, wouldn't you?

By the way, I'm sorry about scaring you with the rattler, like some damned fool adolescent boy with snakes and snails and puppy dog tails. I'd had a fight with Carl that morning—remember all the blood?—and he'd as much as come out and admitted he knew the truth about Laddy. I was scared of keeping you around there, scared of what you might learn, or even of what might happen to you. So I pulled the old dead rattler trick on you, and Carl played along because he wasn't so crazy about having you there, either. But it wasn't me who laid those spurs on your pillow, that was Carl. He was drunk and didn't even remember doing it the next morning. After that airplane "accident," and then when my sister got killed on a night when Carl just happened to be gone from the ranch, I had to face facts. I hope you can find it in your heart to forgive him. Or maybe to forgive us all, especially yours truly.

I apologize. I didn't mean to land a woman like you in all this trouble. Hell. I landed a lot of people in trouble in my lifetime, more than a few of them women, and I never thought I meant to do it.

Anyway, as far as your getting rid of my ranch, I don't think this letter will do the trick for you. Sorry, but if you want to have me declared alive, you're going to have to find me first.

Sometimes, well, some lonely times, I think I'd like that. I like to lie awake thinking of your coming for me. And if you don't ever? Then maybe I'll have to find you. I'd cause a stir, wouldn't I, riding into Massachusetts on Buck?

There rides the last free man, they'd say.

Ain't nothing free, I'd tell them.

The signature was typed:

Cat

I read the letter three times.

How like him to not quite think things through.

On the basis of that letter, I could probably get Canales to have the real Slight Harlan's body exhumed and prove Cat Benet wasn't dead. Then we could unload the ranch, and maybe Lilly Ann Lawrence could buy it in partnership with her cousin Laddy. . . .

But do that and I'd cheat the Railing twins, Mark and Suanna, out of their "inheritances." And their mother out of hers. And Marvalene and Freddie Sue. Do that and I'd horribly complicate the lives of the heirs who were already several months into spending or investing "their" money. If I turned over the letter to the authorities, they might start looking for the real Cat Benet, who might just end up in jail. On the other hand, Lilly and Ladd, who had lost their inheritances by going to the ranch, would get their own back one day.

"Slight," I said aloud, for I had a hard time thinking of him as anything else, "I could kill you for this."

Except that he had an uncanny knack for coming back to life when you least expected him.

I shoved the letter under the car seat, in about the same place where his gun had been hidden in his truck, and I started back down the drive. All the way to the house I was convinced I was going to leave his letter there.

Then I saw our cabin, and I woke up.

It was all a dream, a dream of freedom in a wild man's head, and maybe for a while in mine, and now it was time for me to extricate myself from his dream. These were decisions I didn't have to make, decisions that were not even mine *to* make.

I parked the car, pulled out the letter, and stared for a while at the postmark. Then I walked down to the beach, making a wager with myself: If there happens to be a cop swimming in the ocean today, I'll turn over this letter to him; if there's not, I won't.